THE
HUMORIST

Russell Kane was the first comedian, in 2010, to win both the Foster's Edinburgh Comedy Award and the Melbourne International Comedy Festival Barry Award in the same year. A regular TV and radio presenter, Kane has also written plays for the RSC and Soho Theatre.

You can follow him on Twitter at @russell_kane and on Facebook at www.facebook.com/officialrussellkane.

His website is www.russellkane.co.uk

THE
HUMORIST

RUSSELL KANE

**SIMON &
SCHUSTER**

London · New York · Sydney · Toronto · New Delhi

A CBS COMPANY

First published in Great Britain in 2012 by Simon & Schuster UK Ltd
A CBS COMPANY

This paperback edition first published by Simon & Schuster UK Ltd, 2012

1 3 5 7 9 10 8 6 4 2

Simon & Schuster UK Ltd
1st Floor
222 Gray's Inn Road
London
WC1X 8HB

www.simonandschuster.co.uk

Simon & Schuster Australia, Sydney
Simon & Schuster India, New Delhi

A CIP catalogue copy for this book is available
from the British Library.

Paperback ISBN: 978-0-85720-925-2
eBook ISBN : 978-0-85720-926-9

Printed and bound by CPI Group (UK) Ltd, Croydon, CR0 4YY

To my various Queens:

My mother, my Great Aunt Eileen,
the poet Maggie Butt, the novelist Sue Gee

Long may they reign

The beauty of the world, which is so soon to perish, has two edges, one of laughter, one of anguish, cutting the heart asunder.

Virginia Woolf

1

The Punchline, 2003

In the Comedy Store, Leicester Square, London, lay three hundred and twelve people in various poses of death, none of which were natural. By the cigarette machine I could make out a man dressed as a nurse, frozen on all fours, tongue swollen in silent mouth. Near the Ladies, the crumpled form of *Review* journalist Miranda Love, legs buckled, eyes bulging and popped.

Some of the deceased had fallen like 1980s zombie creatures, forearms prematurely rigored, drawn into their chests, hands splayed, tendrilled fingers stretched in stiff sprigs. Others had limbs and appendages pointing downwards, backs arched, as though on swimming-pool chutes. A few had faces tucked into their own armpits, dead-bird heads, coy in death – flirting. But all of them, every one of those three hundred and twelve stiff lifeless forms, had a curious thing in common: tears rolled down their cheeks. Thirty-seven minutes post mortem, with faces cold and vacant, every cheek continued to wet.

I watched the first detective arrive. A corpulent middle-aged woman in pale cream trouser-suit. She spent her first few moments futilely fending off the stench, but a few lungfuls later she relented, delivering a compact heave of vomit into a crisp mauve hanky. Yes, I suppose as many as one hundred of the dead had defecated or vomited on the way through it. Steadying herself against a brass handrail the detective clambered into the lightbox, as though systematic exploration was a viable way of understanding something this – unusual. Two pallid-faced men came to her aid as she searched in vain for the controls. They were anxious to stop the lurid halogens strobing across the polished black stage. Another officer busied himself with the knobs and dials on the sprawling sound desk in the imperious technical booth stage-left. But for all their frantic searching and fiddling the whole mess remained bathed in jocular purples and yellows for a good fifteen minutes. Cigarette smoke still eddied around lifeless flesh, the neon diffusing through stale vapour. But more than these ghoulish tableaux, the faecal stink, perhaps the worst thing – was the incessant music. At least I found this the most grating; that ridiculous upbeat ten-second soundtrack on loop, introducing an act who would never appear onstage; a stage upon which lay the dead body of Matthew Hopton, compère to the Comedy Store for over fifteen years. His final act was to pitch forwards, turn inwards his head with spiked 1990s hair, exhale his last breath, weep, and die in a copious pool of his own urine.

This was what the first arrivals witnessed. I know, because I watched the whole thing. I looked on with a strong black coffee almost smiling: though of course smiling would have been impossible. I had waited amongst the casualties, crouching in the hallway with a face of terror; convincing shivers, and muddled looks – the comedy-reviewing journalist who just happened to have been in the soundproofed corridor.

In fact, only one seated audience member had survived: a thirtyish man, completely unharmed but dazed. What had saved him? A combination of two coincidental factors. He was foreign, spoke some sort of Baltic language, wasn't fluent in English; plus he had been looking away during the Simongan Choreographic Stride. Even staff manning the inner door, bouncers and ticket-office lady, all perished. The three chaps collecting stubs at the inner door – Barry, Jacob and Roberto, had simply heard the thing, and that was it for them. The fracas it caused meant the security staff had rushed into the club from their various posts to see what was happening onstage. Even Big Dave Wilson outside on Oxendon Street had gone, perhaps because of his radio feed? They found him in the road in a seated position, eyes blank and milky, a puddle of liquidy faeces spreading away from him in symmetrical blossom.

Don't get me wrong: I am not trying to be lurid about the loss of three hundred and twelve lives. My writing this is not some sort of *purge*, nor is it supposed to represent the maniacal inner laugh of an aroused madman. It's more I see what happened as a sort of necessary proof; just the punchline if you like. Think of the set-up. The long, long set-up. Years of academic coldness, then this: all of it out – out in one big spurt of mirth.

'Nothing at all?' asked the pleasant WPC. She had a gentle face, which seemed ill-suited to processing violence and darkness.

'Lindsay – can I call you Lindsay?' I asked.

She nodded. She could have been no older than twenty-five. A few chestnut hairs had escaped from beneath her pied-rimmed cap undermining any authority. Given the scale of destruction around us, the questioning felt remarkably calm. In fact, I felt more than just calm. Alive. Suddenly alive. I sipped at my coffee, easily batting back answers to unanswerable questions. I winked. Pointed. Each motion of my body seemed important, as though it deserved its own special type of respect – I mean from me, as much as from anyone else. I'd never looked upon myself as fully alive. As I followed her words, a strange liquid consciousness ran through me. For the first time in nearly forty years I existed in the present tense, no yearning – just being. No blushing. Just a human being before me, and whatever I chose.

'Are you sure there's nothing more you can tell me?' she said.

I clenched my jaw, enjoying sensations of cockedness, primed readiness. I bubbled saliva – that thick white nervous type; licked my inner gums, savouring the firm contact of incisor upon incisor. I tensed my tongue.

'As I said, it's hard to recall what happened. It's hazy,' I said. 'In my line of work ...'

'Line of work?'

'Comedy. I review.'

'OK.'

'In my line of work ... I see comics die, but it's rare I'm in the middle of an actual genocide.' I had restarted a joke. Lamely. Also, the blend of distasteful death with my vocal flatness should have made it all supremely awkward, but I knew what I was doing and she laughed loudly, attracting reproachful glares from her colleagues.

'Quite,' she said, composing herself, re-nesting the strands of hair. 'Did you see anyone running out of the club?'

'No.'

'You were, you say, in the corridor?' She heaved as the pungent smell of human dung wafted past us.

'Yes.'

'But no one passed you?'

'No,' and I offered a shade of powerful Humour from my eyebrows.

She paused to uncrease an involuntary smile. 'Was there anyone else onstage when it happened?'

'I didn't see. I missed the whole thing. I was just on my way to check the car. That's when I heard a commotion.'

'A commotion?'

'Yes. I leant into the ticket booth to ask Jean what was happening ... and that's when she just ... sort of ...'

'Sort of what?'

'Died.'

The cause of Jean's death, of all these deaths, cannot be quickly explained – perhaps cannot be explained at all. Why did I lie about who was onstage? What really did that have to do with anything? Maybe in the shock of it all I was trying to re-process reality. Change it. I should have just told her the proud truth.

'Could you wait here, please.'

But she did not move off. She stared at me. I had a confusing moment where I too saw 'me'. Benjamin White, the man who the Comedy Store had laughed at for sixty-one wonderful seconds. Benjamin White: detested critic turned successful comedian, if only for a one-night run. Five foot nine inches, dressed in jeans, even wearing the standard-issue bright Indie T-shirt so well sported by try-hard, 'trendy' London comics. Me: the man with the flat boxer's nose; too long overlooked, unenjoyed, underappreciated, undiscovered – underwhelmed by life. Benjamin White: a soul born with the power to know, but cursed never to practise. And when I say 'know', I do not mean in the same sense as those morons in review sections, those half-baked Oxbridge Fleet Streeters, two of whom I know for a fact kept me at sub-editor level purely through personal vendetta. I mean I *saw* humour.

I had made every soul in the world's most prestigious venue laugh hard. Laugh until their beings folded outwards, came together, and transmuted into something more than human flesh could know. For one night only people arrived at *my* theatre.

The house-lights of the Comedy Store burst into white halogen. Things lost their abstracted garishness. The room took on a mundane, crime-scene reality. WPC Grebe continued speaking but I did not listen. Receiving an ominous gesture from a sergeant she moved off towards a fire exit, asking that I remain in the hallway. I watched them conferencing. I had, at most, minutes left.

Half-heartedly I swept the room for unmanned doors. Under the lights' clinical glare, the whole thing seemed graphic, excessive. My feelings of lightness, of power, slowed to a thick, heavy fear. This was always bound to happen, I told myself. I ran that Monty Python sketch through in my head. The one where Germans die in the trenches at the hands of a powerful English joke. Their skit is our modern rewrite of a perennially told myth. And on it goes, that story of death by laughter; only here for me it stopped.

The sharp clacking of folding chairs and men's voices. No escape, no exit, but none was sought. A prey-like resignation coursed through me. By now six or seven officers were circling, their faces resolute. My final flutterings of fright rose until they resolved back into a dead feeling of doneness, of being finished; a mission fully accomplished; and soon many hands were upon me.

It was this rough treatment by the officers which deemed my negative sensations. As the doors of the Ford Mondeo slammed shut, only one thought lodged in my mind: How? How had I, Benjamin White, come to this?

And then I thought of my mother.

And then I thought of my birth.

Yes. This was the joke. Nothing else – but this.

2

The Set-up, 1964

On Saturday, 30 May 1964, in a private ward of the Charing Cross Hospital, a scrawny baby boy slid slowly from the body of Mrs Sally White. The torturous birth went on for some hours, but at last a crushed, misshapen infant writhed before her, the sound of the boy's father assaulting his ears.

'Boy, oh boy, it's only a bloody boy, my boy!'

Blinking spasmodically, the babe discharged amniotic fluid from his nostrils, then let out a piercing, painful scream. Shocking – for this was not the standard yell of a newborn. No, something much shriller, more urgent, and with enough pitch to alarm both midwife and consultant obstetrician. This was not the usual infant squall of indignation, no clichéd cry for a return to the womb. No, this was a reaction.

Boy, oh boy, it's only a bloody boy, my boy! An alliterative epigram drawing its linguistic force from repetition, and executed with a suburban American accent (as heard in hits of the day such as *Bewitched*), had nurses and midwife alike chuckling. Even Sally White, my mother, afterbirth sliding from her stinging body, let out an involuntary laugh: a long breathy bleat of appreciation for her clever, funny, fertile husband. It was this little exchange, so normal, so natural, which made the baby holler. Mr White's lame first joke sluiced through the infant's brain forming a white bolt of dopamine which flashed in the baby's minuscule frontal lobes like a firework stood too close. Memories such as these should not (*cannot*) be stored in such a tiny brain. But from the first moment, it seemed that all experiences of humour were charged.

It's a strange condition, mine: a perfect, harrowingly precise perception of humour in all its forms, but coupled with an inability to laugh – even smile. And worse, from that first moment, the merest hint of someone else's joke could scorch like sunshine on a redhead's skin. They laughed, I cried. Life had begun.

Human history has seen a small but steady parade of the gifted: wild-haired composers and basement musicologists; freakish absorbers of concepts, visionary linguists; mathematicians spinning skeins of formulae that change the way we know our world; paradigm-shifting painters; messianic weavets of tales which transform human consciousness into a finer moral substance. In fact, most forms of human endeavour, creative and scientific, have their talented, who function, if it can be called functioning, in a stratosphere unknown and unimaginable to those who savour everything they create.

Has there, however, been another like me? I do not mean a practitioner of humour – a gag-smith, a 'stand-up'. Neither do I allude to those creators of humorous, sublime tales (I am thinking here of Lee Fraser-Jones and other comic-narrative artists). No, I mean a true seer of humour. Has there? The answer is of course no. I am a one-off, and the thing that . . . happened, was my way of proving this. There may never be another – nor should there be. I am an abomination of art. An aberration of mind. A crippled crossbreed of imagination and geometry who should have been chloroformed at birth.

I don't even have stock tales of rejecting parents upon which to pin my self-loathing. No, it is worse than that. They were perfect parents. Perfect, loving parents. The trouble with love and perfection is that it needs a recognizable form of radiance in return. To see humour as I do can hardly be called a gift.

My whole 'myth' is as old as the world. It's been recycled and attempted over and over, each generation imagining itself the first with enough audacity or wit to realize it. But the myth, like all enduring myths, has been fattened by truth. Greek and Roman fable, Old English tales, ancient Indian poetry, sly references in Chaucer, right up to the Monty Python German sketch. The idea is to compel through contradiction: laughter is a form of dying – a forgetting of self. Laughter and death: the contraction of both into story or joke seems almost lazy; yet our best poets and playwrights, the profoundest philosophers cannot resist it. I did not either.

The idea of genius in comedy, this imprecise art form, is a paradox – or more simply – a joke. Yes, one can paint precisely, yes, one can strum a harp with inhuman exactitude. One can jig word order to create a celestial narrative. But humour? Intangible, ungraspable, subjective humour. The idea is a nonsense. I am a nonsense.

A too-vivid memory: I was four years old. We went to my darling cousin Becky's house to watch the birth of some spaniel pups. Two of them, horrible mangled conjoined things, should have been stillborn, but came into the world wriggling and yelping. My father took charge of their 'humane disposal'. The soaking of the cotton wool, the sealing of the plastic bag. The image is still so clear: those wretched slimy mites writhing, fighting against fumes, dying in pathetic tiny convulsions. Should that have been me?

Eleven years later, when I was at the Centre, I was the only one whose 'gift' had no fixed numerical, linguistic, or spatial quality. Take Richard Gott, numbers maestro/genius and my best friend. He had a way of squinting when formulating thoughts, as though blocking out strong sunlight.

'When you leave here. What will you do?' he asked one day as we carried our plastic plates to the bin.

'A levels. And then university.' I was lying. The idea of 'uni' – all that laughter. No.

'I think so too,' he said. 'We could study together.'

'Will your mum allow it?'

'I'll be sixteen in a year. She can't stop me studying with you.'

'She didn't seem that keen last time.'

'That was my fault.' He looked down at the floor and fingered a bumpy scar on his left wrist.

'We can laugh at it now,' I said. I almost meant to make this joke.

Richard laughed and for a moment made eye contact. Very rare for him.

'You idiot, Benjamin.'

I'd chosen for my best friend someone who could not look directly at me. I won't pretend that this was an accident.

'Shall we do something later?' he said.

'I've got a fishing pass left.'

'Have you?'

'Spot Four on the lake is free. I already checked.'

'Excellent,' he said.

'Shall I meet you at 3 p.m.?'

'Three thirty,' he said. 'I've got Pastoral from 2 p.m.'

And we went too. Two boys double-crossed by blessing, whom talent had deceived, sitting in silence, lifting wet dappled creatures from warm clear water, taking simple solace in stillness, in the quiet sense of a slow race which for once could be won.

Richard was not what you would call clever, nor even 'extremely numerate', yet his gift for numbers was undeniable and it marked him out as one of us. For Richard, each number had an individual colour, a texture; every sum, digit and multiple its own topography. He called it (as we all did when we learned this important term from Dr Rowe) 'synaesthesia' – the production of impressions in one sense while perceiving with another. The smell of grey, the sight of odour. I have it occasionally with compact jokes. I can almost feel the surface of a pun with my left thumb. Once, when we were again fishing, I thought I had a carp on the line.

'It's huge. It's ... it's massive!' I was about as excited as my voice allowed. Then the line went dead. The reel stilled, and the rod straightened.

'Pull the other one,' said Richard, laughing. And he pointed to his rod.

The other one. The contraction of the metaphorical 'other one' into the solid, banal reality of Richard's fishing rod was so dense, and quick and solid that instead of my usual cerebral processing I felt the coldness of a stone in my hand. My thumb pushing against it. All that language, all that happiness boiled into quick tight wordplay. My thumb felt it.

Richard could have counted the letters in the pun and

given its multiples in a moment. His talent was extra-ordinary. He perceived some numbers, especially prime numbers, with many senses at once – sometimes all five. Seven, all of its multiples, and any number whose last two or three digits could combine to form seven as their sum he saw in 'angry purple', and experienced metallic pop-ping noises in his left ear. His left thumb and big toe would heat at the tip, and he would testify to a smell of rotting blackberries in the room. All this within seconds. What I'm saying is, this should not be labelled 'genius'. His daily functioning was poor. He couldn't tell the time, read a shopping list without getting anxious. The only intellectual benefit was that he could instantly tell you (note: not calculate) a multiple's root simply by how he sensed it.

I cried a lot during those years. Not that I ever wept for my own fate; I mean, not in that direct sense. Not boo-hoo, I'm a freak child who lives at the Centre. No, I wept for others. Almost. Being honest – it was a kind of proxy too. A covert, sneaking self-pity. Looking back, maybe I was trying to express the last drops of love from my system. I failed, of course. It took cousin Becky for that. So I would sob: for Richard, for the nurses, for my grandmother – even for my mother after her weekly visits.

For years, when I heard the epithet 'genius' I took sharp offence; sometimes I would verbally attack the person who had used it. It was an insult as I saw it. A more physical person might have punched, but I live in my skull, not my body. 'Genius' – what does that really mean? For me it signifies a kind of nerdish loner monk. In these days of comfortable mediocrity, people use 'genius' in a mocking sense, implying the uselessness of being too clever – neurologically overqualified for life. As for genius together with humour ...

I will admit there have been, perhaps still are, a few brilliant comedians. The gratuitous phrase 'comic genius' can never truly be used. It's merely a comforting hyperbole for the flat-sounding but accurate 'very good comedian'. Comic and genius. Ha! The two concepts are mutually exclusive. Comedians imagine it's the material, or even more deludedly some sort of 'technique' that makes them funny. But even at the Centre, before the Centre, I knew. It's material plus the tiny secret parts of them, the parts they are blind to. This makes them what they are. No 'great comic' has ever been able to *see* all that. Anyone who could would not be a comedian. They would implode, or dissolve – simply not be, and never have been. Or be me.

The Centre could find no record of another genuine Savant Humour Perception case, and if the Centre had no record, there had been no case. By the way, when I say the Centre, I really mean Dr Rowe. He was, is, the Centre. I was 'of interest' to Dr Rowe, my ability being indivisible from my condition, or let's not dress it up – my disability. Benjamin White: for thirty-nine years, two months and fourteen days possessor of the most ridiculous and useless gift. I suppose my life has made no sense, and as now I rot,

I reflect on how natural it is that genius is mirrored by emptiness. No, never been another like me – and it was this fact that made those first five years so hard. I was an illness as yet unrecorded; a new type of blight. An uncategorized animal here to ravage the domestic nest, and it began right there on a green piece of towelling, that first instant; mewling and stretching my vernix-covered limbs, my father's wide grin gaping over me.

My father kept speaking. The room crackled with other people's laughter. Imagine: I could sense the nature of laughter before I knew what it was. These first seconds on earth, the same pattern as my next forty years: everyone else laughing, I understanding down to the last particle why and how they did so, but utterly unable to share in it.

I'll admit, some memories have been refreshed using old photographs, Granny Davids' stories and recollections – but the fact is (Dr Rowe's attempts to convince me this is impossible notwithstanding) I recall much of these first few days. I clearly remember for instance the squeaky feel of polyester-cotton around my body, a soothing antiseptic smell; fleeting sensations of comfort and safety, disturbed if someone so much as sniggered. Then, as now, human joy made up a large part of a maternity ward's atmosphere. Lots of comfortable, in-for-three-nights new mothers with plasticky flowers and brown-papered fruit. Just as many chipper gents bearing gifts and weak witticisms. The 1960s father: the last vanguard of male separatism, lauded by a horseshoe of seated family at the foot of my mother's private bed. My father churned out freshly minted anecdotes about my difficult birth, my 'adorable' squidged nose, the hilarious dropping of forceps, the shameless Indianness of the consultant – cue: comedy accent.

For the first six hours, my whimpers that followed each burst of their laughter were ignored. Occasionally a maternal finger soothed. I did not cry constantly, just reactively. This kept my mother's fears on hold – perhaps I had sensitive hearing – an unknown yet normal fluid to be expelled from my ears within twenty-four hours? The next day, however, she began to worry. Her son seemed genuinely distressed by sudden noises. She hushed unruly admirers. But it was not the decibels of their laughter. It was the very fact of laughter itself; not just that, but the sequence of sounds and movements which preceded that laughter. These invaded my cot from all over. The worst offender from my family was Uncle Jeff. He died early. The only one who never really seemed bothered by my problem – and he was the one to go first. A quiet soul – an outsider. Still, his poor jokes made his actual company intolerable.

As Uncle Jeff wrung out his comic posturing, telling the story of his little Rebecca's birth a few weeks before mine, I wriggled and bucked. I could not even control my eyelids, yet I somehow sensed the coming paucity. I could not understand language, but my instinct, though I was only two days old, was perfect, but who can easily love perfection? My mother would always smile as she described my father's flaws: his attention-seeking ego, his forgetfulness. He'd return the favour, savouring her senti-mentality – her inability to finish anything. Faults, the humanness of imperfection.

Uncle Jeff worked his jaw, lowering wrists and hands, loosening them, miming his uselessness during Becky's birth. Later on, as I heard this story again (and a-fucking-gain) I realized why I had been so agitated at its first telling; a horribly hackneyed tale of male morphine-inhala-tion and loss of balance; a pathetic attempt at making himself vulnerable for comic effect. Uncle Jeff's 'routine' made me scream.

I found the smug good humour on that ward unbear-able, as though a noxious gas were being pumped through the air-vents into my mother's private room. No one knew this, and I could do nothing. I just inhaled antiseptic and waited for stories to finish, and then the laughter came, and I screamed again. *I am here*, I screamed, I am in pain. Thus it was, less than seventy-two hours after my birth, Sally White, for the first time in her contented life, found herself overwhelmed with worry.

How strange, after all my boastings about memory, something drifts back for the first time. Lullabies. I had completely forgotten. What was this, four or five years later? Sometimes, in one of my bad moments, my mother would just hold me and sing. Cling and sing. Don't get me wrong, mostly she would cry or panic, phone my father or worse Dr Rowe, but once in a while, she would scoop me up and hold me against her chest, and just sing. I squirmed, kicked, bit – but then the smell of washing powder. The close-up macro-focus on each green stitch in a winter pullover; and the song, words inaudible – only vibrations from deep inside her. These moments of parent–child tenderness grew more infrequent, ceasing altogether by the time I was nine. In the end, an analytical mind always defeats the good intentions of the heart.

I remember once we were discussing Jane Austen. I ended up punching the wall so hard that my little finger broke.

'Criticism is not the same as being critical, Benjamin,' my mother had said.

'You mean mollycoddling?'

'No – just ... being – positive.'

'While at the same time being negative. Pah!' How old am I here? Nineteen, no – sixteen, just turned. I inverted the '6'.

'But it's good to keep a healthy attitude,' she said simply, as though righting an ornament fallen on its side. 'Dr Rowe ...'

'Yes, looking at things with love. I know.'

'Well ...'

'Mother – you sound like a Born Again.'

'Some things they get ... right, Benjamin.'

We stirred our teas waiting for words. I watched the corners of her mouth contemplate uplifting sentiments.

With each movement of her cakey hands, crumbs showered everything in a sticky confetti.

'Your father and I had that positivity, Benjamin.' She smiled. 'Sometimes just hunting for the positive ...'

I tuned out. Violence, as it so often did around this time, bubbled. A mint dropped in a Diet Coke. The neatness of her merge, the appallingly twee segue into something 'relevant'. I cannot bear any form of conceptual high-fiving. I mean – when the tidiness of a punchline or link is so crisp that the story-teller almost slaps the palms of his audience. In my opinion, adroitness has the opposite effect. It doesn't make an audience flow with the 'seamlessness' of the wit. No. Quite the reverse. For a moment, we all pause and admire the cleverness, the odious capability of the story-teller. And in that stop of admiration, we lose the illusion. We see the cocky little shit or shitess sitting at their fucking smug desk and smiling to their cunt selves. 'I'll try that later onstage,' they think, then go for a reward wank in the toilet. It's a cheap watch with the back removed.

'Mother, admit at least that *Hamlet* was awful,' I said, referring to an abortive production at the Guildford Seal, bringing the discussion back to more comfortable terrain. But this was a mistake.

She smiled, taking a long slow breath – a Socrates with rouge. 'What do you mean "awful"?'

'I mean wooden acting, and bad direction – all the reviews said it. It was complete shit.'

'Benjamin!'

'It was bad. Waste. Shit.' I savoured the coarse bark of the swear word.

'But does that change how one can love their efforts?' She lifted a fat slice of Battenberg onto a side-plate, crumbs sprinkling the cover of her mauve leatherette notebook.

'Love "effort"?'

She nodded, chewing loudly, cake mushing in her sated mouth.

I wonder: how many people have felt this? The deep irritation brought on by an optimist – worse, a cheery, cake-eating optimist. Is there anything more annoying than a self-satisfied person eating a sweet snack? Imagine the primal pleasure of snatching the cake of an optimist. Watching all their self-assured rightness with the world vanish under the imperious heel of one's boot as their treat is squashed into the carpet. Wouldn't it be something? Wouldn't it in some way be just – at least poetic?

A ball of chewed cake slid down her throat.

'Enough,' she said.

The roof of my mouth itched. I could feel irritation upgrading to violence. Clearing the tea things, she missed my reddening face, the backside squirming in the seat. As she turned away I pushed my chair backwards so savagely it hit our vomit-green kitchen wall making a deep gash in the plaster. Yet she smiled, a facile smile. Still, now, in the heat of it, she met my frustration, my boiling over, with a smile. That single semicircular flesh-symbol for everything I lacked. I think I leapt at her, screamed something bad into her face. I punched the wall just to the left of her head. My middle finger crunched – a fracture. The clearest memory a silver fleck of phlegm landing on her chin as a curse word snapped from my tongue; that and the smell of cakes and home, the tick of Granddad's old clock. This outburst seemed involuntary, but really it was being away from the Centre. I mean, knowing that no Yellow Room could get me here. Sometimes after these bouts of rage I rather enjoyed, even cherished, my parents' attention. I couldn't win by meeting their Pollyannaism with reason, and certainly not with my own joy – so I broke theirs. I smashed it, crushed it and soaked myself in the attentive aftermath.

The Guildford Seal's *Hamlet*. My God. Anyway, I think my comedy reviews over the years have proved my case – that bad art *must* be unequivocally criticized, erased from history. Why patronize (and therefore mislead, hurt) the untalented?

Considering my condition, it was extremely unlucky that my parents were a colossal exception to the rule of opposites attract. Both witty, both charismatic, both loud, outgoing and 'fun'. Sounds fine, but who would choose to be the po-faced outsider at a perennial party?

Usually, when two loud people attempt serious love, it's not long before initial sparkles give way to fiery clashes. Normally they split. They seek out new, more introverted partners who will better complement them.

Not so with Sally Davids and Graham White. Their love was instant, deep, secure – and loud. Rather than stifling each other, boundlessness and laughter somehow held them together – a bright putty. Their arrival would warm up any room. Their confidence and conspicuous mirth blossomed quieter friends into life. Sally Davids and Graham White were dinner-guest A-listers from day one. Surely any children produced would be cut from the same vibrant cloth?

What might explain the tedious happiness of my mother? Safeness. No pain. Her memories of World War II in deepest, loveliest Surrey (near Godalming) were marinaded in cloudy lemonades, hide-'n'-seek and a secure thankfulness that Granddad Bernard had been one month too old 'to kick in the Teutons'. Her liberal, book-filled girlhood was stacked with chubby Bernard Davids' handmade toys, and Granny Davids' aromatic lardy cooking. As bombs fell fat and undeniable all over unlucky Britain, the guest bedrooms filled with inner-city children, each one of them 'fun', a 'real character'. My mother kept in contact with seven of them right up until January 2003, when everything came to a head.

In 1954, brimming with everything from Wollstonecraft to Woolf, my mother enrolled at Edinburgh University, where insipid contentment continued. Closely bonding with Adrienne Grineaux and Molly Devonshire (yes, they remained lifelong, ruddy-faced companions, obsessed with bridge and hearty country things such as rambling and wild flowers), she sailed through her English lit degree. It was a time just before drugs, and just after total conservatism. A saccharine window of pre-feminist idealism. Two amicable flings with tutors. Two atrocious but safe nights of drunkenness, yielding just enough anecdotes. She attained a respectable 2.1. Her dissertation was an analysis of 'suppressed optimism' in the unfinished novels of Jane Austen. Later on, when I myself was a teenager, this thesis was something we debated. Anything that got me talking or making contact, my mother pursued. Our intellectual chats usually ended sourly, sometimes in violence, but I suppose she felt this better than silence. Up until I was sixteen, she still mooted my going further than A levels. I reckon I might have enjoyed a literature degree – just to throw spanners in literary works; but beyond A levels, outside the bite-size, the definite, I rebelled; saw too much, let in too much light and spoiled the exposure. More than all that: the laughter. It was the dread of all that studenty laughter.

In 1959 Sally Davids, with jolly outlook and sparkly good humour, found herself working as Entertainment Previewer for the *Surrey Comet*. Very quickly she had her own page: *The Weekend Ahead!* She pronounced 'ahead' as in 'ahoy'. Enthusing about things imminent was the perfect job for my mother. Even in her sixties she would still fizz at the simple prospect of a nice meal out, a rented film. In 1961 her sparkling 500-word anticipations of the Guildford Arts Centre's latest productions were relished and believed. Her nuggets could make a real difference to a production's success, its chances of 'going to London'. Even now when I reread her fripperies in my scrapbook, their conversational charm warms me. For all my esteem as a writer, charm was something I struggled with. I had the technical, but not the lights, the music.

The *Surrey Comet* also let her experiment with the trickier art of *re*viewing, but she never took to it; failed at it, in fact. She tried reviewing for a couple of months, but when she attempted negative reviews, arguments seemed to fold back into a sort of love. She saw the positive in everything. It was one of the reasons we clashed. She tried it with my views, adding in some sunshine, but I didn't want to be warmed up, loved.

Love. I suppose I'm scientific proof that love and joy are different things – neurologically speaking anyway. You see, love is a thing I understand well – I have felt it. Maybe, and this is pathetic, I still feel it. Tongueless and in my own shit, locked up in here – I'm still in love. Yes. It's something I have known – from initial sexual desire right through to violent upset; smashing up the kitchenette of my first-floor flat, sobbing – the works. Joy is not love. Joy is merely one possible by-product of love, not its consequence. Look at the worrying logic: *I* cannot laugh, but *I can* love. conclusion: Love is not necessarily fun. It's something beyond, or rather before. Or maybe laughter came before love. Yes. Looking at chimps it's likely. The callous cackles of the primate as he murders a member of the clan. The loveless laugh of the killer.

At the *Surrey Comet*'s office in Kingston upon Thames my mother met the person she called 'the funniest man I ever did encounter!' – a slim cartoonist, Graham White. A comical, rangy 'chap', clumsily fop-haired and partially deaf in one ear (yes, enough to exempt him from his 1953 National Service call-up).

Months before Sally Davids arrived, my father had already outgrown his provincial incubator. As he put it, 'The *Surrey Comet*'s solar star had risen high above the county, celestial tail of galactic mirth exploding its witty ions in an astrophysical cartoon-caption storm from Dorking to Staines.' Surrey's best satirist and captioner had amused so brilliantly on everything from Tadworth's priapic heraldry to Banstead's halogen traffic lights that Editor Miles Gericho offered him a features position. He was twenty-two, and he turned it down. One week before my mother first 'burst through those revolving doors', my wearingly successful father snubbed the *Surrey Comet*. Why? He had found himself approached by both the *Morning Express* and the *Telegraph*. Yes, perhaps it now dawns that my father was *the* Graham White – 'Gwhite', as it was often scribbled in jokey script. *The* Graham White who, in 1961, drew the now iconic cartoon of Harold Macmillan as a walrus wearing three coats and four bobble hats, standing next to a grossly fat Rab Butler clad only in pants and vest, but with a tie on, the captions:

HM: 'How are you finding *this* war, Rab – rather Cold, isn't it?'

RB: 'On the contrary it's rather hot under *my* collar.'

The cartoon saw my father almost sacked, and the *Telegraph* sued. Mockery of ministers in this way was deemed inappropriate back then. However, it was this near-death reprimand which elevated my father's (let's face it, barely passable) cartoon quip to cult status. Inside the *Telegraph*'s office, he more than held onto his job. In fact it was they who cramponed his steady climb from young satirist to national institution in five short years. I'm sure my father's subsequent work in the 1970s and 1980s for the *Review* and the *Saturday Mirror* respectively needs no description here. We shall also leave well alone his 1999 work for the Carnegie Medallist lady, and ignore altogether his embarrassing exhibition at Tate Modern in June 2002.

My mother frequently recounted her 'first ever eight-minute walk from Kingston train station' to the *Surrey Comet*'s offices in Grey Lane, Kingston upon Thames. For her, it represented much more than the morning she met my father; more than her coming of age as 'a modern 1960s woman, it was rare back then, Benjamin'. Rather, it set up in this one marked event a symbol for her whole peach-coloured mode of existence.

'I walked out of Granny's house, and caught the 8.27 from Godalming. I'll never forget the feeling. When I disembarked at Kingston – everything had changed.'

'This was how we fell in love!' my father would often put in at this point.

Graham White had been working the required one month's notice in his little local nest, readying to spread his satirical wings and flap off to Fleet Street. During that time, 'a rather gorgeous midget your mother' Sally Davids settled into her corner desk which overlooked Frank Bentall's Victorian county store, 'a red-brick building flanked by buffed rows of Morris Minors and colourful trees'. Mother bumped into Father on her first day, her first hour in fact. There was 'no courtship to speak of', they told anyone who would listen, especially me, over and over again. My father would never allow a story which featured him to be in any way conventional (the trouble being that his techniques for achieving a non-conventional story were themselves trite clichés). No – there was no romance, no seeking; just an instant joyous friendship; a brotherly-sisterly rib-prodding bond. Within days, functional drinks for my mother's welcome and my father's farewell grew into boozy after-work chats. Pub lunches stretched out along with the truths of where they said they were, as Graham grew *fin de siècle* and Sally cottoned on to Miles Gericho's disregard for timekeeping. My parents were a fortuitous criss-crossing of ambition, change, and sickeningly upbeat demeanours. By week three they were '*platonic* best friends', yet both felt a dread at the connection being severed.

'We honestly didn't think it was anything like this,

Mummy,' she said to her own mother the day she announced her engagement (and then almost identically to me fourteen years later). 'We genuinely believed we'd found a good friend in each other – for two bright people we were fairly dim not to realize ...'

'... that what was going on was ... we were damn-well in love!' my father would put in at this juncture whenever the story was told, no – *performed*; always presenting the word *love* as though plucking the Perrier Award from a cabinet.

It wasn't until my father had left the *Surrey Comet* to lampoon politicians for the *Telegraph* that they chose to meet for fateful gin and tonics. He had lured her to Luigi's in Soho for a matter-of-fact confession of love.

'Look. It's quite simple,' he said.

'Go on.'

'I love you. Put that in your pipe.'

That's how he had said it. Put that in your pipe. A transposition of the everyday onto the sublime; of the masculine onto the feminine – an alchemy of good-natured self-deprecation and down-to-earth British good sense.

'Graham!' she had squealed. 'Fill up my pipe!'

In no time at all they were engaged. Within a few years they'd have a savant son who could not smile. Five years more, a normal son would arrive: the perfect little Cooper White, ticking all filial boxes with a cute, bright crayon. Another five years, the strange son would be packed off to live with one Dr Rowe.

The very day my mother made her conjugal announce-
ment to her parents, Nazi-dodging Granddad Davids died.
Look at it from my Granddad's angle. His daughter was
marrying the young man who a few months earlier had
been accused of political heresy in every British newspaper
(except of course the *Telegraph*).

Mother's syrupy revisionism began straight after her
father's funeral, continuing right until the end: 'His weak
ticker just kept him going till the day he knew his special
girl would marry well. It was as though he'd been waiting,
Benjamin. Oh ... I miss him.' No, Mother. Shock killed
him, you silly cow. I would love to have told her this.

Finally, April last year in fact, my Grandma Davids told
me how it really happened. She's the one human being I
have left now. A fortyish man and his Granny: it must
seem pathetic, I know, but do not underestimate how close
we are, how she loves me, and I love her. With the media
interest ebbing, she's my only regular visitor: a ninety-
seven-year-old spry pensioner. She is a rare thing. Even to
look at – a tall unarthritic old lady with smooth papery
skin, dyed-black hair, and misty, fey green eyes. She even
smells pleasant. She somehow embodies both sets of old-
lady virtues: snappy feistiness and kind patience. Given
that these days I only communicate with pad and pen, I am
lucky she never tires or becomes annoyed. Sometimes it
takes three or four minutes' scrawling to get the simplest
thought straight. But she just waits, reads it through, then
responds as though we were conversing normally. On the

day of her mini-revelation about Mother, we were chatting in the Visiting Room about the Guildford Seal. It was a Monday cleaning morning. The blended odours of formaldehyde and unclean men were particularly strong, so we had immersed ourselves deeply in chats about the past. I mentioned how much Mother had supported the theatre's ghastly refurbishment, and it was then that Granny Davids just came out with it.

'You see, Benjamin,' she said, closing the scrapbook with a young woman's vigour, then index-fingering it back across the yellow plastic table, 'the truth is, my husband, your grandfather, died of shock – you understand? I don't mean worry, not even slowly, not a broken heart, you know.' She paused and fixed me with one of her mean, milky truth stares. 'It was a straightforward heart attack – later that night, you see, a direct bloody connection. Your mother would never admit it to herself, Benjamin. And that's why *you're* here, my boy, you understand? Too much self-deception. *It's dangerous!*' She shouted the last words – loudly enough to draw a glare from Staff Nurse Nguymbe. I biroed frantically, pushing her for more, but she simply shook her head. The subject was closed. She drew the scrapbook towards her, and again flicked through, stopping at the montage of my Jay Conway reviews from 2001. Unbelievable how that little fraud-fuck has gone on to to bag a historic double in the comedy awards world. Postmodernism is dead, long live trite autobiography and cuntish haircuts.

Granny Davids and I are very similar. Come to think of it, I haven't seen her laugh for at least a year, maybe two. Yes, the last time I saw her smile was in 2006, autumn. Anil Bhupendra, my 'neighbour' from Room 21A, was enjoying a visit from his wife and toddler son. The toddler had been disruptive the whole half-hour, disturbing everyone in the Day Room. We had hardly been able to think, let alone speak or write. Then, quite accidentally, the snotty infant tripped on Granny Davids' walking stick, hurling forwards and smashing his chin open on the hard metal leg of his father's chair. I felt an instant pity for the mite, but not Granny Davids. She laughed, deep and basso, the hearty belly-guffaws more like those of a woman in her forties. She quickly blended her laughter into apology, even helped the child stand again, but the timbre of her amusement had been unmistakable. The child's pain entertained her.

One day, I got her onto current affairs; no greater diversion than hearing a nonagenarian rant about George W. Bush.

'May I swear, Benjamin?'

I nodded an 'Of course, Granny.'

'The cunt's a fucking monkey.'

It's times like that when I experience what Dr Rowe urged me to 'spot, label, and savour'. Specifically, he taught me, and yes, it's a mouthful, the 'Laughter Cathexsis Substitute' for these fleeting seconds when I sense near-laughter. It's extremely rare for me to distinguish laughter-emotions before dissecting their content. The Granny Davids incident is particularly illustrative. On this occasion a sort of warm atomic haze came fractionally *before* this understanding:

> *The juxtaposition of frail sociological entity*
> *(sweet old lady) with linguistic ad nauseam utterance*
> *('cunt's a fucking monkey').*

Dr Rowe explained that when a quick stream of 'pleasure' bottle-necks and almost pushes through my processes of dissection, I must open my mouth and speak the words 'ha ha ha' very quickly. I suppose it gives relief, but it sounds somewhat sarcastic, as though pointing out *un*funniness, lack of wit. Still, it's strangely satisfying, a sort of emotional trepanning.

As usual, Granny Davids was delighted at my delight. She has always been the one person who takes my prosthetic noises for the real thing. Her own genuine laughter settled into a beaming smile, and taking a breath she fished from her wheely-bag her standard offerings: powdered coffee, jam, and permitted magazines. She stood, kissed me on the cheek, shuffled across the Day Room and gave her usual salute goodbye as she disappeared through doorway Y2.

I wonder if my brother Cooper would have visited me? I feel terrible about him. It was wrong he had been there. Yes, OK, I have always had a hot liquid hatred of him, but

I have never believed he wilfully did me wrong. What am I saying? Perhaps, none of them intentionally hurt me. It's just the way it turned out. I was born this way, and their kindness, their attempts at a form of love, unwittingly injured me. Excluded me. I resented the way they tried to love me and failed. I think you remain a child for as long as your parents live. That fire of resentment does not cool with age. It bakes down to its white-hot embers – sooner or later it blackens. It burns you or someone else, and it's not until you've hurt them back that you realize all anyone wanted was love. If then no one was to blame, I couldn't even blame Cooper. He was younger. He didn't ask for an older brother with this condition. Yet it was I who resented him. Hated him. Poor Cooper. At least he was gay – no children, I mean.

Am I trying to place too much emphasis on cause, on nurture? Perhaps I need to be known to myself for everything else to make sense. Is it guilt? Again, it's love probably. A way of loving those who could not love me because of who I was. A way of loving them, once and for all, for who they were – not what I wanted them to be. Does any of it justify what I went on to do, or how and why I did it? Well, this is the point. I do not wish to justify anything. I just somehow need to . . . see the thing – the full canvas – to understand the making of it. Just pull back the curtain a little, but not disturb the act. This is why I keep returning to before; prior to my existence – looking for hints.

Before they wed at Sutton Town Hall, according to my mother, they respectfully mourned Granddad Bernard for a few months. This was followed by three weeks in Tuscany and Venice, and the commencement of cosy married life. They purchased the house in Tadworth, and began two years of unmitigated, nauseating happiness. The pre-Benjamin years as I like to call them. Those years must have passed quickly, and then there I was.

'Boy, oh boy, it's only a bloody boy, my boy!'

During my mother's post-natal stay on Kanty Ward, Indian consultant Dr Khahindi assuaged her nascent fears. There were content newborns, there were grizzlers. She held onto the standard 'women fret too much' rationale, grateful for any blitheness with which to blur worry.

As for my first months at home, here my memory uncharacteristically fades. I must be honest: I cannot testify to any more real recall till at least two or three years later. This surely signals that for my first couple of years at least I was relatively content. Why? Maybe because of my father's quick wits and my mother's self-deceit. According to Granny Davids, within a matter of days my mother started requesting people not to laugh around her son. This was easily explained away. My father spuriously opined that laughter came from a lower part of the larynx; perhaps something in his new son's ears was extra-attuned to low, bassy noises. At this stage he would not have dared posit joy itself as the problem. No. Not his son. Not the offspring of 'dangerously witty Graham White' (the *Telegraph* Obituaries, 2003). This other explanation, this laughter-as-noise theory, seemed to work – for a time at least; while the baby was a baby and not a little person.

Although I neither smiled nor giggled, I was regarded as 'satisfied'. Worry still stippled the mind of Sally White, but before long it blended back to a rosy canvas. The day when she should phone for a specialist's appointment never quite arrived. New excuses were made, fresh observations of my normality. After all, her baby lived – grabbed index fingers, gurgled, interacted, vomited, shat, ate, wept and slept – everything worked – except that one thing: her baby never smiled, no matter what she did: silly hands, comic animal babbles, contorted face – nothing elicited a twitch upwards at the corners of my mouth. On the contrary the harder she or anyone else tried, the more grizzly I became. It took another week or so for my mother to realize that, as well as laughter, people clowning or japing even near my Moses basket produced tears and tantrums. Again, my parents extenuated. They made themselves feel comfortable in the form of, well, a joke. They said I was a proud little baby who got upset if I sensed people might be having fun at my expense. They rationalized the same way in which owners anthropomorphize their haughty cats. This technique enabled them to suppress the evidential facts: any laughter, humour, or animated happiness made their firstborn wail.

Around eighteen months old, so I'm told, it all changed again.

Ten years later, Dr Rowe explained to his 'little student with a thirst for medical language' that a baby's prefrontal cortex alters dramatically around this time. In layman's terms, rather than just being a passive sponge, I began 'interfacing'. From my parents' point of view, this meant humour and laughter could creep back into the house. I no longer cried, nor was scared or overwhelmed by humour or the various noises laughter makes. Fascination replaced fear. It's around this point, two years old or so, that hazy memories fizzle and hiss. I can mark it in my mind because of my red football blanket. Curious: my father detested football, as I soon would. Looking back it was probably a vain attempt at implanting regular boy behaviour, diluting what I had become: a serious and strangely adult toddler – at least in their minds. I stared now, you see. Not just in the way a two- or three-year-old watches adults with that sweet innocent fixation, no, more like a steel penetration. I can't pretend that remembering it doesn't give me satisfaction, but at the time it did me no favours. It scared people.

Granny Davids described it well: 'You know – it was the sudden laughter. When it broke out in a room, your head would ... wrench round,' she said one Visiting Saturday a couple of years ago. 'I've seen a lot of babies in my time, you know, a lot, but I have never seen one move like you: just your head and not a muscle of your body. I found it sweet, it was, you know, like a little owl or something. That's what we nicknamed you – the Owl, remember? But, crikey, it did put the willies up people,' and she laughed, 'but sod them!'

We shall call this then, courtesy of Granny Davids, my Owlhead phase; the phase which led to my first meeting with Dr Rowe.

The axis of my Owlhead gradually increased, neck muscles stretching, allowing more and more rotation – nearly 180 degrees in its final stages. I did all the usual, sat, played, or crawled, just never laughed. This could have been ignorable, but if someone made a joke or joyful noise my head would violently revolve, clicking to a stop at the exact location of the source. Needless to say, this phenomenon tended to chill the mood for the adults; some people took genuine fright. After six months of Owlhead, my Auntie Lena stopped visiting altogether. Uncle Jeff used shit jokes to make himself feel comfortable; but of course that only made me swivel towards him even more. I'll say this for Uncle Jeff and Auntie Jemima – as spooked as they were by me, they never stopped visiting, and the best thing about that was Becky.

I think I can use the verb 'enjoy' to describe those early memories, sitting together in my bright blue playpen. My first image: our nakedness – our innocent associations and exchanges of pre-word prattle. I cannot have been older than two or three, but metallic sensations of savouring her were already sharp. Some would have it that certain types of love are for adults only. I know what I felt, and I mean in a physical sense – a version of actual Love. Straight away, something very like it at least.

When my parents, Uncle Jeff and Auntie Jemima tickled and prodded us, I found myself absorbed by Becky's reactions; in fact, she was one of the few anomalies of my Owlhead phase. My head did not swivel to the jokers themselves, but fixed on their audience: Becky. Maybe it was these first experiences which branded a lethal ambition deep in my consciousness. I did not know it then, but I was very different. Bestowed with something. A gift which in effect was negative: to know the precise causes of the laughter and joy which I could never myself provoke. I had to find a way to create; and more powerfully than anyone before me; teach all those who toyed with the candle-flame of wit, who wasted and puffed at it; those who let it flicker and die.

I run ahead. For now, it was about Becky. Maybe I had taken laughter and changed it, swapped humour for her. But I don't think so, for I have no memory of not being in love with Becky; and we sat in our nakedness, she smiling and giggling, and I watching, the little owl, the strange lonely bird.

If it had been only a swivelling head and blinkless staring, perhaps I would have been tagged with the less stigmatizing label 'gifted child'. I could have even settled for 'troubled child'. But my mannerisms, coupled with an inability to smile, unrelenting no matter what they did, however many hamsters, puppies, kittens, or toys were plopped at my feet, left people repulsed, fearful. I became a 'problem'.

I was certainly younger than ten, when I realized exactly what it was. People were repelled by me as a thing essentially inhuman. Later on, when I began writing and reviewing, I came to realize that, however painful, their reactions were quite reasonable. What? Is it pitiful that I loathed myself so much that I empathized with those who rejected me? Laughter and joy are not just components of a full person. They're fundamental building blocks. Smiling is one of the basic evidences that a *being* is indeed *human*. A one-hour-old baby will already give proof of its emotional fullness: looking, grabbing, and within weeks – smiling. If one of those functions is absent, especially that most sapient one, parents may reject the child. Not being able to smile made me a robot creature; a simulacrum, almost everything there; but ultimately a sort of cold nonthing.

From my fourth birthday, the bad memories begin. By bad, I mean that incidents were watermarked with a burgeoning self-awareness. Relatives' arms would reach out to embrace me, faces smiling, buffooning, but the warmth faded when people were met with my blank, head-jerking stare. Most would physically recoil, a pure tactile denial.

Perhaps because of our identical ages, afternoons with Becky were a double pleasure. There was the emotional rush I experienced from simply being in her company, but through her I also enjoyed a kind of vicarious acceptance, thrilling fugues of belonging. I could go so far as to say she helped me feign what I *should* be. The more we sat together, the more we played (yes, I did play, just never smiled as I crashed Tonka cars and danced dollies), the more I would ape her. Inevitably though, this shadowing moved me from enjoying her into dependency. She *was* amazing with me. She must have noticed the contrast with our other young friends, yet we were inseparable companions for our first five years. Of course, when school started, and certainly by the time we were ten, it all changed again.

Things were not helped by the coincidence of two massive events: the birth of Cooper, and the start of my formal education. It took less than two years of state school for me to take the predictable role of 'lonely child'. We were at the same primary school, same class; yet my relationship with Becky began to cool. Not that this made much difference to me. I did not know the phrase, but I was 'in love' with my cousin Becky, and I stayed 'in love' with her; all through my teens, my twenties, and right up until the end. I still love her now.

The Owlhead phase stopped suddenly one morning over Ready Brek. My mother, heavily pregnant, had been on the phone joking with a friend. She let out a sharp piercing laugh, cupping her mouth as she realized her slip; but my head did not jerk. Instead, I slowly turned my whole body towards her and simply blinked, a slow, eloquent blink. She dropped the receiver, launched at me, sobbing as she massaged my flesh into hers. That happiness. A magic. Unreal, amazing. That was a good day. It led to some good weeks. I'm not sure I fully understood what I had done to please them – but the new control I had over my body, over their smiles – it thrilled me. Even my father began interacting. For a cruelly brief period of time, we pretended togetherness. The thought of the coming baby, my 'progress' – these were weeks in which harmony was easily counterfeited. It was the last month of my being the capital of their empire. 'You're our centre, Benjamin.' Yet – and I may only have been five – I felt the real course of their energy. Both of them kissing me, yes, loving me, and I loving them back; but I could feel the flow. It went unremittingly towards the perfect stretched hill of my mother's abdomen and the unborn brother inside it.

3

The Stage

Dominic Wray sucked the dregs of his usual latte from a brand-embossed styrofoam cup; not to efficiently drain the vessel, but to simulate the air of a tense intellectual. He flicked his eyes from his cup to Miranda Love, hamming at power, bating. I, as usual, had been almost invisible during the meeting.

'But is it based in actual fucking fact?' he said.

He rocked his chair back onto two legs, spreading his thighs in full alpha male display. His belt had ridden higher than usual, its tawdry buckle clipping the edge of his solid-wood desk.

Dominic Wray was a squat yet dapper man; a compact, buffed autocrat in his late forties. His office was a glass cube, the centre of Ents – our department within the cultural dissector, and often mean journal, the *Review*. Clear panels of logoed glass enabled the infantry to look on and witness Dominic Wray's greatness from a clinical distance. He possessed the only real furniture on the floor; no doubt all part of his scheme to contrast his domain with ours. On one glass wall, a printed cut-out of a fireplace; above his desk, real antlers. He enjoyed being perceived as kitschy and off-kilter – a free-thinker. Everything else on floor seventeen was a bland version of late 1990s Scandinavian minimalism, just the odd concession of etiolated yucca or doomed bonsai.

On Dominic's oak work-station only a square-inch of wood remained visible. The surface was covered in an orgy of writing briefs, photo contact sheets, and piles of CVs which kept pace with the stream of broken rookies who leaked into the lift and flowed out of the building for ever.

Dominic licked his lips and removed inch-thick Cutler & Gross frames from his pudgy exfoliated face. I found the juxtaposition of obesity and grooming really a sort of injustice against nature.

'Agh!' he said, trying for his usual cancerous cocktail of doubt and apathy. 'Do you see? Isn't it just bollocks?'

There was a dangerous pause in which Miranda planned her response. She had to get this article away, a simple, sparky-yet-weighty, write-itself sort of assignment that would ease us into the New Year. Breezy discussion soon blew into a storm.

'Not this, Dom, please,' she said.

'Not what? Have you seen the effing circulation fig-ures?' He did this: put felt edges on swearing.

'No. I've been in twenty minutes this year.'

'Still in Crimbo mode?'

'Eff you, Dominic.'

'Let's start the New Year with a blazer, shall we?'

'Please, Dom. Do you want to go with it or not?' This was almost shouted.

Colleagues stared in. Chaz and Ali openly smirked, leering and gesturing when they could get away with it.

Whenever a Dominic Wray meeting went this way, I found our lighting made it worse. A misguided attempt at minimalism in 2001 had plunged the whole Ents floor into an era of strip-lit epileptic glare, and Dominic's glass den had come off worst. It also just missed the edge of a much-needed air vent, and this morning the odour of bad-mood breath, secret farts and toner ink was potent. His little room was a bad place within a bad place.

'But ... is ... it ... factual?' Dominic pushed.

He replaced his spectacles and crushed the styrofoam cup. A bubble of milky froth landed on his amethyst cuff-link. He looked at it – looked at me looking at it. He knew this was the sort of thing I would observe. I absorbed every molecule of the potentially humorous, that's why I had the job, why he found me sinister and essential in equal measure.

'Come on, Miranda,' he said, softening slightly – a little

irony maybe. He flicked away the latte globule with his index finger. 'Of course it's not factual: it's academic toss. All I'm saying is this: January stuff should be about ... home truths.' He always did that – made up crap rules and spoke them as though they were axioms.

'Yes, Dom ... but it'll make a bloody interesting feature ... and funny,' said Miranda. (I thought then of how I had fucked her in the research corridor at the Christmas party.)

Why the recent strengthening of the link between funniness and sexual attractiveness? It's got worse (or better, depending on your hard-on) since I've been in here the last few years. This pathetic attempt to make jesters into rock stars. The glib use of the word 'gig' – when what we mean is show. I think it's the paranoid attempts of middle-brow comedians such as Jay Conway to elevate their pedestrian ejaculations to art or iconic status. The magazines suggest that the girls fall for it. Horrendous. This is why the critic is essential. History will thank us for our corrections.

Miranda recrossed her legs. I felt a rush of lust, like icing punched from a piping-bag.

'Dom ...'

'You do understand, Miranda. Upstairs laughs in my effing face when we print tripe like this – there's no ... substance.'

'But it won't be tripe.'

'Well it's not real, Mindy, not *real*.'

'Yes, it is bullshitty, but it's not bullshit.' She shrank

back into the leather chair. Many times had we all suppli-
cated from this seat. 'I thought we take the urban fable
angle – acknowledge it as myth and all that, research the
arse out of it.'

'What's the idea?'

'"Fatal Amusement" – that what it's called, apparently.'
She shot me a glance, showing Dominic the concept had
boffin accreditation. 'The phenomenon of dying from
pleasure, laughter in the original myth – but fuck it.
Anyway, laughter is a biggie this time of year. Comedy
clubs do massive business with seasonal depressives. We
could take it off on a whole New Year resolution, over-
indulgence tangent via comedy.'

'Go on ...'

'Well, there's the ancient history for a start ...'

'I'm not saying it *can't* work,' said Dominic, sensing
potential, backpedalling.

'We chart the history of it. We *could* go to Aristophanes
and all that – but I reckon we focus on modern touch-
points.'

'Writers?'

'Writers and comedians.'

'Comedians as writers,' I put in, but was ignored. I was
always the passive character in these scenes. I had learned
this was expected of me.

'Most famously,' continued Miranda, 'you've got the
Monty Python sketch at one end, the Foster-Wallace novel
at the other – then we could go—'

'Who?' he barked, ready to bad-mouth upstarts or unknowns.

'David Foster-Wallace, the novelist, essay chap.'

'Shit. Yes. Of course.'

She slid her backside forward in her seat. I found myself pondering whether she had fucked me two weeks before out of sympathy or curiosity or both. It would definitely be one of the two. I'd had sex eleven times in thirty-nine years.

She tucked a strand of red hair behind her ear. 'He wrote this massive novel in '96.'

'About?'

'About a film that puts people into a coma when they watch it.'

'Hmm.'

'He's an American.'

'Exactly.'

'I could probably get an interview with him,' she said.

I felt an irrational spasm as I wondered if she'd slept with Foster-Wallace at the *New Jersey Review of Books* party. Strange I should have felt jealousy – the thing with me and Miranda was truly stillborn. It had been a silly escapade. Sex was a trinket. Yes, I knew love when I felt it, but sex, the physical act of joining bodies, was so gimcrack, so foreign, that to practise it was a sort of extreme sport; now and again, for the rush, just to say I had. Well, maybe it went further than that – almost; but Miranda was so normal, so harmonious. I felt like a small stone around her. A dead boy. It was a Freudian fuck.

'Maybe John Cleese too? But we can, er, well, forget Palin,' she said.

'That wasn't my fault,' said Dominic, lips whitening. We all had the same flashback of Palin's outstretched arm, the closed fist, Dominic's bloodied nose, the commotion, the legal complications.

'Cleese'll be better anyway. He led that sketch,' said Miranda.

'Effing great silly walks and all that – bit of January bathos for the punters,' blush receding, 'with a smidge of cultural toss lobbed in, a nice bit of that.'

The utter charlatan. Silver-spooned fake fuck.

'Uh-huh,' she said: victory.

'OK, OK. Sold. Run with it, just sprint with it, Mindy. First draft?' He returned his chair onto all-fours and stroked his return key. His inbox began boasting his workload in cold beeps.

'Tuesday – no later than Wednesday.'

'Possible to make this Saturday then?'

'Precisely.'

'OK – coolio. Coolio.' This was the type of language which did him no favours. 'Two days. Make it funny as well, Mindy. It's about humour, *humourrrr*.'

At last, Dominic looked at me.

Miranda followed the gaze. 'I mean, naturally I'm suggesting Benjamin and I work as a team on this. The Stiller thing's ready to print. I'm happy we've wrapped copy and legals.'

'You don't need to give it the old Mindy glaze?' Dominic asked. And again I was invisible, insulted.

'No, I think Benjamin nailed that one,' she lied. She had already tweaked my copy.

'Yes, I bet it's full of your android warmth, Benny boy – did you write it in binary code?' His joke misfired, too harsh and spiteful to catch the small audience. I watched it hang there for a moment undetonated before vanishing.

Miranda was embarrassed. 'I'd really like him to help me on this, Dom. It's one area he knows inside out.'

'Yes, yes, OK – take the Ben-bot 5,000 then. Load him, program him in,' Dominic chuckled, gently herding the gag through this time. Miranda joined in with a perfunctory snort. I watched the joke unpack itself before me. I experienced the thing as I sometimes do – in a clear visual way. The suffix 'bot' spelt itself out in a sort of green vapour; actually floated up onto the ceiling where my name was spelt out too. The gases fused and data streamed through me like this:

Subject: Benjamin White
Description: a full human being known for inability
to express emotions of happiness.
'Bot': a word-part indicating an android, a built thing.
'Bot': suffixed to someone's name creating a neat,
compact, nounal feeling.

A commercial-product-type sound.
Processes: sudden condensation, contraction
and wordplay.
Result: amusement. Humour.

Doing what I did, I had learned to control and suppress this sense. In my early days at the *Review*, if someone made a good-enough joke, I would almost relapse into Owlhead. It became essential to occlude the visual part of my gift, but some days I would still feel it a half-dozen times. It wasn't exactly painful, more shocking, breathtaking. Even office banter could cause it; quick and twisting through me like a screw on the end of a drill, and in a moment, in a second, gone.

'Look at him, he's *loving* that, he's loving it,' said Dominic, pointing me out as though I was a disabled child building a sandcastle. I fantasized his house burning, or perhaps a lump on his testicle.

Finally, we escaped the foetid cube. He shouted after us not to spend too much fucking money; another endearing trait, his obsession with cost-effective arts correspondence. To Dominic Wray, art was a commodity, and our commentaries upon it, the shop in which art was displayed for consumption.

'He's such a tosser,' said Miranda.

'He is,' I confirmed, 'a tosser.'

She smiled.

I did not, could not.

'I'm sorry, Benjamin.'

The apology was as much for Dominic as for her; her going along with the status quo: Benjamin produced the dull data, Miranda made it sparkle. Well, I suppose Dominic was right. My comedic insights may have been the most technically dazzling on Fleet Street, perhaps I was the most feared man in comedy, but without 'the Mindy glaze' my reviews had a surgical, automated feel. More simply, they were bad writing. Take the biologist Bill Hamilton. Never heard of him? That's because he couldn't write; yet he was the most talented post-evolutionary biologist of the twentieth century. Ask Dawkins. It's strange, even though I was the one who wrote the reviews, I didn't struggle to see exactly what was wrong when I read them back. Yet I could not *fix* the pieces. My inability to *feel* humour continued through to my writing.

One cannot write about humour without feeling. Another odd thing: when I write in my diary about love, if I rant about anger, I'm a more than passable writer. But when I attempt to explore the very thing I see clearly, that makes me breathe and is my life, the words come dead and mechanical.

For what it's worth, I believe British comedy needs no more punk-jeaned boys with chrysanthemum-hair strutting their vacuous stuff on some channel or other. I always saw it as part of my calling to disperse these egotistical and fatuous belches of cable television gas while they were still at the live comedy stage. As I say, technically I was perfect at marking out what was wrong with an act, but it took Miranda to make it palatable – publishable.

Take the Jay Conway (bleached thistly coif, Indie T-shirt wearer) review. The gig was at the loathsome Comedy Bat Night, the Cricketers, Tooting. I typed my version on the evening of the gig in six minutes flat. Miranda's edit took half an hour the next morning. I'll admit, as a reviewing team we were the fastest, perhaps the best. But it was me who was the feared and the hated, and my power was great. It feels good to remember that.

12 March, Benjamin White

Can't deny it. The deafening noise as Jay Conway finishes his set indicates one thing: the room has great love for him. And this in a way is the problem. What is the aetiology of that attachment? Is it his use of objectively defined comedic skills; or is it his annoying prancing? Very much the latter. During his set he has used only the mere rudiments of observational technique: Socratic false observation, sub-Jerry Laycock re-observed call-back, and Eltonian sociological pointing. He supplied a cheap 'upper' to his audience, drugging them to provoke laughter. That drug was choreography. Not comedy. But mime. He certainly did not *stimulate* my laughter, certainly not when he used his Easyjet call-back *four* times – a basic error, contravening the structural rule of three hard-wired in the Western symbology. That fourth time, he sensed the clumsiness, and drew a studied Indie-boy fringe across his face as though to undercut the budget-airline routine. His final routine about the female orgasm was so unashamedly textbook that its success was entirely down to his by now banal 'manic' energy and face-pulling, and even then its vacuity rudely poked through. Alas, of course, this worked on the audience. His elastic attempts to mock biology caused the usual cathectic laughter from the onlookers, resulting in them closing their ears to the gaping flaws of his logic. His final goodbye was this reviewer's biggest disappointment. He did not bid the audience farewell but instead looked into the middle distance, as though practising for a cable television camera. I rest my case. B.W.

March 13. Miranda Love

Some comics you love, others force you to love them. And meteoric Jay Conway (*Stars of Stars*, *Comedy Raffle* and so on . . .) is defiantly the latter. Wild energy and fierce facial contortions had the audience in stitches within his first few syllables. It's this innate funniness, however, that lets him down. Beneath his orang-utan prancing is a dearth of original material. Easy clichés and tired stereotypes colour his stock offerings on Easyjet and the female orgasm, but the audience just didn't seem to care. As his set progressed, technical errors crept in too, with an amateurish over-egging of his punchlines, but once again, with a knowing look and a toss of his tousled coif, the charm won through. The fact remains, however, that underneath the silly, latexy grimacing is a little boy begging us to put him on MTV. You know what – perhaps that unoriginal portal should suck him in, because for all his hilarious raspberry-blowing, here is a comedian completely lacking in originality. M.L.

Oh, Miranda.

Miranda Love, a thirty-six-year-old almost-married woman from Tunbridge Wells, living in Clapham. Neither stunningly beautiful, nor satisfyingly ugly; not even plain, just female. Brash, clever, extremely red-headed, erotically fat without being wobbly; breasts enormous enough to have been multiply christened with sexist euphemisms. She smoked too; often ate three hunks of cheese at lunchtimes, and had dogmatic addictions to pretentious Italian films (for gender-bending effect), Martin Amis, and London musicals – most unfathomably, *The Phantom of the Opera*.

I joined the *Review* in 1982. She was my instant companion, mentor, defender and eventually 'fuck-buddy' (her noun, not mine – a classic Miranda attempt to diminish real feelings with jokey vernacular). I think part of it was the toneless gaps in my personality – she found these 'quirky': the way I stared at people when they laughed, the way people laughed when I stared. But what endeared, perhaps impressed her most, was my 'boffin weird ability' to deconstruct a joke or comedic routine in seconds. As well as being the only reason I had a job at the *Review*, it also made for a rather good party piece.

At the Christmas do, the Ents team had been huddled for some time. People throwing anecdotes above the music. Chaz Gladwell was finishing off yet another story in which he had sex.

'I didn't even want to bang her.'

'Christ,' Miranda barked, but with affection, 'and the intern was dying for you, wasn't she.'

'I don't go for consent, I go for attrition.'

A roar of laughter. Rape more or less. Laughter at rape. I spat an olive stone close to his square-toed Ted Baker shoes.

'Lovely Benjamin,' he said, 'give us a joke.'

He meant take a joke, and pick it apart.

'Go. Just one.'

The group jeered, dancing on the borders of peer pressure and larks.

'Come on, Benjamin – old lady on an icy dog poo,' he said and return-fired an olive stone into an ashtray on the table next to me. His pointy purple Christmas hat twitched to a pissed angle.

I placed my punch on the floor, closed my eyes, and staccatoed: 'Old lady, extreme end of sociological groupings; walking, strong expectation of perambulatory normalness; slipping undercuts our projection of old lady's walk and surprises the brain energies resulting in a cathectic release. Dog shit, comic symbol – strong associations with childhood mishap, intense socially rejected stench. Slipping – quick, clown-like motion when lower body precedes the upper. All of these elements converge to produce a synaptic charge that demands release, release as laughter.'

I opened my eyes. The small crowd exploded into drunken applause. They had seen me do this many times, but alcohol heightened by a mild desire to mock boosted its reception. The clapping subsided, and without warning Ali Kemal-Collins, a man educated to MA level, stood up with just one testicle pushed out of his fly. Highly literate adults were reduced to tears of laughter. Not me, of course. Miranda, shaking her head in faux disgust, swallowed her giggles and pulled me aside.

'Hey. Benjamin. You're bloody brilliant, you know,' she said. And after that, we fucked.

I do not apologize for my Miranda-esque use of the verb 'fuck'. It's an area of comedic debate I take seriously – use of fuck. Not only is it the correct word here, but I will brazenly continue with it whenever neurologically appropriate. Yes, 'neurologically'. Dr Rowe once explained the reason swearing had such strong resonances for me. Profanities promote neural activity in a different part of the cortex. Recently, in one of my permitted magazines, I saw fMRI images from Peter Singer's research. They more or less prove Dr Rowe's assertions. It seems the brain's language centre has evolved its own escape valve – a whistling aperture which lets off pressure in an attempt to avert physical violence.

So Miranda and I had a nice *fuck*. It certainly wasn't 'love-making', nor was it a biological 'sexual intercourse' just for release – this was a violently charged erotic encounter; even if the eroticism came with sympathy, pity. I'm sure it was largely alcohol which promoted her compassion to desire.

As we lay upon my padded winter jacket behind the 1998 archive, she climbed onto me telling me, once again, that I was brilliant. Brilliant. It was this icy word which marred the experience. 'Brilliant' is a loaded word for my sort, you see. In its nicer colloquial sense, in that teenagerish northern cutesy sense – someone can be 'brill'; someone you love, laugh with, take joy from. Brilliant in its other sense is like a diamond – flawless, hard and admirable; clever, neat – fascinating. I am sure this was what she meant. At the time of course I just lay there, my silent gratitude neutralizing her pity. Sex which could have been carnal ended up maternal, tender. She must have regretted it straight away. I expected as much. After the Christmas break, however, she was open and affectionate; not a cloaking niceness, not fake or compensatory, but a straightforward, warm acknowledgement that things had altered. We had fucked. It did not mean we were in love, but we were closer. Things would be different, but not too much. It's a shame that she had to go in the end. As I write this, it occurs she may have been the one to save me. As it turned out, *I* released *her*. I released all of them. The main appeal of Miranda was how refreshing she was. By refreshing I mean the opposite of Becky.

Miranda coughed, bringing me back to the present moment. I'd been staring at her breasts.

'Hello ... serial killer.'

'Sorry.'

'You're cool with doing the doggy work on the fatal pleasure piece?' She stabbed at pieces of ready-prepared pineapple and Cheddar with a midget fork. 'It's well up your street, nay?'

'Yes. It will be fascinating. Home ground,' I said, nodding my head diagonally. I used this gesture where others would use an everyday smile for mechanical reassurance.

'Keep it real world – but use literature for consistent examples, background stuff – rather than vice versa. Don't let the old dissection dominate ... Benjamin-bot.' She smiled, breaking eye contact a fraction too slowly.

It was a vain request, we both knew it, but I told her I agreed.

Oh, the Research Chest, that lovely box of useless details which made me feel secure. Its books, files, and preliminary notes had been moved in preparation for the Christmas party. This would mean poking around Chaz's work-pod on my first day back. Not good. I felt a familiar social eczema prickle over me.

Catching my expression, Miranda panicked – I might be put out because of Dominic. 'Ignore the turd,' she said and went into one of her set-pieces about his pig-headedness; a diatribe that also threw in the repellent image of piss-dribble often observed on his pristine grey Paul Smith trousers.

'He is a wanker of the highest order, Benny!'

Tuning out, I found myself drawn into the criss-crossing narratives of the large, framed family picture on my desk. I played an old game. Pretending the group were strangers. What would I make of this congregation of six motley humans standing in front of Tadworth Chapel on Christmas Eve? My willowy father in Christmas sweater and corduroys, sporting oppressive grin, arm around my brother Cooper (matching sweater, warm smile), the oily closeness of their bond leaking from the tableau. My portly mother in pressed cream trouser suit, a concessionary arm reaching around my waist, a firm grasp on my father. A minute gap, and to our right Uncle Jeff, thin, bland, frightened (and not that he knew it) with two months to live, his head slightly turned towards solid Auntie Jemima, looking like a strong Russian peasant, and in a Sutton high street khaki dress. And then of course, just in front of them, laughing, open-mouthed, moistness of lips visible, dark-chocolate locks cascading over festive purple woollens: Becky. My Becky, or rather, Pierre Fourier's Becky of eight years' happy marriage, ten years' love. Cliché conglomerate Pierre Fourier, tall, handsome, maned, did-things-in-the-City. Pierre Fourier, owner and purveyor of all that is firm and forty-something and certain and male, including in fact the camera which he was holding when this shot was expertly captured. I would often use this family portrait as a stealthy way to stare at Becky. Even editorial assistant Benjamin White could not be attacked for having a family picture on his desk. No one would suspect me of being in love with my own cousin, and naturally I never spoke of it. Especially not to Miranda. It was the kind of thing Chaz and friends would have gone to town on. The kind of in-joke that even Dominic would have surreptitiously enjoyed.

As Miranda semaphored about Dominic's prejudice against musicals, I studied Becky's green eyes; her small triangular face, her nervous grateful happiness, her tiny hand clasping a red-felt tote bag (it had generous slices of Waitrose chocolate log inside). As for me, I'm not smiling, obviously. But neither am I completely *un*happy; my outfit, green and bright, flat red nose.

Now and again I see a photograph of myself and spot an ambiguity in my face; not much of course, but nonetheless a sort of fledgling happiness – I find it there sometimes, I'm sure I do. I want to.

My head is angled, rather pathetically, I suppose, towards Becky. It reminded me of a ridiculous phase I went through in my late teens; when I was first out of the Centre, shortly after the trip to Venice. I used to have a formally scheduled weekly weep at Becky's beauty, at the impossibility of fully knowing her. Can you imagine: a man that cannot smile sobbing over a woman's loveliness. Do you realize how obscene that is? My crying was dismal. Not that I ever wept before her, God no, nor in front of anyone else; but my mawkish air must have been noticed, repellent. I repulsed myself. Maybe I was simply in rebellion. You hear it all the time. The posh kid who wants to blacken his elite family by smoking crack at Eton. The lefty son born to the racist father – making ethnic friends just to spite the fat alpha that spawned him. Well, I was surrounded by love. By a smiling encouraging love which could not fix me. I think over time I came to associate unconditional love with sadness. My mother rocking me back and forth, telling me all would be well, when the opposite was true. All happiness came with an assurance that nothing would change. The safety followed by the big wide world.

I was doomed to be in love with someone who could never love me. The winter of my great depression. Luckily, the Argentinian invasion of the Falkland Islands saw my father called into journalistic service, saving my crisis from being detected, or even worse discussed and fixed. Even my mother's usual scrutiny abated for a while as scribes and academics gathered in the kitchen to talk shop. It gave me the space I needed to recover. In the end Mother went off freelancing for the newish *Greater London Reads*, turning out some surprisingly sharp yet chirpy cod-liberal commentaries about Borges's work. Father began ejaculating a series of Galtieri cartoons; their narrative lynchpin being a crudely imagined divorce sex comedy between Thatcher and the General.

'Benjamin ... Hello ... day-dreamer ... Where's the Stiller copy saved?' said Miranda.

'What?'

'I've asked you three times.'

I emailed it, volunteering to proofread any amendments.

'No. Get started on the research for this new thing. And go easy on the ancient stuff.'

I argued 'ancient stuff' might just be the perfect way in. I was being modest, I *knew* it, felt it. She baulked, I stood firm. The usual dance.

'The piece needs just a touch of the Greeks. I've had an interesting philosopher suggested by Senate House, a Stoic chap.'

'A what?' she demurred, only half-heartedly.

'Chrysippus of Soli,' I explained – an easy and colourful way into the meat of the feature. How did I not ask myself: why this Greek writer? Why drawn to his name? Why not the more obvious Aristophanes – something about *The Frogs* perhaps?

'Yes. The all-famous Chrysi-something. Who the fuck?'

'He fed wine-soaked figs to his donkey and then died laughing at the consequences. It's where the whole myth started.'

'Riiight. Yes. Hilarious. OK. Well our lot love a bit of

pretend clever, don't they? Maybe get your dad to knock out a donkey-fig cartoon,' she said. 'Go on then. Go Greek it up.'

And there it was – a little call to action, combining with my idea, dispatching me to a forgotten corner of Senate House library.

'I'm going with the Senate stuff rather than the British Library – less pillaged section on the Stoics.'

'Go, go, travel by taxi, treat yourself to lunch – collect some receipts. Spend money. The fucker,' she said. Her witticism gave me a mild tingling data-rush. The casual throwaway cosmopolitan tone mixed in with rebellion. The juxtaposition was light, delicious.

I do not entirely know why I did what I did next. Perhaps some weird intuition of the discovery I was about to make. All I know for sure is that I flipped the photograph of my family face-down so firmly that I cracked the glass. And no, I don't think this was just about Becky. It was more. It was all of them. It was everything. This year would be *my* year, for *me*, and damn everyone else. Perhaps it was this electric egoism which caused things to get so out-of-hand. I refuse the category of 'unrequited lover gone loopy'. Christ, I went thirty-six years holding it in. And anyway, our connection had been violently broken the previous Christmas – when that accursed cracked photo was taken. Yes, I admit, by then the worst of it was over, but what happened on Boxing Day was the crushing, awful final act.

Thirty-six years of biding my time and enjoying her secretly; of sustaining myself on sisterly hugs and kisses; the coconut smell of her when she leaned in and ruffled my hair. I ruined it, disgraced myself, gave away my secret inner passions. I shall never drink sherry again.

It would have been easier to forgive Becky's reaction to my confession of love if she hadn't geysered those tears and fetched Pierre in scream and panic. The sobs belched forth and she fled the room whinnying. My left cheek zinged with the hot slap of rejected love. I buttoned my cardigan, and awaited the inevitable. There is something awful about mixing violence with cardigans. Thankfully, my parents, Granny Davids, my aunt and uncle were all out in the gazebo in their paper hats prodding at some new gadget of my father's. As far as I know they never did find out what happened next.

Pierre appeared before me, Becky nuzzling into his chest like a broken pigeon. I was frozen, idiotically frozen, purple Christmas hat still on head. He alternated between soothing words for her and scornful noises at me. His lips were tight and pale, like worms being pulled in half by schoolboys. After thirty seconds of Mexican stand-off, he detached himself from Becky, zapped across the conservatory, and frogmarched me into the utility room, angry fingers digging into the sweaty pouch of my armpit.

He spoke in a white-hot monotone. 'Not only 'ave you offended me in the greatest possible way, but what you suggested to my wife – your cousin, is illegal in some countries.' His fake English accent faded, the original Swiss notes swelling up and angering his vowels. I blocked the next few sentences of his lecture, pondering instead on the surrealism of Neil Khan. An artist. He'll take the word 'badger' and repeat it one hundred times until the audience cannot breathe. Some critics attack surrealism. How can simply wearing a horse's head, or referencing a squirrel be funny? Where is the narrative, where is the idea? But they miss the point. The employment of the surreal image *is* the narrative. The repetition of nothings takes on a shape, a structure. Cadence and personality bring the joke to life. Those lost are soon found as Neil Kahn comes on dressed as a knight and gives a talk on jelly. 'Jelly. Have you ever said that word in a lift, for no reason?' Sublime, Mr Kahn. We see it, we feel the incongruity – and against our wills we are in his story.

Reluctantly I was pulled back into the conservatory, to reality.

'Well?' Pierre said, small specks of Tipp-Ex saliva on lower lip.

'Well what?' I could still see badgers, horse-heads and jelly.

'What have you got to say, you cunt?' He pronounced it 'coont'.

'I'm sorry. I was thinking of jelly.'

He took one step back and broke my nose with a single punch. It was a mechanical, peremptory strike. No shouting,

no flailing – a crisp, measured right hook – coolly and fero-
ciously done. I fell into Mother's raffia chair, my nostrils
gaily pumping thick raspberry ooze. Panic dappled the face
of the golden son-in-law. Snapping from his testosterone
trance, he pulled me to my feet.

'Get some cotton wool,' he said to Becky, her mouth
gaping.

Together they patched my face. For some reason I felt
the urge to urinate. Pierre realized what he had done. I
could have shopped him, but of course none of us wanted
my parents to know what had happened, so we hatched a
plan. Pierre took a sodden cotton-wool pad and wiped it
on the glass of a French window. Next, smoothing back his
steel mane, he began concocting a cover story, explaining it
to Becky and me as though we were children being taught
Connect Four. Hearing the others returning along the
garden path, he lifted me to my feet. My mother was first
into the house, gasping with horror when she saw my
swollen purpling face.

'Casualty coming through!' shouted Pierre jovially as he
guided me through the dining room, past the traditional
Boxing Day buffet and into the downstairs bathroom.

'What the hell happened?' said my father.

'The culprit is French not Swiss, Graham,' replied
Pierre – Surrey accent almost restored. He pointed to the
blood-smeared French windows with which I had
'collided'.

It was a clever joke. Even in my two types of agony the

mixture of the political with the everyday produced a firm coarse tickle; like being licked by a cat.

Maybe I was hoping for sympathy, some sort of weird Münchausen's attention, but of course all that happened was laughter. That's all my parents knew: good-natured laughter. The hilarious information passed back to Granny Davids, Uncle Jeff and Aunt Jemima. How they all hooted at the idea of cold, unlaughing, purple-faced Benjamin running full pelt into triple-glazing.

'Oh, Benjamin,' said my mother, 'exactly how much sherry have you had?'

'Too much,' I replied, applying a new clod of cotton wool to my nose.

Another wave of mirth broke over them. Hilarity settled into chuckling before rising once more, building, lifting, then finally thinning into contented chortles. Even Pierre and Becky smiled. I did not. I just stood there. It was the end of the affair.

I crossed the office feeling as though someone had filled my legs with cement. A 4 a.m. feeling. I needed documents from Ali and Chaz's pod. Why should I have to tackle these creatures? They were having a debate, supposedly ironic, but in reality a thin veil for the vile things they meant and felt.

'Why are some men breast-men?' said Ali, festively enhanced gut nudging grossly against his keyboard, even depressing the space bar.

'Because tits are lovely?' replied Chaz, a dry vole of a man. The final shades of japing disappeared from his face and his eyes narrowed to *Crimewatch* identikit slits of misogyny.

Neither had any work to do. The first week of January was notoriously slow for new film. Plus, the pair of quasi-laddish workaholics had written all their DVD box-set reviews in December. Their work-pod smelt of Lucozade, stale bacon and Christmas gift fragrances. A strip-light above Chaz's head flickered, setting him in gargoyle relief.

'What do you think, Benjamin?' asked Ali, noticing me at last. As well as being fat in the wrong way, he had a tremendous hook nose, a genetic bequest from his Turkish father. From my position on the floor it obscured his tiny eyes.

I shunted three boxes of junk. I would extract my research quickly and flee. 'About what?' I said.

'About breasts? Tiiiiiiits.'

I pinched out my document, a dot-matrix printout of sourced-material locations on the sublimely musty seventh floor of Senate House.

'Well?' one of them said.

Standing up, I felt painfully conscious of my cream trousers and formal shirt. 'I have no opinion,' I said.

'He has "no opinion" on breasts, Chaz.'

'I'm a breast-man,' said Chaz, slimy and wry.

'Come on, Benjiii?' pushed Ali. How could a man with such acumen for film be such an unmitigated prick at real life? The answer, of course, was that this was mostly for effect, to bother me maybe. Sometimes they called me the Aphid, sometimes the Automaton.

'Ben-bot can't compute tits,' said Chaz in robot voice.

'What about arse,' said Ali. 'Call me old-fashioned but I love a nice shitter.'

'I thought that was the Greeks, not the Turks,' said Chaz.

'All women are Cyprus to me.'

They both fell about laughing, culminating in a high-five. I suppose it was a good joke – precise, metallic, pointed – with an obverse of misogynistic filth. I processed it quickly, like a cheap mint.

'I'm off to Senate House,' I announced, grabbing my satchel and making for the exit.

'You can't leave us guessing, Benjiii,' said Chaz.

'Yes. Come on, Auto – which is it?'

I rounded on Ali. 'It's an easy question to answer, Ali Khemal.' I aspirated his surname.

'Really?'

'It's rather a contradiction,' I said. 'I love the very thing I now loathsomely stare at – a fat cunt.'

If I could have smiled then, I would have. There was the tiniest gap before they began laughing, and a half-unified giggle at that. It let me know I'd stung.

Now and again I can make a good joke. It's always probability more than design, but still, occasionally it happens. Agh – the paradoxical side-effect of my 'gift'. Not only can I never experience laughter, but neither can I form decent witticisms or passable jokes. I attempt them, oh, I attempt them – but it all just rushes and confuses in my mind; thoughts pile upon thoughts, endless permutations and possibilities fan and fray any chance of precision. Given the chance to be colourful, my patterns mottle and I'm left with a dull brown. Before what happened, I mean when I could still speak freely, any attempt at verbal humour was pointless. Words and intonations would resolve themselves into a functional bland monotone. I have great sympathy for stammerers. When they manage to squeeze out a stutter word, the result is ruined by idiotic facial contortions.

My role was to watch. My job to observe the amusement of others. But on that day, something would change for ever. I was completely ignorant of it as I boarded my bus, but I was about to become the funniest being on earth.

4

The Props

I'd acquired my library-resources list by phone on 24 December. I always try to keep busy on Christmas Eve. Jules Morris, Senior Corporate Librarian, had been on duty that day. She picked up her extension, taking her trademark pause for reflection before speaking.

'Hello, research and corporate.'

'Hello, Jules?'

'Benjamin! Fellow denier of days off. What can I do for you?'

'Death by laughter.'

And she laughed.

I remembered once receiving a Folio Society email flogging a volume of Greek anecdotes, a picture of a laughing donkey as its lead image. It had lodged in my mind, and I suggested the Chrysippus fable to Jules as an excellent starting point.

'Excellent. Yes. You know we have a little collection of essays on the subject,' she'd said, keys clicking away like fleeing insects.

'Get me all you've got.' I had not the irony to make this sound polite. But Jules was a friend of the cause; of laughless knowledge. She understood me well.

'No problem. Have an excellent Christmas Eve, Benjamin. I promise to break your back with the quantity of tomes I call up for you. Give me a few hours.'

Senate House library takes corporate care seriously. Private-sector clients such as Western News Corps pour massive amounts of money into these institutions. Jules Morris was one of its best – a total librarian. I cannot recall her ever making a mistake. Everything about her grey and intelligent and predictable, as if she were printed information transmuted into flesh. The only thing which spoiled this was her passion for sculpture.

She did not disappoint with the quantity of 'tomes'. Starting with Chrysippus she had generated a nexus of more obscure works. The email took five or six scrolls for a full preview. Rather than devouring the information there and then, I tore it from the printer, and folded it into the dog-eared jacket of Miranda's *Infinite Jest* by Foster-Wallace. I placed the book into the research box destined for bastards Chaz and Ali's work-pod. This was uncharacteristic – my not reading a list straight away. Why did I do that? Booze? Perhaps the excitement of the Christmas party just hours away; I'd already had three 'stubby' cans of Heineken, more than enough to get me tipsy.

Perhaps the wrong word. It carries connotations of merry wobbling, lubricated fun. Being drunk was something I did for other people's comfort, never for myself. Colleagues, pseudo-friends – I think they enjoyed seeing what might happen if I got high on anything. They were disappointed quickly enough, but it never stopped them trying.

Stimulants merely calcify my inwardness; hammer my flatness. I admit I've never tried LSD, not even at the Centre, but other drugs, yes: alcohol, cocaine, marijuana, Ecstasy; they all simply quieten me down; worse, they suppress my intellectual gift and accentuate its emotional side-effects.

Once Dr Rowe experimented with nitrous oxide, laughing gas. The effects were interesting to say the least. Each inhalation made me weep. A profound sadness swelled up in me, exactly in proportion to the fullness of my lungs, each exhalation bringing with it thick, salty rivulets of tears. Much later, I realized this was not irony, but science.

Or maybe I was drinking at the thought of Christmas Day. Everyone trying so hard; me included. All these wishes of well-being, reaching out but never quite grasping. Emotions running alongside a train that would never slow. That's how Christmases were. A blur of noise and steam. Laughter, love and happiness all around me, a mute jester.

I'm not cold. Just locked in. Like jokes that misfire even though their construction is perfect. These puzzle even me – for a moment at least. The surface gag, flawless in its make-up – tonally honed, delivered with the right inflection to a room full of attentive people. Yet it falls flat. That's the part most critics cannot understand. They cannot see the knots and strands around the idea – how it hooks onto the mood and matter of a room – its shape, its light. No joke is perfect, you see. Environment shapes even platinum material. It's my favourite type of joke. The perfect imperfect. It's me; it's a version of me. That is why my parents, people in general, found me hard to accept. No matter how many times it was explained. This wasn't evil, it was lack. But lack always breeds disaffection; and affection, love, is oxygen.

Christmas. Keeping busy. That's why I had immersed myself in my January project. And I was sprawled out in a capacious disability seat on the bus when the cataclysm began. The actual moment an instance of magic.

My finger, steadily running down neat columns of dot-matrix text, came to a jerking stop. My other hand involuntarily pincered my overfilled Brie and cranberry sandwich bought a half-hour before at Luigi's (yes, the same Luigi's where my parents had their first date more than forty years before). I visited three or four times a year with a sort of masochistic sentimentality. I never told my parents when I went to Luigi's, even though it was the kind of thing they would have enjoyed. It was my boyish secret; like visiting an old forge, or a disused railway station.

My appetite died. My mouth fell fully open. A ruby globule of cranberry dropped onto the printed sheet. I smeared the sticky blob away with my thumb, and to the surprise of a Jamaican pensioner next to me, read out loudly, *'The Greek Philosophers' Joke: The Ancients' "Quest for the Metaphysical Formula of Humour"*, Leavey, Professor David, Handsworth-Hartrill, New York, 1st Edition, 1950 – Senate House Loc-*ref* 8HT7-B.'

I closed my mouth, clenched it. Two things here were staggering. For the first time in thirty-nine years I had read something relating to humour and felt absolutely nothing, not a pinprick of sensation. I waited, and nothing. I felt nothing.

'Does this bus stop at Holborn?' asked my neighbour with a soft Caribbean lilt.

'Metaphysical Formula,' I said blankly. He moved away from me, quickly.

The printed line of information was appalling. I'll be the first to admit I've missed out on a lot of what you might label 'a normal social existence', but I will not have it said that I do not know humour. So, reading the name of a formula in inverted commas of which I was entirely ignorant, which provoked no instinctive intellectual response, outraged me. In fact it went beyond outrage, it was an impossibility. It was a set of stairs in an Escher illustration.

I have, and always have had, an almost physiological reaction to theories and forms of humour. Does that sound implausible? I have an organic feeling for what something is. It's not that I understand right away in a straightforward cognitive sense – no, it's more that I *know* it, feel it; the same way in which one knows love, lust, or anger without needing a dictionary to define them: some-body's bad joke, a businessman slipping on a crisp packet, Socrates, Diogenes, Apuleius, Chaucer, Fielding, Austen, Arthur Askey, Amis Snr., Amis Jnr., Lenny Bruce, Bill Hicks, James Byron, Jay Conway ... I feel before I know. And once I know, I feel as though I always have, as though within me every possible manifestation of humour lies latent, waiting for call-up into my con-sciousness.

So when I read the words 'Quest for the Metaphysical Formula' and felt nothing, I gasped into a hot panic. Worse than the panic I experienced blankness. Never had I encountered any form of humour or humour theory (including false or bad theory) that had produced such a terrifying nothing. This free-floating unknowing: how could it be possible?

I tested whether it was me. Maybe my 'gift' had gone into abeyance? I placed the printout on my knee, and pulled my notebook from my inside pocket. I found what I was looking for, a silly note written by Miranda that

morning: 'Nice bot, Benji-bot. Happy New Year.' The
words twisted through me instantly, a child's straw in
cola:

> *Pun, sexual language diffusing android*
> *implications of non-humanity.*
> *Warm greeting grounding statement in*
> *emotive humanness.*
> *Juxtaposition with main counter-contention:*
> *boring man has nice posterior.*

I replaced the notebook and stared ahead turning my
mind to Freudian Condensation. The whole theory, the
notion of language fusing with opposite meanings, double
meanings fusing again, all of it boiling into an intense bolt
of mental energy, electric brain activity, efficiently discharged as laughter. In a moment, in a second, I
understood not just this, but the whole Freudian schematic
for *homo sapiens* humour.

No, it was not me. It was this piece of data.

My fingers jerking like an ECG, I retrieved the printout,
which had fluttered from my lap onto the filthy bus floor.
I again read aloud the volume's title.

'. . . *the Metaphysical Formula of Humour*.'

Still nothing. I heard a wet thud. My sandwich had
fallen to the floor. I'd forgotten my other hand, my body,
myself.

This entry was awful for a second reason: the Senate

House reference number, or rather the rubbish masquerading as a reference number.

'It's shit, it must be shit,' I whispered to myself. If I allowed myself to think otherwise I would jump through the bus's window and outrun it to the library.

'*8HT7-B*?' I knew the department codings backwards. There was no '8H'. No such location.

Christ, it must be an error. The whole fucking thing was a misprint – incompetence, that would explain my blankness too – a freak typo. Yet, in all my years of using Senate House I had never once seen an error such as this. Understand – mistakes of this type were simply not seen; just as the idea of a Jules Morris with her own carefree stubby can of Heineken on 24 December was inconceivable, like Hitler in drag (I can see this is an amusing simile, this will happen sometimes). In eight years of weekly visits, I had never experienced laxness such as this.

As the bus slithered into Holborn, a smudge of low grey cloud hovered over Central London. My waves of discomfort subsided, replaced by a surging impatience. What if this were a real reference? Two implications ran from this. One: somewhere within me was something normal; it was, after all, possible for me to encounter written humour and react as Miranda did, or golden boy Cooper, or anyone else for that matter. I could read, look up – feel the delight of discovery. Perhaps there were some jokes out there that could work this way too; this might mean I could one day laugh, smile. I reproached myself: don't ever imagine that, fool. The other possibility was that Senate House had some unexplored corner, a part I had never seen. Yes. Instead of dread I should feel hope.

The shower gave one gust then died. Traffic lights, cars, pedestrians – intolerably slow. I scowled at the old man as he disembarked with slow movements. He hobbled nervously from the bus, not looking back. I began jiggling my feet, softly punching the wall. 'Cunt cunt cunt cunt.' It just felt right to say it. The driver glanced back in his mirror. Perhaps I was his first nutter of the year? Unlikely given London Transport's New Year's Eve service. 'Fuck fuck fuck.'

I lasted as far as Goodge Street; hammering at the bell with the ball of my sweaty hand. I power-walked from the bus, finding myself in Bloomsbury Square I broke into a mild jog, then a run, only slowing when I turned into Malet Street. Forcing a feigned version of my usual calmness, I approached Senate House's side entrance under the shadow of its towering modernist façade. Yanni Adasolglou was on duty behind his ugly functional desk. I rang the security bell, and he waved affably as he buzzed me in. I did not return the wave, instead ramming open the massive brown door like an American stockbroker onto the deal of the century.

'Good morning, good morning to you, Mr White,' said Yanni.

'Morning, Yanni.' No eye contact, could not risk sticky webs of chit-chat.

'Happy New Year to you, sir.'

'I think it might be, Yanni, only time will prove whether it is or not.'

For some reason I performed a bizarre backwards walk into the waiting lift.

Yanni's ancient face crumpled into confusion. 'Yes, Mr White.'

The doors swished open on the fourth floor and I swiped my electronic pass on the inner gate – closed to lesser members until 7 January. The intoxicating fumes of journals and old books rushed into me. The dim 1930s lighting streaked my face; massive windows, cathedral-high ceilings, paintings, tasteless old brass things. I floated in. It always felt more like returning than arriving. These 'closed days' in Senate House were special. There would be a maximum of ten or twelve staff, maybe a few fellow professionals, though perhaps none so early in the year. There's a sadness now as I reflect on this; that I felt so at home there, loved – an abstract love. A warmth in its cold-ness. It's because it wanted nothing from me, this library. It asked nothing, it cared not if I cried or laughed, there was stability. There was history: the walls opened me up in a way my mother could not. Flesh let me down, you see. Flesh let me down.

The reception desk was unmanned, so I rang the brass bell three times. Annoyed rufflings and whisperings came from the tiny inner office. I waited, primed to greet Jules, panting with excitement, but hot anticipation melted to cool dread. In place of Jules Morris emerged Ed Austen, a twenty-three-year-old part-time librarian/semi-professional stand-up. He was clutching a wodge of multicoloured tatty papers, and his manicured nails pierced the outer sheet when he saw it was me. The atmosphere was instantly malignant. He wafted towards me, bringing with him clouds of tar soap and citrus fragrance. I imagined him opening the aftershave on Christmas Day, applying it this morning, walking confident and perfumed through the streets of Acton. His glasses pinched the end of his nose like evil assistants. He smiled, a bad smile tightened by the grudge he bore. Rightly so, perhaps. I had gangrened his Cambridge Footlights-fostered aspirations with 100 words of pure (perceptive, I'm afraid) and somewhat vicious deconstruction in the *Review*. The morning after its publication he had emailed me one solitary word: 'Wanker', with a link to a website demonstrating different ways to kill yourself using household chemicals.

'Benjamin White,' he said, his spectacles jumping a few millimetres more along the bridge of his tiny nose as he nipped at the syllables of my name.

I stepped closer to the desk, monitoring the barely perceptible ripples and muscular adjustments as he primed himself for fake civility. He puffed his chest, shook out his fingers – a hybrid of comedian in the wings and bantam-weight boxer.

'Ed Austen, how are you?'

Of course, at that moment we were both remembering the same incident: Ed onstage in Maidstone, a few years before, when a dildo had struck him fully in the face. Dildo-gate had happened exactly one week after my review. His emotional wounds had still been gaping, so his anger cubed his shame when this performance ended in assault.

In the six days leading up to the thick purple mock-cock striking his cheek, he had been steadily emailing me hate-filled messages. It was mere coincidence I had been assigned the Comedy Bunker show in Baker's Bar, Maidstone, that night. I certainly wasn't there to review Ed again. I was there for Canadian political surrealist Ricky Nyborg's headline appearance (which masterfully mixed bizarre imagistic wrong-footing with the most incisive political deconstruction witnessed since Lenny Bruce; so inspired and mathematical was my break-down, that the next morning Miranda had to completely rewrite my copy).

Ed Austen was in the amateur ten-minute slot straight after the interval, just before Nyborg. The audience, a particularly feral Maidstone mob, were dominated and coxed by a group of fifteen or twenty screaming hen-nighters. The hen herself was by far the most boisterous of the troop, dressed as a slut-bride in labia-chafing white leather trousers, frilly push-up corset, and gossamer black veil. She clung to the word 'cunt' as though language itself were fleeing her and this the only prisoner captured in its retreat.

The first performer, the unashamed peddler of filthy post-feminist banalities Sarah 'Lickwell', had stormed the room, serving ladles of intellectual fast food which the two hundred-strong audience swallowed down without tasting or chewing. At first the hens were dubious about conceding to the grossly fat comedienne, but as soon as Lickwell began dishing up menstruation, penis width, and the weakness of male tempers in IKEA the hens clamorously announced allegiance.

'Go on, girl!'

'Fucking quality. Fuuuuccckkkiiing quality.'

During Lickwell's eight-minute encore, the chief bridesmaid of honour charged the stage and crowned her with an honorary veil. She was more or less carried off, a gladiator of smut victorious in the arena of cliché.

It must have got about backstage that Benjamin White was in the building.

'Mr White. How goes it?' Sarah Lickwell slid up to me, obscenely winking and gesturing.

I never enjoyed the sycophancy of performers. A lot of critics thrived on it – arrogantly believing that the comedians were made by them, needed by them. Fools. The true critic was above and beyond the performer. To latch yourself onto individuals was tragic and a little tawdry. Analyse and dissect in privacy. I certainly was long past the stage where I cared whether I extracted praise or respect. I just had to do the job. To use what I had to some effect.

Look. I'll admit – I could be passionate, vehement – angry even when I watched an act; but my words were never supposed to be vindictive – although they were often taken that way. It wasn't supposed to *be* anything. It was simply my childhood silence breaking for a sensed truth. It was my way of feeling.

'Hello, Sarah.'

'Cracking night.'

'Yes – all work for me though. The *Review* have sent me here for Nyborg.'

'Brillo.'

Odious abbreviator. She seemed unfazed, happy perhaps simply to have shown her talents to the most loathed man in British comedy. There was an awkward interlude while she chugged a Budweiser, seeming to chew the beer rather than swallow.

'You want some beer?' she asked, offering the slavered neck of her Bud.

'Don't think I'm being rude but ...'

'Cool, cool – it's cool, mate.'

It was not cool though. She was dying to give me some advice. Her tone was matey and inappropriate, a retarded Iago.

'Everyone says the same, mate,' she said, pulling her jeans from her bulging bisected crotch.

'Really.'

'I'm not saying it to be funny. It's just the way you do it.'

'OK.'

She polished off the beer, confidence bubbling.

'It's not though, is it, mate? It's always a bit fucking personal.' She spoke blithely, as though circling a disarmed opponent.

'It's got absolutely nothing to do with "being personal", Sarah,' I said.

It was then that Ed's head popped out from the backstage curtain. It looked detached and comical. He found what he was looking for. He fixed on me maliciously. There was perhaps an earthy hand-signal.

'Classic example, Whitey,' she said, gesturing towards Ed's floating head.

I relented. 'All I'm trying to do is get at the artistic truth in routines.'

'You called Kev Unsworth "barely a GCSE thinker".'

'That was not *my* metaphor, it was my editor's. And I believe the phrase she used was "as useful as a BTEC".'

'He's a nice bloke. Good comic,' she said. 'Three kids.'

I followed a milky sweat bead, tracing its foetid path through stretched flesh into the chasm of her cleavage. 'With respect, what has that got to do with the comedy? All I did was analyse down Kevin's substandard routine about 9/11. I didn't come up with the BTEC analogy. My original metaphor was something like "when one scrubbed away the glistening mud, only a potato remained, not a jewel".'

'I'll tell him that – he's a fucking spud!' She laughed and lit a cigarette, smoking it as though the paper, the butt itself could be inhaled.

Any aggression was mitigated by her blunt good humour. She has that, Sarah, an ability to transfigure the nasty into the amiable. In 2008, I was unsurprised to see her guest-presenting 'Hellsy' Smith's ITV3 chat show.

I had had that criticism a few times, even from Miranda. Make it less personal, Benjamin. It did explain however why I was so hated. The comics found my reviews personal, malicious in some way. What they were really reacting to was my tapping into their metaphysical and psychological core.

It's because stand-up is the most personal of the art forms. (And yes, I do believe it art, regardless.) Look at Sarah Lickwell, Ed Austen. They are not really 'acts'. For most performers there is virtually zero artifice in what they present. It is, for all intents and purposes, their selves, the ineffable centre of their Kevin Unsworth or Jay Conway, which they present to a random collection of strangers for validation or rejection. When a critic gets a bull's eye (I do not mean subjective stabs at appraisal, I'm talking about objective discoverable truths) it is the performer's very essence which is broken down and sometimes destroyed.

It wasn't this power I grew to love, but the quest into truth. Yes, OK, as well as bringing neglected visionaries to the fore, I enjoyed administering artistic justice to the untalented; but what they never understood was that

justice was neutral. Sketch-troupes, comic actors and character comedians disliked me less. Whenever I unpicked
one of them, it was the idea, the script, or the character I
obliterated. Directors and writers would be annoyed, furious even, but they would never feel that dull existential
ache inside; a pain I am told can last for weeks. That's why
Sarah Lickwell fawned; why Ed peered with such black
hate through the stage curtain. Understand me, I no way
wanted his act to go down badly. Christ – to have seen
him transformed by my words would have been wonderfully fulfilling. Nor did I see his humiliation as proving
my review from a week before. I just told as I saw it. And
I saw it.

Sarah Lickwell and I settled into a comfortable silence,
and the second part of the show got underway. A fatuous
compère (Jamie McAllun – thirties, Irish, faux whimsy, all
mannequin smiles with venom beneath the veneer) held a
quick, raucous caption competition, before formally kicking things off. It was a short section. Then it was Ed
Austen's set.

His performance died within a minute.

The mood soured as soon as the audience detected the
unmistakable vocal traces of privilege. After his initial
'Hiya' he had perhaps thirty seconds to self-deprecate or
diffuse sociological prejudice. He needed something like
Harry Baxendale-Ellis's self-mocking public school persona, but all he had was his opening routine about his
mother's addiction to jam making. This very cooking act

itself, redolent of detached-cottage middle-class comfort, was enough to heat the atmosphere. We (yes, I almost became part of that audience) turned to our coxswain: the Hen.

Chatter frothed. A few tentative heckles tried taking flight, but the Hen – she was the leader, and the room looked to her. It did not take long for her call of duty to win through. She climbed majestically onto her seat, funnelled her hands at her mouth and screamed, 'Cunt. Fuck off. You're shit.'

The reverse-scale triple blasphemy had its desired effect. The revolution began. Shoots of drunken banter sprouted in the remaining silences; any silence left was awkward. Then, after sixty seconds, it happened. A missile, a streak of luminous colour through the oppressive fug: a purple, veiny dildo hit Ed fully in the face. For a moment he was frozen, stupefied. Blood trickled from his right nostril. Raucous laughter mixed in with chatter and the room swelled into a poisonous soup of noise. He hooked the microphone and stepped backwards looking like Carrie in her gory closing scene, but he did one final thing before leaving the stage: looked straight at me. He needed someone to blame, and standing amongst the wreckage of hollering bastards and flying objects, he blamed me.

Now imagine the awkwardness this January morning as I handed him a green piece of tatty, cranberry-stained paper and said, 'Ed. I need some help finding one of these books.'

'Help?' Not so much anger, but incredulity; a liberated black Southerner being asked for a loan by an old Klansman. How rarely I needed assistance; and now from him. It was almost too good that I sought his succour, and he glowed as he pondered his next move.

'You seem keen, Benjamin. It's January the 2nd.' He moved his spectacles to the very tip of his nose and inspected the list. 'Long list ... Long, long, list.'

'Yes.'

'Of course, there's no way I can source all these today.'

'Well, just one of them's essential, actually.' Why did I show weakness?

He followed my finger, his breathing calm, nostrils belying his true excitement.

'I think the reference is wrong,' I said, 'but it's the one I really want – sod's law.'

'Yes. Sod's law.' The casting of me as sod in the aphorism was blatant.

A long pause. Losing the will to pretend, he removed his glasses altogether and looked straight at me. I honestly thought I was about to be punched in a library; a pathetic place to be struck.

'Look, Ed. I am sorry about the review, but you can't—'

'Let's not, shall we. Let's just fucking-well not.' He had the misfortune to sound more middle class when angry.

'OK.'

'I will help you find your fucking book, you arsehole. You can then leave and ruin someone else's fucking day, year ... or perhaps their fucking career. And that rhymed – or is that a cliché too?'

'Thank you,' I said, necessarily without humour, but this seemed to annoy him more. He wanted this spikier, more belligerent; he was disappointed with the play of his big confrontation – probably rehearsed many times in the bath. He replaced his brown-rimmed specs.

'Benjamin White,' was all he could say, bile leaking through the vowels. He wanted truly cutting, perhaps brute insults, but ambition applied the brakes. See, the reality was that he still, despite it all, aspired to my critical sanction. He imagined a day when the benighted comederati would grasp how wrong Benjamin White had been. He probably lay awake at night clutching at an imaginary Perrier Award over and over again. He could not see that I had no plan against him, against anyone.

'May I see *8H*?' I said.

'*8H*? *8H*? I'm sorry?' His eyes, and only his eyes, moved.

'That's the Store. It says this Professor Leavey work is in the Store?'

'No. It isn't actually.' Fangs retracted, antennae out.

'I thought I knew this place inside out.'

'Yes. You would.'

I ignored this. 'But it's not the Store?'

'No.' He savoured a saliva-sucking pause. 'How very

odd. Haven't seen one of these for ages ... the Safe Store.'

'Safe Store?' I prickled. It was something then, not an error. No matter what this little shit did next, I could enjoy the buzz of discovery. Blood rushed to my cheeks. My penis twitched, balls throbbed, the works. I shammed calm. I couldn't let him see how much this meant. He was exactly the malicious type who might find the item and destroy it just for the thrill of scotching me.

'I've not heard of it,' I said.

'Even you wouldn't have.'

'How many books are in it?' I asked. Here healthy people would have smoothed their question with 'jokey charm'.

'None.'

'None?'

'It is a literary Russian doll, a little library within a library without books.' He laughed, and a minute speck of his phlegm landed on my lower lip. I'm sure he meant the cackle to underline my disability, my silence. I suppose in his mind if one is mocked by a cripple, then a tap dance next to his wheelchair is justified.

'Without books?' I played along, giving a laugh-surrogate nod.

'Yes. It's a hold where we keep the James Hartrill manuscripts.'

'James Ha—?'

'James Hartrill and this Yank Louis Handsworth ...

They had some sort of doomed publishing venture in the 1950s.'

'Could I get in there? Have a little poke around?'

'Could be difficult before the 7th. Why don't you phone after two. You have my direct line. If I'm busy, I'll get straight back to you ... of course.'

We held eye contact, clock ticking, testosterone pumping, lips bit.

The impasse was broken by the Victorian lift heaving into life.

'Jules,' I said.

His eyes narrowed into a needle-white hate.

The lift doors creaked apart; modest female heels on parquet flooring. Ed shuffled at papers on the desk. I snatched back the printout, paranoid he might burn it.

'Happy New Year, Jules,' I said, turning.

'Benjamin,' she clipped, swiping herself in through the solid iron gate. The bad atmosphere was obvious, and she looked at Ed with suspicion. She knew of our feud, or rather his feud with me.

I nodded another greeting and she thinned her lips into an asexual smile. She wore a dusty pink suit jacket with large gold buttons and a hessian-looking peach skirt so long it chafed her flat brown pumps. Clouds of Obsession arrived with her.

'Thank you, Ed,' she said in her neutral voice. He vanished into the office like a spell, repulsed but not diffused. 'How are you, Benjamin? Good Christmas?'

We exchanged more New Year's banter, swapping vignettes in which we always had ourselves beyond the banalities of wasteful days off. Jules Morris was one of the few people with whom I could properly chat.

After a few minutes' vapid jawing, we moved, as we always did, onto interesting new journals and her addiction to Greek sculpture. She extolled an Argive aesthetics book, a gift from her blind dotty grandmother, but I could not focus. Ed's spiteful reticence about the manuscript had made the whole thing more intriguing. Eventually my impatience poked through our small-talk. She looked offended when I cut her off midway through an interminable reflection on Polykleitos – whoever the hell he was.

'Sorry, Jules, but – you'll appreciate how odd this is – well . . . I'm at a loss for a reference.'

I held out the piece of paper. She let out a compact, nunnish giggle of disbelief.

'Benjamin White needs a manual shelf-check. Wonders will never cease. Allow me.'

She pincered it from me delicately, a master surgeon at work. I don't know what I expected; some sort of dramatic pallor – shock, maybe subterfuge. But instead she flushed ripe strawberry with delight.

'Oh yes. *Yes*. I thought this might interest you. It came up on the manual system, almost an accident.' I assumed this to be modesty.

Opening the *guichet* in the mahogany counter, she

passed through the desk and settled into the official requests chair. She looked like a wartime code-breaker.

'You see, Benjamin, there was surprisingly little precisely on "Death by Laughter". One would think there'd be reams of the stuff – but other than the obvious Greeks, not much academic material really.'

She reached under the desk.

'Apart from this. The Safe Store.' She winked, and handed me a large silver key. For me, this was Narnia-wardrobe stuff.

Hartrill and Handsworth, she told me, were two very unimportant and incompetent characters in the history of publishing. James Andrew Hartrill, born 1890 to a tradesman turned titled cotton magnate, was a dilettante Scottish psychologist – a Jungian of the crudest type. Louis Handsworth was a New York publishing entrepreneur born the same year in Rhode Island into an equivalent milieu. The two met in Vienna just before the war, hatching a project to publish groundbreaking academics from both sides of the Atlantic. The timing, obviously, was awful. Their choice of texts became more about their whims, and had no relationship with academic trends. The obscure works never made it to the shelves. Hartrill evolved into a benign patron of Senate House.

I ascended to the eighth floor in the rickety 1960s trade lift. This excitement was odd. I was more accustomed to calm doggedness. I forced myself to breathe steadily. This was just paper, a book – remember your earth, your resting point. But I knew I wanted chaos; needed it.

The eighth floor. The Safe Store. Row upon musty row of books stacked together behind eerie mesh-gated shelves; each case with its own combination lock, as though untamed ideas might break from shelves at any moment. A sad place of forgotten writers, outmoded thoughts and neglected masters.

I located the thick square door which Jules had described as 'mock-rococo', and lifted the cumbersome key from my denim pocket. The mechanism turned easily with a smooth multi-dialled clunk. I felt the satisfying obedient weight of old movements, histories spinning and turning. The ornate grey block sprang open to reveal a dank cube of a room. The smell was rotten, yet exquisite – damp paper mixed with tar and mystery. I flicked a fat metal switch to my left and a dim green light reluctantly spread through the room. The space was surprisingly sparse of bound material, more papers and journals really. One corner was piled to the ceiling with a strung-together stack of mouldering papers labelled '1989 audit'. I drew a tight breath as I heard the trade lift whinge into life behind me.

Disorder presided in this damp, foetid place. A visitors' book lay open on a heavy stained desk; the front cover had almost detached itself, the frail cord of the binding trailing from spine to cover like a thin gristle of rotting flesh. I picked it up and flicked through. Pages and pages

of signatures and comments starting in 1960 and continuing to 2000. James Hartrill's old desk? Other items and
bric-a-brac, all breaking off around 2000; perhaps they
cleaned this area away in a fit of millennial sprucing. I
slid the visitors' book into my grey satchel (a bag constantly mocked by the fat Turk for being 'geeky') and
rifled through the drawers; old pens, pins, an ancient
receipt in shillings for a boozy 'luncheon', the pitiful detritus of a failed man without a real role. In a small inner
drawer I found a once-cream 1973 leather diary. I flicked
through it. The yellowed pages smelt good and damp.
The entries ran until June (the month of Hartrill's death).
Some pages had been ripped out. I held the diary up to
the weak bulb looking for impressions on the blank pages.
Nothing. I placed it on the slimy floor and moved into the
murkiest corner. It was home to an unlocked bureau-
bookshelf hybrid – all split dark wood and Edwardian
impracticality. Inside it as Jules had described were the
Handsworth–Hartrill manuscripts. Their existence
shocked me. Just to see them, a pile of ordinary old
papers – it blasted away the air of suspense. I ran my fingers along the spines, seeking Professor Leavey's work
within the unalphabeticized stack. It took a few minutes,
but even in my feverish state I found it – a slim, dog-
eared, twenty-page document, no more than a typed essay
really. The title page was handwritten. There is something
pornographic about seeing an author's handwriting;
information is denied its objectivity. I pulled up an old

stool with a disintegrating green leatherette cushion; possibly the fossilized indentations of James Hartrill's buttocks. I heard the trade lift wheeze to a stop, manual doors being slowly concertinaed open.

Professor Leavey had neat, methodical writing – astringent even. It was all a bit too carefully laid out, as though he had shallowly fantasized about the typography of a finished, published thing.

The Great Philosopher's Joke:
The Ancients' 'Quest for the Metaphysical
Formula of Humour'
Revealed and Explained
by Professor David Maurice Leavey
New York City 1948–1949
Livingstone 1949
London 1950–1951

It seemed an ostentatious roll of locations for such a slim volume. I brought the shabby bound leaves to my face and inhaled; nursing home and old tea towels. Even as I held it, as I read his words in his handwriting, I had none of my usual instincts, talents. No savant categorization which had been instant and standard my whole life. This was more than odd; it contradicted my reality. What was this? Perhaps his ideas were so bad, so incorrect, so pathetically skewed, there was simply no kernel of truth in them. Unlikely. No way. Besides, many times I had read things that were flaccidly worked or completely false, and I'd still experienced something, some flash of what it longed to be. Something quickly occurred to me. This 'Professor' David Leavey might have been a young man when he wrote it; might be still alive even.

I peeled open the first jaundiced page.

1. Introduction

This essay will explain and elucidate upon the formula of pure humour, or rather, coalesce and emend the multifarious erroneous formulae to produce a cohesive theory moving towards an empirically provable theorem.

This first sentence wobbled me on my stool; a boast, a waffling piece of idiocy so ridiculous it needed flinging at the wall. Maybe he actually wrote it up in the 1960s, high on mushrooms. I couldn't get through his hallucinogenic ranting. That was it. He was a junkie. A junkie prick. Pah – to make a *theorem* for something metaphysical such as wit. I should know. I spent eight years at the Centre trying to show others in 'empirical' ways what I felt. It cannot be done.

... and conclude with an original theory as to the neurological methodologies at work, examining possible sub-formulae and corollaries of this original aggregation.

Only fascination with someone so obviously deluded and drunk on abstract theory drove me deeper into his turgid nonsense. My own style might be technical, but I rooted all I saw in truth, not in a fucking test tube.

There have been many oblique references to Pure Humour Formulae throughout the history of thought, but no text has before laid down in systematic language the Ten Step Columns alluded to by Xenophon and Chrysippus. The distillations of this document are largely supported by my recent discovery in Northern Rhodesia of Xenophon's 'Terpsichorean Lock', or colloquially 'The Simongan Thrust', fully culminated in Movement Eight.

A NOTE ON AMALGAMATION
The Ten Movement piece has never been assembled in one text before; in fact has never once in history been fully explicated. Using a number of new sources and through assemblage of extant materials this accretion will be made explicit for the first time.

This 'Simongan' discovery in Northern Rhodesia will be of interest to Greek scholars as well as philosophers of the phenomenon known as Fatal Hilarity.

Another new sensation. Boredom. I didn't even feel compelled to read on. I forced myself through the rest. The disappointment was so bitter I could taste it, like eating instant coffee, like swallowing someone's puke. There were very few crossings out or amendments. Odd for a draft. In the last few pages I found the Ten Movements. At first glance they seemed silly, basic, naive – lots of ridiculous drawings and examples of what one must say and do to 'fully *achieve* pure humour' – the fool!

A noise.

'Anyone there?' I called.

I brought the gaping manuscript to my breast. I would take it home, study it in privacy.

'Hello?' I called again. Nothing.

I closed up the thing, like a dead bird. The back leaf fell loose at its top right corner. That's when I saw the scrawl. The mark. To look back now and think of that ink, that flash of red. At last, I felt some familiar sensations: excitement, fullness, clarity mixed with instant visceral, electric perception. I folded the page back on itself, focusing, processing. Red pen, different handwriting to Leavey's. And what writing. A smooth hot charge twisted up through me as I read aloud.

'Schneidy wasn't fucking about. This is Alfie's key – follow it the fuck up. I ain't gonna make it.' W.H., December 1992, London.

This was addressed to me, I did not doubt it. Or rather, to someone like me. It had been put down in order to be found. Here was something sparkling concealed inside a clod, only recognizable by a jeweller.

I again speed-read the opening passage by Leavey – again not a twitch. Brown confusion. The red scribble, simmering, inscrutable things lay beneath the words. I knew this person? W.H.? W.H.? W.H.? No. And yet something in the satiric loops of those o's and f's which so confidently scythed at the page. This was humour beyond the courier of its handwriting. Power and passion spilled from the writer. A man, I thought. Masculine i's, dots tearing left, then right, here running into preceding letters, there kicking them in the face and ass. Ass. An Americanism. An American male, bitter, biting handwriting. W.H.? W.H.? W.H.? No.

'Cunt it!' I shouted. I mean roared. I heard a jangle in the next room. 'Who's there? Who's there? Hello!'

A lot of nonsense is written about the use of the word 'cunt'. Most critics have a small-minded reaction to it; it's laziness on the part of the speaker and all that. But they miss the truth, the poetic possibilities. It can be the putty of humour. What of intonation, conjugations? What of the C word in the present participle – yes – what of 'cunt-ing'? So I swore. I swore in C. I belted out profanity.

And the letters: *WH!*

I tried saying them loud. Whispering them like a medium. I thought the words: Ha and ha. WH, WH.

Placing the manuscript on the floor, I pulled the visitors' book from my satchel. Keys and mints cascaded across the floor as though ejected from an eager fruit machine. I rubbed the sweat from my forehead, and began sprinting through the pages. Beyond 1973 and Hartrill's death, entries jumped months at a time. The 1980s. 1989. January 1990 – Raymond Saddler – that prick who calls himself an expert in Freudian humour.

And then I saw them.

Two entries: 14 November 1992 and 1 December 1992. Same pen. Identical red writing.

DATE OF VISIT: 14 November 1992
NAME: William Melville H.
PURPOSE: Research

That exclamation. Such confident assault of the paper. Only he could have had the self-aware irony to use such a clichéd strike. I traced the mark's violent lineal path towards a subscript bloodspot of ink which had nearly pierced through the paper and Saddler's name on the previous page. I savoured a slow ten seconds' inhalation. No more info needed. There was, only could be, one William Melville H. with this handwriting; let alone the circumstantial fact he was indeed in England at that time, that very month. Half voluntarily I let go of the visitors' book. It dropped down next to the Leavey manuscript, cover finally detaching and sailing away from my foot on a cushion of slime.

With relish, I enunciated the name of the 1990s master: 'Bill Hicks.'

But by then I was not alone in the room, and a swift

reply came with a spiteful hiss. 'No, Benjamin. Only me. Can I give you a hand with anything?'

Ed Austen stood in the doorway, a goblin, a conjured thing. I thought we might charge each other and wrestle. Instead we fixed eyes, moving our heads, only our heads, millimetres at a time, towards the same object. The manuscript of Professor David Leavey.

The following document was discovered and unsealed in the presence of DI Kirsch, DI Lamont, and DI Solie on 13 March 2003, and as such has been marked confidential level 3, and filed within the Bruce Case/1.1964./A

Agent J.S. Candy. Dusting/3BLYN/NY
Central Intelligence Agency
03/20/03

Arthur J. Hamilton Jnr.
7 March 2003
New York City

Tomorrow is my seventy-sixth birthday and I intend to blow my fucking brains out, for I am tired.

Too dramatic? Well take a look then. What do you see? A dead old man. Or a sad son of a bitch with a drunk's aim, a note full of bullshit. What do you see?

A pause to drink. There'll be some drinking from now.

Yes. That was a good hard burn. Now I'm ready – Jackie D. will help get down the bullshit I gotta say before I leave.

First of all, some housekeeping and some sad-ass clichés. My darling baby daughter Margie: I'm sorry, OK. I'm sorry that I was 'an absent' but I'm more sorry it has been ten years, four months and eight days since I saw you and the boys all dressed in black and each one of you looking like you wished it was me in the coffin being carried by Vernon, Kyle and Mickey. That's right, ain't it? I am sorry your mother died with a broken heart and a mad head, but I'm more sorry that every person thinks it was my goddamn fault. That was part of the problem with me and your mother. People always saying it was Art's fault. No, Margie, it was not. It very rarely was. Sorry to remove that easy little label for you, but I can't put a hole through my sorry fucking skull without setting you straight on that. I was a workaholic – worse, unsuited to the work to which I was addicted. That's messed up. Sure, I was a pig-head, a drunk, and away a helluva lot. But, you know – I tried. She didn't though, baby. She was a mad old bitch for a long time – secret, sneaky with it too. People never wanna admit that the mentally defective have personalities too. Someone can be mad as a box of rattlesnakes but underneath all that pain they can also be a right bitch and it has fuck all to do with their madness. I don't wanna hurt you but I have to let you know. Sure, I didn't help things, but trust me, she was nasty as well as crazy. It was always gonna end that way.

I could have retired us to a village in the Litchfield Hills and kept goddamn goats, and it still would've ended the same way for us. I'm sorry to break it to you, Margie, I was a useless son of a bitch, but I was not a bad man; not bad enough to cause her death. That's kinda inconvenient, I guess. For the labelers. Well, again, I'm sorry. I'm sorry too I behaved like such an asshole at the funeral. But everyone was blaming away, and that's what this note is about. It's about what I will and will not be blamed for.

See: I have this fantasy that one day you actually get to read this note, Margie, then maybe one day explain it to Rusty and Ricky. But of course. It ain't my Margie reading this note.

I plan to get very fucking drunk while I type this.

I want you pricks to know the real reason you're staring at a dead old man. The compounding factor is you went for me on the Lenny Bruce thing. Me. A retired, crumpled-up piece of old meat. Think of this wound as a work-related injury, Al. Ten years outta the fucking business, and one of my dumbest fuck-ups comes back to do me in the ass in my final days! That ain't nice. It really ain't. Well fuck you.

Let's take this from the beginning.

People should have done their jobs BACK THEN, that all should have gotten dusted down forty years ago; dusted old school, dusted properly. Shouldn't have even needed goddamn dusting if you recall my advice at the time. What pains me more, the worst bit, is that I respected Lenny Bruce. What Bruce was putting out in those clubs made sense – made too much goddamn sense. That's why we hit him, wasn't it? Least that's why he became a target, the Leavey thing took the hit to the next level. Lyndon B. Johnson was a goddamn secret Republican. Heresy?

Try this – he was a fake and a fascist and a cunt. He made me sick, Allan. The hypocrisy of him walking round in a dead black preacher's robes making out they were his own – wearing good Kennedy's smile, and Harlem and Watts all in flames. Yeah – so what, so what, you say. Well I agreed with Bruce, that's what. That's what I say. And I agree with Michaelson too, it wasn't just that Lenny Bruce fanned those riots, that turmoil – he was directly responsible for it going off. I know it now – the truth always comes out, and that's gonna be your problem, my friend. At the time I thought, no, can't be that direct – but I got that evidence three years later, which made me see different. That's when I realized exactly what we'd specialed. Bruce was directly involved in the Harlem troubles. He did that nigger set and three hours later it was all going off. I might as well tell you now, Allan. I suppressed – I was ordered to, I mean – what I learnt later on – intelligence on the Negro kid Panalo who sparked the whole fucking conflagration. And guess what? Sitting down for this, you fat treacherous fuck, Allan ... Not only was he a Bruce fan, but him and his woman (none other than Delia Compton – does that name ring a bell too?) were at the gig. They didn't want anyone to know Bruce had a direct link with Panalo – it would have made martyrs of the both of them; and that's why they sure as hell didn't want him working any more New York clubs in 1964 and 1965, or anywhere else in the world for that matter. That's why we were called in to shut him down, seize his papers, passport, all that shit. That wasn't surveillance, that was to shut him up. Lyndon Johnson was full of it. There's only Republicans, or Republicans with a college education in leftiness. That's your choice. There was only us; only the dirty us. No happy niggers, no peace – where'd have been the buck in that? Back to the old ways. That's what they all wanted. But you see, this pus and guilt has really started stinking lately. Seems the scars and injuries I did myself were waiting a long stint to get good and infected. I'm eaten up, bad and twisted more than ever. I've listened to this 'new' bullshit since 9/11, the same fucking shit more like – barely re-edited. After you dried the tears off your scales, you guys rubbed your hands together. It makes my fucking brains hurt to realize how goddamn right that little junkie Jew was in the 1960s. They muddled the whole thing with that Leavey document. Or maybe they did that on purpose – so we wouldn't know how important it was. But what he was saying – that in itself was good – and that's the truth of it, Allan.

I drink to him. Lenny Bruce. Truth-sayer.

Remember how tough he was? We thought a tired-out scrawny mad bastard would go down easy. He nearly killed you in the throat with that fork. Ha!

We worked together thirty-five years, and I reckon just about every day I looked at those three little dots on your neck and remembered what we did. You got off easy, man. Your tattoo was on your flesh. Mine's deep in me. I was the one that held him down while you shot him up with that hell-load of junk. I crushed that poor little fucker's arms as the shit hit him good. He crapped his shorts and died smiling. Shit and piss and giggling. I reckon that's how a comedian should die. Funny and pathetic. I couldn't strip him naked though.

Fuck, he was tiny.

Nothing left of him.

But fuck, if we didn't dust it badly.

We thought we did it. We thought . . . You enjoyed being smug about it, Allan, didn't you? But the fact is, though we got spoons, needles, and the naked dead little junkie, and we set it up all nice for Kimsky, Malone and all those other flashbulb vulture fucks, we got one thing wrong, badly wrong. We didn't find that goddamn document. They didn't brief us right, but the first thing they wanted after the Jew dead, was that goddamn Leavey document. That's why Michaelson went, I reckon. We treated the doc as a prop, as some sort of confidence thing – right up until '69 we were still saying that, or we were told it, I don't remember which now. MacGillon replaced Michaelson and I don't know if he was even briefed on it. After that it was just you and me. How could we have known what that fucking thing could do? I spent longer arranging Bruce's furniture for the crime scene than I did looking for those fucking pieces of paper. I still wonder if it was even there. We should have told Michaelson it was missing from a known location. It's probably the truth. Think about it. If somewhere in his fucked mind Bruce'd gotten a hunch about what that thing might be, he definitely would have gotten rid of it. He couldn't take a leak without one of us watching. Would he really have kept a thing like that in his apartment? He was on the junk but he wasn't stupid. We know now he'd already perfected Leavey's Thrust and the Brow and the Lean – that's what panicked them. Leavey must have shown him that himself – one on one. I swear they were closer than just posting shit to each other, never proved it though. I think Leavey picked him out. There's no way Bruce could have gotten those Movements so right.

That's what they got obsessed with when we were tracking Hicks in 1990. There's another tricky bastard that was onto it and us. In what he was saying, I mean. But Bruce started it – he must have had direct contact with Leavey – I know it. Sure enough, what he was saying was the truth; that's why Leavey went for him. But even without Leavey,

the words on their own would have given a few
Village liberals hard-ons. But he didn't have clean
enough blood to make it truly political. It was
Bruce's words with Leavey's technique. That made
the results explosive, and they would have been
lethal too if Lyndon Johnson hadn't called on La
Pearl to brief out dear Michaelson. I don't think
Bruce fully worked it out though – he certainly never
realized what it did, regardless of any fucking rants
about 'coming'. He probably treated Leavey as some
sort of guru-type freak. If Bruce'd known, he
would've stopped turning up to court. There's no
way he would have hung round. He'd have planned
something big, in the way that mad-ass tea-bag Brit
Benjamin White finally did. Benjamin White who
has signed my death papers – and yours if I have my
way.

8th March 2003
It's 10 a.m. Happy Birthday. I'm already half-cut,
and by the end I'll be cut fully. I think I made a joke.

How will it go? 'Arthur Hamilton, rogue agent.
The secret white-supremacist pro-Vietnam right-
winger who went against his directives and killed a
liberal icon.' A bit like that, asshole? I refuse to be
alive to stooge that for you, you jelly-ass fuck. You
can nail me while I'm in the grave, I don't care shit
then. Do what you like, you yellow bastard. That's

what we did to Bruce anyway. Laughed at him dead, and then fucked him over. Used him. Corpse pissing. Only he's laughing now, isn't he, Allan? I bet he laughed his ghostly ass off when you filled your shorts for the fourth time on the Leavey case. Do you realize how powerful that thing could have been? I know it don't come easy to you, but have you actually sat yourself down, and had a good fucking THINK about what Benjamin White just did – what he might have done next? Someone who could use it got it. It is pure failure on our part.

I got one question I cannot fathom on this, just one that's bugged me for years – and I got a few theories: how the hell did Bruce get the document out of New York? He never left the Village, let alone the city. How the hell did it get to London? That was the start of the end for us, my man. Who was working with them? It must have been Leavey himself. That fucking poltergeist. You should have made sure he was dead, Allan. Made sure you got him.

Maybe Leavey got out of New York when he realized he'd picked a junkie for a gerbil. Maybe Bruce got it to Hicks through Chapman? How that little Brit faggot Python Graham Chapman got his hands on it in the first place, we checked it all out – he never was in the States, not in the 1960s anyway. Again – must have been Leavey – directly involved, somehow. Cambridge/Berkeley contacts maybe. It's kinda weird that Chapman sat on it for years, but c'mon, Kirsch – he had it '69 – you must admit that now. No one believes that Python German sketch was a coincidence. It was fucking naive how we all convinced ourselves (and MacGillon too) that it was a freakish play. It wasn't, man. That was David Leavey and Graham Chapman saying fuck you. I still don't believe he didn't tell the rest of them. But they all passed – even Gilliam checked out OK. I still can't believe that. Chapman, that sly little fuck, waited nearly twenty years. Maybe he was just chicken shit. Maybe he had it but didn't believe it? He had it though. He was a loose ass-fucking cannon. He didn't have the balls to use the Formula himself, not for real anyway – but he was hellbent on getting it to someone who could. Smart enough to know the thing was bigger than his balls and I suppose he felt a kinda duty to bequeath it. And again we were late. He got it to Hicks before we could intercept. Hicks certainly knew how to start working on it, hid it in London. I suspect a Handsworth or Hartrill crony. It's tricky as hell working with 'Her Majesty'. That's how it ended up that Benjamin White found one of the most powerful weapons we've ever known filed in its CORRECT FUCKING LOCATION. Of all the places not to check! Do you realize what pricks we look for that? Whenever he was in London, that's

when Hicks was banging Morris. She followed his
instructions, and when the heat cooled she quietly
filed it for the next freak who popped up in history –
stuck in the one place incompetent Yank fucks
wouldn't dream of looking. Only this last time it was
a goddamn Rain Man who works five times as quick
as Bruce or Hicks – and with protection. Shit.
Chapman sure did good getting it to Hicks. Hell, we
could have allowed Chapman to live, but he just
couldn't shut his smart mouth. Yeah, I admit that
one was needed, I admit he had to be specialed – all
that gay rights shit – I see their point – but fuck. I
admit it. He was too much. Too fucking vocal. He
had one loud cock-sucking mouth. And if I may suck
my own cock at this juncture: that operation was a
touch of genius. Allow this drunkard a bit of
arrogance at his gallows. Only thing we got wrong
there was we should have specialed the 'dentist' too
when he left the Service. I heard he got wasted one
night and starting mouthing off to a few ex-agents in
London about how he was the big-shot who took out
Graham Chapman. You should check if he's still
alive – Hinkleman or Heinklemen, something like
that. But as for Chapman, well turns out the clever
little faggot didn't tell anyone after all, did he?
That's why he was clever. Got the document away
and did nothing with it. Saw what it was, what it
might do, and got it to someone who could use it.

Somehow got it to Hicks – someone with the balls to take it all to the next level. Had to have been '87 – the Dangerfield CBS show. Definitely. Not that it's my problem, I'm just getting it all down, showing what you missed, before I fuck myself up one last time.

Just stopped for a morning smoke. Had a think. These are difficult things to get down straight before I ride my final metro – and I don't doubt it'll be to hell for me and you both, Allan old boy. Cast your disloyal mind back to 1966. It's all so clear right now for me. My first year, your first month. We were in at the deep end. What did I say to Michaelson at the time? WHAT DID I SAY TO YOU, ALLAN? I told you Bruce did not have the whole Leavey key. Well maybe I was wrong. Maybe he had the whole goddamn thing. Turns out whatever the case, the thing was real. Without it he'd have been nothing more than a junkie-ass speech maker getting people riled. They never would have told junior agents if there was a bigger truth. They just wanted that document. Bruce had it – at some point he had it all right.

Now: what did I say when you fucking amateurs hit go? Remember, Allan? This shit will come out. It's comics. They ain't fucking Harvard researchers, they ain't Kennedy conspiracy nerds. These are shallow, pig-headed ego people. They ask the wrong

questions, in the wrong way, and if you thrust your
hands in shit often enough, sooner or later you'll dig
up what no clean-handed motherfucker ever
would – the filthy truth. Whatever it takes to be the
funniest, and the by-product is truth. They'll fucking
kill to do it, man. It was a matter of time till one of
them was gonna find where Hicks had hidden it in
1993, which would lead back to the Hicks hit, and
then to Bruce. Hicks and Bruce were too fucking
clever and God-complexed not to leave the right sort
of clues. Especially Hicks. And so this Brit prick
Benjamin White – that Asperger's Rain Man fuck.
You really think that even locked up and with his
tongue surgically removed to the root by us he'll be
silent? Get rid. I refuse. It's gonna reverse all the way
back to Bruce. To you, Allan, to the CIA, to the
American government. Even if you use my dead ass
to meet the debt, you assholes will do the paying of
it. The dog work. We should never have hit Bruce.
Fucking ridiculous amount of kudos combined with
very little power. That is a dangerous cocktail. More
dangerous than power mixed with respect.
Weakness and cool, makes a fucking martyr every
time. A 126 lb junkie who couldn't get a show in
town; he got Leavey purely by accident. Or by
Leavey approaching him. Yeah. I think that actually,
for sure now. Then we should have hit Leavey. We
should have found Leavey. He could be alive. I

wouldn't be surprised if that fucking loon's back in a mud hut in the Congo or wherever the fuck he disappeared to before. It weren't Northern Rhodesia. I tell you that. I combed every fucking mud hut in the south of that country. He's dead this time. Maybe. But watch out for him, Allan.

Hicks, Bruce, White – only the one who never played a club in his life could understand it quick enough to do real damage. Hicks was close. Close to building it. We were right to special him. No question there. Smooth, tight operation. Clever. That was dusted and tidy. He went clean; it was perhaps a little fast, he a little too young for it to be believable, but I was happy with it. The agent did well there. Just a little quick for a cancer, but clean nonetheless. The trouble is, Allan, old boy, if Bruce comes out, then Hicks will. Then you got some real shit on your fingers. So get rid of Benjamin White. Bruce is a historical icon – Hicks is as good as current. They'd make a Messiah of him both sides of the pond. You'd get nailed asses for a Lyndon B. Johnson signature, sure – and he did sign that off, Allan. But triple all you'll get for dead President historical heat. Conspiracy theory shit. Imagine if from the grave someone can produce a little Willy Clinton squiggle from March '93. It's gonna look real bad. Two months in office and he pointed the gun at Hicks, the geeks' fucking hero. It's gonna be

THE HUMORIST

real awful, especially for Mrs Clinton. Real
awkward.

So. Fire away. Scoop up this old man's brains and
throw them in the garbage with the rest of the
fucked detritus of his life. My advice to you: special
Leavey if he's alive. Make sure that the British target
has a bad accident in his cell. But don't call on me
too heavy. I'll be a scapegoat, but I won't be more.
Don't ask me that. I've got no cares beyond the
grave. But don't overstep it, Allan. I still got friends.
If the Bruce thing comes out in full, take it. And do it
properly.

That's all I've got to say. This is my piece. My will
is with the lawyer, and go with the secret words I'm
too chewed up to say locked in my heart. Don't
throw me under the bus, that's all I ask. Peace and
love in the end, peace and fucking love. Amen.

5

Call-back

I have just one memory of Father reading to me. He rested me on his lap, a fleshy prop for his own happiness, such hope in his strong face – a gaping, dreaming smile which he tried to sear into me; that's what I remember. In his long hands, some sort of farmyard tale, a colourful pop-up book – silly, papery and bright. But from me, nothing in return. No yelps. No gasps of delight. And the moments slowly bled of colour. I met none of his joy with my own. I could not, so it drained out of him. His boy would never laugh. Never smile. And to him this meant unrequited love.

The first concerned phone calls to our GP Dr Hamish were made when I was four and a half – just before I started school; just before Cooper was born. I admit I don't fully recall those first informal appointments (initially with Hamish and then by referral with a newly qualified Dr Rowe). The health professionals took a 'let's see, give him time' stance. My primary school teacher, Miss Hathaway, was not so willing to let time take its natural course. As I passed my eighth, and then my ninth birthday Miss Hathaway wanted me out of that school, but she couldn't get rid of the 'devil child' just like that. I presented no real behavioural problems. I did nothing wrong in the concrete sense of the word; but I was bad – perhaps I mean – evil – in her eyes. She had a puritanical rejection of me and what I was.

I remember Miss Hathaway as being old (and yes she was, this not just a child's poetically misremembered image), with a wire-wool bun, and facial features retreating behind her skull in four different directions. She leaked a pious gas and hissed a voice full of silver asperity. She disliked little boys intensely. For her, the child was a sacred innocent thing, therefore boys were not really children. In religious lessons (the inculcation of Protestant Christianity, naturally) she would watch me intently, looking for some sort of twitch or reaction to confirm her suspicions. I wish I'd been a more devious child. When the rest of the class laughed in unison at one of her soulless jokes, my face did not move. Maybe I should have given her a bit of a show, rolled my eyes or waggled my tongue. In some ways I think it frustrated Miss Hathaway that I never manifestly misbehaved. No tantrums. No malicious acts of pinching or biting. No laxness in my schoolwork, just an unnatural inwardness; a small implacable stone.

By ten years old, I was deep into my ideas and observations about the very fundaments of human wit. I had no words yet for the things I saw: language folding within itself, double meanings leaping upon each other, fusing themselves into mental space-saving definitions, contractions; the illogical narrative directions of my classmates as they made their mothers laugh; teachers' stories with characters, their authorial wrong-footings which I could sense a mile off; the called-back joke from earlier on between friends at an adjacent desk, blinks and noises blended into current strands of a story like egg white into dark chocolate. Yes, I could taste these things. The head-twitches, Becky's eyebrow raised during kiss-chase. I felt, saw in luminous colour all they meant and all they could mean. So it was unsurprising that when we sat down for stories on the mat, and Miss Hathaway made lame witticisms about her parrot, that I would become even stonier; partly out of boredom at her basic offerings, partly in stunned analysis of her unimaginative delivery. She sensed this. She keenly felt the little killjoy in the corner of the room, and she hated him. We were at undeclared but raging war.

From time to time we were called up to read to her. My final session was unforgettable. She creaked open the spine of a small brown book called *Who Were The Romans?* On page fourteen there was a joke about the Spartans with an 'amusing' image of a Spartan soldier standing in just his underwear. Briefly forgetting hostilities, Miss Hathaway laughed. I did not join in. Worse than that, I had a momentary remission into Owlhead. It had been years since this had happened – this quick unnatural swivel. It was violent enough to hurt my neck. I don't know why it should have happened then. Perhaps it was being so close to her shrieking metallic cackle. She checked her laughter and any trace of colour in her face drained away.

She craned into me. 'You're not normal, Benjamin White. I see you. I *ssseeee* you.'

But, of course, it was I who saw her, and she knew it.

And so that was that. She closed *Who Were The Romans?* and I never had another personal reading session. Shortly afterwards my parents were called in by the headmaster Mr Dory. He told my mother that I made the other children nervous during play sessions. This was a lie. The fabrication could only have come from Miss Hathaway. True, laughter from the other children sometimes made me stare unnaturally, but they were too young to know. I would have been bullied for it had they noticed. My memories of primary school are all loneliness and exclusion, not of oppression, no satisfying trauma to whinge about.

Becky moved classes after Miss Hathaway deemed my relationship with her 'unhealthy'. She wanted a proper crucifixion, but had nothing tangible. After all, she removed Becky from her class and not me. As our fourth year of primary school drew to a close, Miss Hathaway became a vocal opponent of my attending normal second-ary school. (I just noticed my tendency to use the gerund – strange, as I like my stand-up deconstructed and informal. 'Me attending', not 'my attending'. Odd – some of the finest humour hates rules, but hates them in excellent grammar. Maybe it's just the contrast. A clown in a dinner suit. Or maybe it shows a master hiding behind a glitter curtain.) Why should Miss Hathaway have done this? It was of no consequence for her. It could only be spite; at best misguided missionary work.

Miss Hathaway had several meetings with my parents and Mr Dory, counselling them to send me to Barker's, the expensive residential 'special' school for troubled children in Hampshire. They all disagreed with her. Until I did something explicitly bad she could do nothing, and nor could anyone else. But I never did, and I almost – almost, made it to the Sutton School for Boys.

Yet not quite. Cooper's fifth birthday changed it all.

I looked down at Leavey's document. I had a glass of nice Pinot Grigio on the go, an expensive chicken dinner from Marks & Spencer. I was celebrating. It was this which had brought me back to Cooper.

The act of celebration is common; but think – it's much more than just commemoration or cheering significant dates. It's a weird mix of achievement and gaiety, a semi-gas state, a lucid moment of self-loving, back-patting cheer – often lubricated by friends and family. With me, half the metalloids are missing, always were, will be. I do not function. That piece of me is wrong, dark (literally so on an MRI scan).

Birthdays, Christmases, exam passings, all were marked with suspicious over-attention to tinsel, cake, music, and gift; the paraphernalia, the shadows of joy. My mother was especially good at the pretence. Painstakingly, the ingredients of merrymaking would fill the house, from surprised morning greeting through to chuckling presentation of candled cake or framed certificate. Yes, Sally White always made the effort, but it was the making of 'effort' which hurt, the feeble stabs at festive occasion; straining at normality. My father joined in too – albeit egocentrically. If a celebratory song needed singing, or flushed-faced speech needed orating, irrepressible Graham White glittered through; tight-lipped mouths prising open, following his lead, obediently emitting song or laugh or joining in ritual. I always knew their offerings were nothing but paste. Credit where it's due though, for the first five years they acted through every script thoroughly. They truly *wanted* to feel it, they did; wanted Uncle Jeff and Auntie Jemima to feel it; willed it through primal human song and dance. Then Cooper came along, and of course that all changed.

See, once they had the real thing, as soon as they possessed that fat pink ball of gratifying reciprocal happiness, the pretences with their firstborn grew rarer, faded – eventually ceased. My inability to laugh or celebrate was taken as lack of feeling. In turn I also quieted my sadness.

I became emotionally invisible. One half of me, the smile, broken, the other trained into silence. Maybe that's how I came to feel so empty, spiteful; soon I had not even my sadness – everything removed. It was a matter of time until I snapped – bit, grabbed back something for me.

Cooper's fifth birthday. This was the day Mother would pick up the receiver in the hallway, and instead of calling our GP with her trademark warm concern, shakily dial 999, mouth gaping, sobs suppressed, initiating the chain of events which led to the Centre, to the *Review*, to all the chaos, and to the secure ward in which now I type these words, a firm gristly stump of muscle pressed resolutely against the roof of my mouth. That evening was the first time in my childhood when my disability showed a violent side. Looking back, and I am cursed to look back with an unusual clarity, perhaps my parents should have been happy that finally I displayed some sort of passion.

I was ten years old. A decade of laughless staring and quietude. We had settled into a rhythm. It's a common one. The large dribbling syndrome brother to be included but never blended. Cooper satisfied Mother and Father's true parental needs. Their generous dispositions plus his well-balanced, artistic, kind nature meant that I could be indulged and petted, like an ill dog. That's the wrong image. A large incontinent cat. Loved, yet involuntarily regretted; love with roots firmly in obligation.

Each and every meal, it was as though I were in a high chair, or a bib, or sitting slightly separately, in another room, another world. And now a laugh, here a snort. Jokes surged up around the table, all three of them guffawing, and just as the crests of mirth rose and swelled my presence would pierce them, their trailing after-sighs stained and spoilt with a tacit sadness. Often a cloud of guilty shame would follow the gusts of a family giggle. It took me a while to come to terms with why; simple really. When the three of them joked together they felt as though they were rubbing my nose in it, tap-dancing in view of a landmine victim. I made them uncomfortable. I made cheerfulness immoral; and the more merrymakers there were for dinner, the greater the pool of reflective dark.

It had been a very difficult day. My brother's birthday fell on a Saturday that year, so we were all at home. The sense of *his* occasion was horrible for me. (I had no trouble experiencing full jealousy in the normal way.) Mother burst into his room at 6.30 a.m.

'Five today, fa la la, five today! You're a big boy now,' rang through my wall along with his giggles, bubbly conformist laughter. I thought my solar system poster might fall from its sticking place. I willed the universe to fold in. I knew right away this day would be bad. I counted down on my yellow Timex Ironman wristwatch – exactly eleven seconds – and my father's singing filled the hallway. As usual he paid too much attention to vibrato and the ditty somehow became about him, about the applause *he* received from Cooper and Mother. I floated out of bed and down the stairs to eat some fun-coloured cereal in silence.

Having no real friends except Becky, and still too shy to go out alone, I was forced to attend the whole of my brother's birthday party. Gifts, song, joy and laughter filled the house. It's not that I resented Cooper's happiness. What hurt was the palpable sense of relief, of their letting off steam because of me, which accompanied it. I'm afraid Uncle Jeff and Auntie Jemima were included in this. All of them compensated for the tiring pretence of celebrating my milestones by over-enjoying Cooper's. I consoled myself heavily with sugary lemonade and pink cake, eating and drinking until I felt jittery and sick.

It happened in the evening.

The guests had left. The house was a wasteland of bright, screwed-up wrappings, trod-in sausage rolls and used paper plates. A heavy cloud of cigarette smoke hung in the air mixing with the residual cocktail of suburban wives' perfumes. On the kitchen side stood a pile of 'Happy un-Birthday Presents, Benjamin' (my father's idea) which relatives were told would cheer me up – note my father's default assumption: lack of smile = depression.

It was seven in the evening, and the four of us sat around Granddad Bernard's big pine table playing Junior Mastermind, Cooper stretched erect in his small plastic chair like a meerkat. My mother and father drew cards from the pack. Cooper and I took turns naming things beginning with the chosen letters. I knew my parents invented questions, keeping it fair for our respective ages. At the end of each three-question turn we had a round-robin in which Cooper and I could in theory steal points. The questions, however, were ridiculously skewed so I could never steal his points, nor he mine.

'Which cake beginning with *c* did Cooper eat too much of at lunchtime?' asked Mother, smiling.

'Choc-lit,' said Cooper.

'Choc-lit, correct!' said my father, merry, complete – his face puckering at the pun.

Another turn completed, and it was my round-robin.

My mother went through the pretence of drawing a random card. 'What *j* did Benjamin read out to everyone at the party which made them all giggle a bit?'

I paused for a moment, savouring the respect for my expertise. It was true, I had been given the dubious honour of reading aloud from a novelty card. It was a bad joke of course, but the partygoers had laughed good-naturedly enough; it was the only point in the day at which I'd been content. I was so busy reflecting on this tiny glory that I didn't notice Cooper raising his meer-head.

'Joke!' he barked, a Chihuahua, a pup. 'Joke, Mummy, joke!'

The idea I might be put out never arose in my parents' minds. Why would it? For all my strangeness, I was a placid, stoic child; always OK to stand back while comic incidents at my expense ran their natural course. A moment passed; they fully absorbed the delicious irony of Cooper's answer. Was it not Benjamin who wanted only joke books for Christmas; books about comedy for his birthday; who ogled and squinted when others joked? Was this not the one question, so babyishly phrased, to which Benjamin should have known the answer?

The open-mouthed tableau burst into animation. 'Yes, darling, joke!'

My mother fell laughing into my father. He kissed her softly, making warm animal noises into her thick fudge hair. His hand massaged the fat folds of her waist through her cake-stained polka-dot dress. Cooper clapped and laughed, looking wildly from my mother to my father and then to me; not understanding, but enjoying his moment of glory.

'Joke, Benjamin, joke!' my father said. His eyes bulged at me. Into me. I only realized afterwards what he had meant. I had heard 'Joke-Benjamin'. Me as the hyphenated joke. The semi-person. The half-thing. I looked at chubby little Cooper, his chimp mouth hooting its happiness, its simian connectedness. My next actions were automatic, somehow unwilled. I thrust my bent index finger into his wet mouth and hooked him like a fat perch at his right cheek. All laughter ceased. The wetness of my brother's mouth felt good.

'Benjamin, stop that at once,' said my father quickly. I could see his chest moving rapidly under his garish festive pullover.

Cooper's eyes widened, then, in a clean procedure, I dug my fingernail into his cheek and sharply yanked my hooked finger from his mouth. It tore easily through the delicate pink flesh where top and bottom lip met. A fine vermilion triangle of boy-meat disappeared, replaced by a trickling redness which ran along his lower lip and dribbled down his chin, soon pumping steadily; and then my father's hands, and my mother's noise – and two hours later the custody of a social worker named Tom.

Tom. The social worker. A pudgy collection of cells with balding head and face scarred by kindness and his bad salary. I did *not* sit with this Tom in a state of confusion. Nor did I stare blankly into the middle distance with 'cold psychopathic detachment'. My capacity for guilt and fear was as good as anyone else's. I was terrified. I wept in fact; that *was* rare for me, but I wept into his green cable-knit sweater, which smelt of Ariel soap powder. I remember nothing else. Tears, words, a few white rooms and then Tom was gone. Within a few days, a few spoonfuls of this and that, I had been processed.

Maybe this 'event' saved me – with my family, I mean. Naturally, there were a few days of alienation, shock – but all too soon their synthetic jollity, their noxious calm returned. Negative consequences were suppressed. Before I knew it, Cooper had forgiven me too. I can't lie, part of me was disappointed; not disappointed – frustrated. Even this decisive smash had produced no echo. Their default joy was an emotional padded cell. I could scream and holler and foul the wall; but it would be cleaned up with a smile; my buckles calmly refastened.

The best warm-up comedians are like this. Hard units of mirth. It's a division of the art all on its own. Most would dismiss it – or sneer loftily at it. I do not. To create an impermeable wall of good nature – an art in its own right. Again, the material is irrelevant. They cast spells of goodwill. Winks, tics and smirks – songs even; all hypnotize the apathetic into a trance of happiness. Then, and only then, does the headline act take the stage.

I found myself back home within seventy-two hours. Cooper needed two stitches in his cheek. He bore the small tick-shaped scar until the end. My mother and father resorted to self-help. They chose understanding. They 'cared'. They 'worked things through', bought therapy books. Appointments were made. They 'got on with life'.

Their saccharine could not, however, stop the educational peacemaking consequences. My hopes of attending the Sutton School for Boys were extinguished. We fought the decision, but Cooper-gate proved pivotal. We had a victory of sorts over Miss Hathaway. She had been zealous about sending me to Barker's in Hampshire. This place had a good reputation for healing damaged or troubled children. Sending me there would have been a double admission, so my parents were strongly opposed to it. Barker's was also fully residential. My father had boarded as a child, and would not have me endure it; certainly not at an institution with psychiatric mandates.

I managed my frustrations. At first things improved if anything. We were closer as a family; certainly my mother and I. What I'd done had made the thing a Thing – a palpable problem. She took up the challenge. I became like one of her weaving patterns, detached from a perforated page in a glossy magazine. She started writing about 'early adolescence' for the *Saturday Mail* – the women's section. My father acted chipper, but I could detect a backlight of pessimism behind his alacrity, his 'research into possible disorders'. He did try though, he did – I must not allow current bitterness to distort. Cooper was so young – within a year all was forgiven, within five years, more or less forgotten. Much later he actually thanked me. He was a good-looking chap, my brother, and it turned out his boyfriends found the tiny scar somewhat sexy.

I must try not to run ahead, so many fronds of story tangling for position. That's a fine image for me. Why should anything be linear? This singular impulsive act of violence was a leap forward – into something. Miss Hathaway. She needed it to happen. That old bully. That crisp, malignant witch. She knew she could not force Barker's, but there was enough time left to ensure my exclusion from the Sutton School for Boys. Mother negotiated for the best of both worlds. She 'liaised' with Dr Rowe. She met with the social services and my primary school. My father pulled a few favours. He was enjoying success at the time (it was the 1974 election debacle with Wilson just inching past Heath, a time of vehemently witty cartoonery). Soon, we received that brown envelope loaded with partial victory and declaring my fate.

'... from 7 September 1974, Benjamin White will attend the Russell Square Centre for Children, on a residential basis, Monday to Fridays, being released into his parents' care for weekends, Easter, Christmas, and each August, until 31 July 1980. He will receive a full syllabus-based education plus occupational and psychological therapy under Dr William Rowe MD, MEd. who is a specialist in this area ...'

Area? I was an area now, no longer unknowable or anonymous. My mother edited as she read. I could tell. Now and again her eyes would narrow and she hummed instead of speaking. She probably omitted the nastier terms such as 'problem', 'psychiatric', 'sectioning'. Who knows. Still, she smiled and we declared it a 'victory against the system'. I brim-filled my cup with milk enjoying the vulnerability of the meniscus. I said it: 'meniscussss'. We quietly toasted my rosy future. Mother then told the story of her first day at work in 1959. The day went on like any other.

It all passed to Dr Rowe.

He took control of things. The growing me up, I mean.

My parents found this handover somewhat liberating. During the week, I stayed in Russell Square. ('The heart of Bloomsbury,' Father would chirrup, literary sketchbook in hand.) Each weekend they 'had me'. They hugged me. They touched me so as to assuage their feelings of parental incompetence; soothe abandonment-guilt – then handed me back. I have to be fair. Their interest in my progress certainly didn't wane. Not at all. I would never imply that. If anything their curiosity became stronger, yet ... more abstracted. Mother colourfully wrote her mainstream psycho-babble (for the *Friday Express* now). My father obsessively ordered books on Jung from Foyles. He devoured them in his study with lashings of Ragnaud Sabourin brandy and once again the whole thing became about him. The Centre helped my parents compartmental-ize the challenges. The day-to-day practicalities of making me into a real person had passed to an expert. I would be dressed by a servant. My parents were now merely diners at the fully waited table of my childhood, picking and choosing whichever interesting pastes and grains charmed their palates.

Is this incident with Cooper really the start of the whole thing, my story, I mean? Is it funny? Can I really tell? Humour's certainly at its strongest when blended with a good story. The old lady slipping on the icy dog shit: it's funnier if we know her accent, her name, her views on life. Why? Because the unpredictable and inexpressible become fused with the concrete. The contrast is greater, the humour more real. That's how good stories work – character plus incident. A joke is the same. A joke is the smallest story, an emotional haiku. Ripping open Cooper's cheek was just a tawdry emotional lynchpin. It was the event that began the narrative. The real story. My chapters at the Centre.

My first day there was shockingly untraumatic. I needed drama, pain – hollers at my unjust fate. Instead, I folded easily into the mixture, this gentle madhouse. Of course, I'd built the thing in my imagination – lots of febrile spazzes rocking back and forth; maybe a hunk of excrement thrown in my face by an autistic boy as I crossed the Centre's threshold. None of that.

'You must be Benjamin,' said a youngish man in a chis-elled Ulster voice. He had a meaty face marbled with friendly colours, one of those men who grey early merely to seem more trustworthy. 'I'm Dr Rowe.'

'Yes,' I said. I looked at my mother. My father was 'waiting with the car'.

'Thank you, Mrs White,' said Dr Rowe.

'Goodbye then, Benjamin.' She gave me a long deep hug before releasing me, arms flicking outwards as though scattering ashes. She disappeared off through the foyer, a benevolent ghost.

'Why don't I show you to your room?'

'Thank you, Dr Rowe.' I spoke in a flat, portentous monotone; accepting, but strangely content. It felt so like home. Within hours, it was.

It helped that the building was gorgeous. Granite, public-schooly and historical – but spruced-up and friendly. Tiny simulated lakes in luxuriant leafy gardens. Yes, there were stained-glass windows and fishbone floors, but people wore casual clothes, chatted. It seems banal to describe the place as 'friendly' – but it's the best word. And it smelt good too. Bread and clean linen, an army of well-kempt bakers.

We drifted along a bright corridor, Dr Rowe pointing things out along the way. In New Wing things were more plasticky, the staff more foreign, walls brighter.

'This is your room,' said Dr Rowe, opening a door onto a modest, clean rectangle of light – two single beds, pine units and some new pine shelves. A thin, serious boy sat on a basic chair next to the solitary circular window.

He came towards me in small steps. 'Hello. I'm Richard Gott.'

'I'm ... Benjamin,' I said, and he shook my hand.

'I'll leave you two to it,' and the doctor was gone; but his alliteration, the comic double-clipping of 'two-to-it', like a mechanical bird stayed oiled and flapping through my mind. Special school had begun.

There are no answers there, back in my school days, only ingredients. Whenever I celebrate I go straight back to Dr Rowe. Not that I toast many things now. Dr Rowe: after all, it was *he* who helped develop my insight into this 'condition' or 'state' as he called it. Within three days of that childish rushed handshake with Richard Gott, Rowe taught me all about celebration. He showed me how I might experience my version of it. He started giving me tools for stand-in happiness; like the artificial 'ha' he taught me to vocalize in place of laughter. He taught me how I might in moments of glory act out joy, rather than experience it in the normal animal way. As the first term went on we worked on social scripts, had countless rehearsals for the staging of happiness.

So, you see, that day of my discovery in the library, had been my biggest challenge yet. I wanted to mark it with joy. I wanted a full party for one. I almost, so very nearly, knew some cells of happiness. The Leavey document had taken me to Cooper, to his cheek, to all the birthdays I pretended to enjoy.

Escaping Senate House had not been easy. Ed Austen proved to be his usual little shit self. Turned out the Hartrill safe was his responsibility. He insisted on booking out the manuscript himself.

'I insissssst.'

I protested. He leeringly stuck to his guns, vanishing like cigar smoke through a fanlight. I made distracted small-talk with Jules Morris about Polykleitos for a good five minutes before he reappeared. I was certain he had photocopied it, sensed the possible importance of it.

'Sorry about the delay, Mr White.'

'It's fine, Ed.'

'We try to give a five-star service – but not everyone gets five stars, do they?'

I was annoyed, but not alarmed. Why would I be? The malevolent little prick just wanted a nose; he couldn't have guessed the truth, and nor could I.

I grabbed the document without thanking him.

'Goodbye then, Benjamin!' Jules called as I dashed down and skated through the lobby. I pushed impatiently against the security door until Yanni buzzed me out. He was offended and audibly scoffed before the door had finished closing. I jogged along windy, wet Malet Street, dropping my mobile as I tried to call Miranda. I took a few deep breaths, then punched in the number.

'What's wrong? Calm down!' She was eating: chewing and speaking.

I broke the news of my discovery. Although by no means a Hicks adulator, she was very excited.

'You abso sure?'

I was abso effing rock solid.

What evidence did I collect? Did I take this 'visitors' book'? I savoured the frantic questions of a sub-editor when they know a rover's stumbled upon something real. It felt good to hear her this way. Ha! It would be published. I was too excited to take in the words. What was said next? We were on the phone some time conversing erratically, speaking over each other and ignoring poor signal-strength as I cantered through a dank dog-shit alleyway into Goodge Street. The whole feature was turning into a 'nature of humour piece' with Bill Hicks at the centre. I had dreamt of writing something like this for years. A draft plan waiting in my head.

'Chrysippus through to the last master,' I said, dodging a filthy puddle. She laughed playfully and I skipped, yes I skipped, home via the shops. Was I about to have the best day of my year over and done in January?

That evening, as I cooked, I threw boxes and bags in the air like a fox raiding a bin. Calming myself to sit and simply eat would be impossible. I laid my dinner things out on a tray and carried them through to the lounge. Many minutes passed. The Leavey manuscript lay at my feet. On my sunshine-yellow plastic tray I had carefully placed a dish of my favourite foods. I reserved my electric-blue ceramic plate (won in A level psychology class at the Centre) for such occasions. The regressive M & S 'feast' was on a bed of carrot and potato mash, with Heinz Curried Beans and Green Giant sweetcorn. One glass of wine had been enough.

I sat enchanted by steam and aromas; a cat's cradle skein of momentary stillness, a hammock of scent. You will think it plain, boring post-war-type fodder. But for me, even now, in here, when I see those oranges, yellows and blues (they allow me the plate) mingling together ... I'm fifteen – I recall the television lounge and Dr Rowe's prematurely lined beneficent face; or I'm eleven again and his Belfast accent is more distinct, his skin smoother, ruddy plump cheeks and fat 1970s hair flecked with early silver. Or I'm eighteen, and I finally believe I'm equal to Cooper. I realize I am at least more special.

The steam rose and I sat there a good while drawing the juice of memory from it until it once more became food. 'Bliss' is a word I am never sure of, though frequently use; I still write it sometimes. For me, more than rapturous happiness, it expresses a fullness of being, filled up until happiness loses its hues; an uncoloured, impartial satiation. Bliss, if you like.

RUSSELL KANE

Me, plus meal, plus comfy chair. Nothing more could
be wanted to 'celebrate' what had happened. This was my
analogue of joy; the perfect reproduction of an inner smile.
Next to my plate I had a blue bowl containing a simple
salad of cherry tomatoes and iceberg lettuce dressed with
black pepper and Sarson's vinegar. The smell of spotted
dick was already wafting into the lounge from the kitchen.

A fine meal needed fine company. Next to the tray,
balanced precariously on my hairy knee, was the CD
case of Bill Hicks's *Live at the Oxford Playhouse*. The disc
whirred in my stereo. I'd long ago grown sick of his actual
routines, so I just let the acerbic notes of his acid wit roll
through me. What's special about this recording is the
audience. Listen out for the progress of the mirth. Unsure
English chortles gain confidence, then burst into hot fun-
nels of full laughter in response to his sardonic Texan
drawl. Yes, sardonic and drawling – that added so much;
the fact his glutinous vowels were at odds with the short
sharp edges of his waspish vitriol.

I dissected the chicken breast, lifting a moist slice away
and building upon it a forkful of vegetables. I did not chew
the food but gently massaged and sucked at it in my
mouth, eventually allowing the hot ball to slide down my
throat and into the centre of my being. I never went more
than a few seconds without eyeing the manuscript at my
feet. I ate my meal gazing affectionately at Hicks's scrawl
as if it were an old cat nuzzling my toes. The only thing I
knew for sure was that I had found something interesting

enough for him, and therefore at least worthy of a few days' study.

'"Schneidy wasn't fucking about. This is Alfie's key,"' I recited after swallowing.

This reference had been simple to decode once I had made the connection with Bill Hicks. Schneider of course could only be Leonard Alfred Schneider, better known as Lenny Bruce, the comic who kicked it all off, who could have been the greatest were it not for his heroin overdose in the 1960s. Indeed, he is perhaps the only comic one might classify as 'as great as Bill Hicks'.

As 'blissed' as I was I still had no inkling of what the thing might mean. I had read through the manuscript by this 'Professor Leavey' and still felt nothing but the faintest glimmer. I discounted these flickering sensations, told myself it was simply excitement at seeing Bill Hicks's handwriting on a document. I had to respect something he'd endorsed. I considered that these stirrings might be a nascent appreciation of a document I could not yet understand. But, no. This document was nothing, surely. Aside from the guff and academese of Prof Leavey's waffle, there was the laughable ten-step formula for the 'foundation of human wit'. Leavey called them 'Movements', because he saw them as music, compositions in which each element must be perfectly executed; plus they involved a lot of conducting. Humour aspired to a physical music, he said, vapidly paraphrasing Schopenhauer. Though, I did agree with him on this. The best humour I'd written about invariably employed the physical. Even the most consummate deadpan raconteurs could never be truly great without choreography of some sort. Bill Hicks, a self-confessed wooden stick with no natural physical skills, always used movement to underpin his scathing routines. The eyebrow, his use of the inquisitive furrow. But I know now this was not his work alone, nor was it really Leavey's. It was no one's. It was everyone's. It was lifted from the ambrosia of Humour in Itself.

I run ahead. As I read, I saw only a combination of showing-off and childishness – a useless mixture for an academic work – an *unpublished* academic work.

The phone rang.

'Benji?'

'Miranda?'

'Sitting down?'

'Standing, actually.' This came out flat. It sounded like a genuine correction rather than humour.

'No, I meant – "ready for this", you fuckwit?'

'I know what you ... go on.'

'Dominic had a complete spunk-off over your Hicks discovery. Wants to see the whole plan tomorrow.'

I could hear clanking and talking in the background, the sound of a lighter. 'Are you still at the office?'

'For fuck's sake, just have the draft plan ready.'

'You're smoking in our office again, aren't you?'

'I smoke, you write.'

'It's done,' I lied.

'I'm sure it is, Ben-bot.' There was a noise, lift doors, maybe. 'Sorry – on my way to a piss-up in Covent Garden.'

'Jackie?' An orange, alcoholic thing – lost and wild.

'Yep. One must shag. Ha! Anyway – ready for this?'

'Yes.'

'I think Dom wants you for the whole damn thing.'

She let the news hang there, an outstretched hand behind a toddler walking on his own.

'The whole ... thing?'

'Run with it, as it were. And the best bit of all ... Goodnight, Terry ... yes, the spookiest bit ... you're gonna fucking love this, you nerdy swot – apparently Leavey's still alive.'

I did not reply.

'Yeah. Living in Zambia. Livingstone. Crusty, but still going.'

'How old?'

'Mid-seventies at least.'

'Incredible.' I did the maths quickly. How old was he when he wrote it? The dates must be wrong. The work read badly, but I could not believe a twenty-year-old undergraduate could concoct a thing which would dupe Hicks and Bruce. 'Zambia?'

'At least that's where he was last seen. He's in hiding.'

'From what?'

'The States are seeking his extradition. Something about sedition, civil unrest in the 1960s.'

'CIA?'

'Don't know. Probably.'

'What, and you can find him but the Yanks can't?'

'Ha ha. Of course. The arts, darling, the arts. I have my ways.'

'What the hell do they want him for? Not related to this manuscript?'

'Don't be a bloody fool, Benjamin. An unpublished joke manual? It's something to do with 1960s race riots.'

'I see.'

'But that's still not quite the best bit ... Taxi! Taxi!! Fuck it. Wanker ... For you anyway, you lucky shit.' Notes of envy polluted her goodwill.

'What's that then?'

'Put it this way. Dominic's got a massive hard-on about this guy being on the run, CIA, arts maverick who knew Hicks, blah blah and all that bullshit. He started banging on about tracking him.'

'You called Kyle in the US?'

'No. Think about what you just said?'

'Ahhh. Bobby Enanda?' He was a legendary bounty hunter-paparazzo hybrid.

'Of course Bobby, you numbskull – Kyle's just had his prostate ripped out through his arse.'

'Yes.' I had forgotten. I had a flash of Chaz and Ali's lurid japing in October. I must have cached the low-grade banter.

'Bobby's been in Zambia for yonks. The corrupt fuck knows everyone in the region, the undisputed master of bringing anyone out of hiding. Plus from Leavey's point of view, it's an ego-piece. It's amazing what an edgy double-spread in a national can do for curing a hermit.'

I remembered the J.D. Salinger interview, sensationally arranged in Gaborone, Botswana. 'I'm not sure, Miranda, if the American government can't find him . . .'

'Don't be a knob, Benjamin. You really are a knob . . . Covent Garden, please, can I smoke in here? Fuck it . . . the Yanks couldn't find the bush on a giant hippy.'

'That's disgusting.' But in truth the overplayed ironic coarseness of her words – conveyed in posh voice; it worked. Not disgusting, but a sublime use of bathos.

'Thank you – the point is this: Dominic's put an enthusiastic call in to Bobby-boy. Now obviously—' The signal cut out and Miranda went Dalek for a few seconds . . . 'But he reckons if he's around Livingstone, he'll find him within seventy-two hours.'

'Brilliant.' I sounded bored. I was deeply flustered and nervous.

'You still haven't worked it out, have you, Benji?'

'What?'

'Get your cunting suitcase out of the loft and start learning Zambian, you moron.'

And with that she was cut off. I tried calling her back, but it went straight through to her three-word voicemail greeting, 'Miranda. Busy. Bleep.' By eight thirty she would be drunk and full of rich food.

I polished off my banquet, mopping myriad juices with

slices of fresh white bread, all washed with another glass of Grigio. I relaxed into my chair and restarted the Bill Hicks CD. I replayed my day, my year, my life.

I reread the Leavey document, occasionally pausing to swear. I took deep breaths, focused. My mind: it felt clear. I was open for whatever the hell Hicks and Bruce had seen. Could it really be the case that I'd spent my whole life in a state of egotistical self-deception? That after all I was no savant? Were there limits to my automatic perception? Perhaps I wasn't really that much like Richard Gott, my best friend at the Centre. My prime numbers had a finite quantity of digits. Damn it. And with these reflections, I felt my happiness dissolve like a Berocca in urine. Bubbling up for the first time in my life were doubts.

I waited a few minutes, then made some tea. I spooned two sugars into my favourite mug and stirred very slowly.

'I must try harder. Must try.'

I returned to the lounge and picked up the manuscript.

'Movement One: The stance is of primary importance. Your buttocks must form a ledge in the Simongan manner.' Why would he use obscure terms in the practical part? I skimmed with disgust through Movement Two which featured a 400-word diversion on the splaying of one's buttocks.

'Movement Three is based on a fundamental archetype of human choreography: lifting your right leg up to a 90 degree angle and swivelling the ankle exactly in the Simongan manner.'

Simongan? Fucking Simongan. Should that mean something? No glossary. The arse. Perhaps there might be a published version after all. No. A twenty-year-old's spurious offerings to academia. It was a joke. This work was a half-finished joke; a set-up without a punchline. Maybe I was the punchline. If this had been published it would have affronted the academic press with its mindlessness. Yes. I'm sorry, Bill Hicks, but this book is a piece of shit. Lifting one's leg up? I stared wistfully at my Hitachi stereo. Bill? Are you there? The CD was still on and he was busy breaking down the first Bush administration with a series of electric analyses animated by spiteful caricatures. Masterly. And yet, here a 'professor' tells me all I need do is lift up my leg. Bill Hicks agreed. Devastating, to have someone defecate in the face of your god, and the god enjoys it.

'... It is important that the ankle is held loose and swung gaily [Gaily!] as you utter your clauses using the syntactic rules ...'

This sentence alone confirmed Leavey as a quack. I told myself that Hicks had simply been intrigued. His quality control had temporarily malfunctioned. He followed a harmless whim. That was it. He had a few days to kill in London so he went for some reading.

'We got ourselves a reader!' fired from the speakers. A famous punchline of Bill's where he mocks ignorant haters of books. I nodded, savouring the quote; still I was unconvinced. The vehemence of his handwriting unsettled me.

Whichever way you looked at it this was bad. Whether I liked it or not, at some point my acidic idol had been a fool. I was forced to choose between him or me. Either I had lived a lie, or he was a fraud; maybe just once. As much as I loved Hicks, I preferred the latter.

I drained my mug of tea, took it through to the kitchen, and I turned off the oven. I couldn't manage dessert. The laughter redoubled from my Hitachi subwoofers, something about smoking, taxes. It was the final insult. I charged back in. I punched the CD player and back-heeled the manuscript across the room. A flap of translucent skin hung from my knuckle. Any enthusiasm had melted under the cold heat of this doubt. My pad was still blank, pencil sharpened and unused. Another first for me. No inspiration, no thoughts, no words spewing out. I panicked for about thirty minutes, then relaxed, and eventually I felt a soupish boredom come over me; a languid lack of interest. Nine p.m. Fuck. Nine. Tomorrow represented the opportunity of my career, yet I longed for the nothingness of sleep. I cleared away the rest of my dinner things and splatted into bed like a used tea bag.

But sleep brought no oblivion, not that night.

It must have been about 1 a.m. when things starting coming at me. In icy shocked sweat, in blank-eyed delirious dream-sleep wonderful things came quick and spiky and with a screaming white heat.

The solution *and* the problem. Me. My gift. I had been staring too mathematically at pure beauty. I had been calculating infinite digits, when the prime number was simply ONE. This booklet was not some tawdry piece of sub-doctoral writing; not an abstruse university manuscript; nor was it simply an academic curio which had piqued Hicks's interest.

No. None of these.

It should never have been called just a document. That was an insult. It was the blueprint of wit itself. It was the archetype of human lightness. And somehow, my eyes were opening.

6

Good Material

I awoke shivering. Freezing. Fucking freezing. Four minutes past something. I gasped, the safe reality of my pastel-blue bedroom seeming a non sequitur. Cloying wafts of vanilla plug-in air freshener aided a fuller consciousness. My jotter with two paltry pages of half-hearted plans sat on my duvet near my knee, my pencil inertly next to the last word I'd doodled an hour and a half before. Stretching my icy forearm from the bed I placed my moist palm against the chipped white ridges of the radiator. Scalding.

The dream had been powerful and simple – a recurring nightmare rooted in a real-life trauma. I had not dreamt it for years. I'm standing onstage, at the Laughing Goat, Camden, 1992, the only other live stand-up performance I ever attempted. I had always known I must try it at least once – see if theory could become practice. The whole thing had been disastrous. Five minutes of hell. The five minutes in which I realized once and for all there was no correlation between the things I saw and the things I might say. I would never decant the nectar of which I was a connoisseur.

I tried blinking away the vivid visuals recalled by the dream. No good. They burnt and they came through and stayed viciously hot in my mind.

Onstage, two minutes, eighteen seconds into my routine about life at the Centre. I knew it was funny. Perfectly, mathematically, funny. But although my material was pure-hewn art, every word died in my mouth. I sucked the joy from every syllable. The marrow of each word dissolved into an insipid paste. During the third disastrous minute, as I continued dying horribly, the audience started their disaffected mutterings. I switched my mouth to automatic. My mind presented the horrible truth. To these shallow comedy-consumers, my material was unimportant, the vapid cult of personality paramount.

July 1992. I was a bad pun away from writing my first reviews. Ents floor had begun to respect its strange older-than-usual junior. I knew my time was coming. After ten demeaning years, the senior critics (Raymond Collins and Jackie Barker did theatre as well as comedy back then) finally saw how my strangely mechanistic observations gave their flaccid pieces the stamp of expertise. I knew material, I saw how it worked. In seconds, in fractions of seconds, I could break things down into precise technical paragraphs of buffed and oiled critical malice.

Sadly, this burgeoning respect from my journalistic peers prompted me, aged twenty-eight, into the Laughing Goat ordeal. I wouldn't have attempted this had I not foolishly believed I could succeed. Though this made it so much worse. I had read and reread my five-minute monologue. It could not have been improved if Aristophanes himself had redrafted it. But my material, it turned out, was not the point. Bad jokes about wanking, good jokes about the Gulf War, neither here nor there. If the audience deemed the comedian a joyless, impassive – let's be honest here, a boring person, he was toast. That's what they saw after all. Yes, comedy 'lovers' needed enlightening. I saw straight away that the truth of 1980s comedy, that coruscating time of politics, venom and raging against the machine, was in its death throes; the era of the dickhead had begun.

In my flat (Morden back then) I had rehearsed into the hallway mirror. I convinced myself that total deadpan (in vogue thanks to new hotshot David Galton) would scaffold the darker meanderings of my routines about mental health. There were logistical problems too: the bottlenecking of my thoughts. How would I control the rush of concepts? By memorizing an exact script. Heckles, I'd simply ignore. Any tangents or rebuttals that came up, I'd wholly disregard. This seems idiotic now. How could I, an alleged savant of humour, have been so naive, so patently wrong? What's beautiful or human about flaw-lessness?

'Good evening, ladies and gentlemen,' and my mono-tone stream of perfection gassed the room. Geometrically perfect call-backs in the fourth minute; six word-play devices (pun, pleonasm, contraction, synecdoche, homo-phones, and bathetic swearing) in the second and third minutes; and fourteen semicircular thought reversals. I had convinced myself this android performance would please the audience. But in 1992, as now, comedy audiences were personality-loving beings. They cared not for the perfectly written. If good material coincided with great personality all the better, but for someone like me, well: I was screwed; destined to criticize or be criticized.

After my five minutes, I tore from the stage, leaving behind my expensive leather satchel stuffed full of ideas for further performances and an Edinburgh show. I bar-relled out of the tube at Oxford Circus. I needed the Nellie Dean pub. I thanked God out loud I'd never told a soul about my first and last 'gig'. Downing three half-pints, I vowed that if I ever achieved my dream of reviewing comedians, I would destroy and crush the immaterial, the intellectually lazy – and champion only true material-genius. This vow I bloody-well honoured.

When I remembered this gig in my trauma dream, it

left me depressed, deflated – full of the remembered horror. It wasn't even really what one should call a dream. What was altered or fantastical about it? It was a cruel photocopy of a horrible evening from my life.

Except not this time. How different this night's version.

Most would assume that *all* my dreams are blunt and literal. Not the case. Mostly they're uplifting and outlandish, just like yours. Even now they're wacky. Flying – I flew at least once last week; magic, transmagnifications, weird erotica, bizarre adventure and adrenalin as far as my subconscious imagination would propel me.

But never had I dreamt the sensation of laughter. I felt robbed of that. Back at the Centre my classmates who had congenital disabilities, motor or mental, all experienced vivid dreams in which they were free from their defects. The paraplegic artist boy, Darryl Paige-Edwards (in Tate Britain, April 2009, apparently); born with two withered stumps for legs and an inability to make eye contact. He had a sublime talent for painting the human face; borderline genius, I'd say. How could Darryl, who had never known the sensation of walking, dream of running? Why did he awake with the residual memory of a satisfying barefoot thud connecting with damp grassy earth? *His* imaginative faculty enabled it. Why not mine? My imagination was undamaged. I played as a child.

I imagine stories now, I've tried to write fiction before. I can imagine a laugh in words – look:

*THE SURGE RISES IN THE THROAT, AND A NOISE
COMES OUT OF THE MOUTH. THE BRAIN EXPE-
RIENCES A PLEASANT SENSATION OF RELEASE. A
LAUGH. HA HA HA HA. HE FUCKING LAUGHED.
HA HA HA.*

See. Why then shouldn't I have dreamt what it *feels* like
to laugh? I wonder if the blind dream in images.

Yes, it alarmed me that after five or six years this sense-
less nightmare should return, but what terrified me, what
confused and ripped at me, was its new ending. It had
been recast.

Trembling, I wiped the icy beads from my forehead
and switched on my reading lamp. My hair was soaked.
The sheets were sodden. My jotter was virtually empty.
There had been two differences in my dream this night,
one small the other . . .

First, the minor discrepancy: I was thirty-nine in the
dream and not twenty-eight. What did that mean? Time
had moved on; the dream was commenting, not replaying?
I eyed Jung Volume VIII on the bookshelf. No – much too
shaken up for indulgence.

Apart from this rather cosmetic discrepancy, the climax
of the dream was different. What a bland adjective to
describe what happened. What a flat collection of letters to
carry the momentous thing. This wasn't just new detail in
a dream.

In this fresh cut, I didn't end by fleeing the dingy

above-pub room at the Laughing Goat, Camden. Instead, as I spoke the last words of my five-minute disaster, the audience began clapping. Not warm congratulatory applause. No, a functional and forced ovation, good-natured nonetheless, but patronizing. I still felt the urge to bolt, but found I could not. I was dream-cliché paralysed. The audience's smatterings died to a trickle and I surveyed them. They were a bizarre, motley selection of humans, gaping and peering like extras in a Kafka adaptation, all of them strangers but one. I gasped, taking in a breath like a cat disappearing through a door ajar. Sitting at a small candlelit table was Becky, my Becky. A contemporary Becky, too. Thirty-nine-year-old Becky. Sitting with Pierre, eight-months-pregnant Becky. His arm grotesquely snaked around her and clamped at her breast. He scowled at me. He flicked his lustrous silver Swiss mane left and right and massaged her milky teats, and scowled. Still I could not escape. I could not move a proverbial muscle. I gawked at the audience. They waited, more than waited. They leaned in, necks telescoping absurdly from shoulders with gristly creaks. They knew that more would come. Yet no one knew exactly what, especially me. I attempted speech. At first nothing; then an alien guttural noise, bestial, an Elizabethan-feast belch, a sort of primal gastric song. To my surprise, a few people chuckled, Becky included. I panicked. I tried to run, but my legs were still locked. I bucked and convulsed but remained rooted to the spot.

Mild chuckles dimmed to awkward throat-clearing, and again the weird semicircle of long-necked strangers craned in anticipation of something no one knew quite what. My right side released from its paralysis. All eyes turned to my leg. Slowly, I brought my right knee up to chest height and began dangling my ankle. I swivelled camply; the swivel was more than camp, fractured-looking. Again, warm smiles and chuckles, even laughter. Becky's quickly surged and drowned out the others'. This was a different breed of noise. She began giggling, rising into snorts, belly-laughing, and swiftly into an unnatural, maniacal screaming, hollering, tears running down her face, eyes screwed to slits. Pierre tried to subdue her, half leering, half pacifying – he himself giggling. She shoved him from his chair so forcefully that he broke a window. Screams from the street. Becky bellowed even harder, turning back and opening her mouth wider and wider until the vermilion corners where her lips met tore open and blood trickled down her chin in a sharp scarlet funnel.

That's when I started lifting from the dream. I sweated and floated into consciousness, but just before the scene dissolved one last momentous thing occurred. As the tableau mosaiced and faded, I did it. I . . . I dreamt my first laugh. A short satisfying black bark of laughter. Victorious, self-praising, yet hot, full, it ran through me like an orgasm. I might vomit, I might die. I might come – I laughed. And when my sweat-pricked eyelids fired open onto my pastel-blue bedroom, the trace of that dream laugh, my first ever laugh, was still upon my lips.

I gulped a pint of tepid water at the kitchen sink. As I swallowed each mouthful I glanced over my shoulder into the lounge. The manuscript lay on the floor by the wall, burning at me, calling like a neglected lover. I strode into the lounge and slowly lifted it, brushing away the dirt from its cover. I opened it on page one. A loud crash. My pint-glass had slipped from my hand and shattered on the laminate floor.

My mistake had been fundamental.

All I knew, all I had ever needed to know, was the art of decoding. From the moment I was born and my father and Uncle Jeff assaulted my sensibilities with vacuous wit, right up to Ali and Chaz's faux-laddish japing: all I knew was unscrambling. I'd spent so long building coherent images from the messy pointillism of everyday humour that I was blind to pure daubs and pictures. That's what this was, I realized. I believed I had gone through life seeing the essence, the unalloyed form of humour; but I had been interpreting the fuzzy shadows thrown by that form; the shapes people made. I had never needed more than people's offerings; the motivations that drove them. I had no knowledge or witness of pure humour itself. I had never seen the ore from which wit was worked.

I rabidly reread the manuscript. Pins of spittle hit the yellowed paper as I read aloud. Sentences, numerals, clauses, illustrations flickered as I poured myself into them. My eyeballs swelled and twitched as when one follows the windows of a passing train. I could not grasp it. It was all loose, all gas. I was raking my fingers through clouds. The stuff was undeniably, maddeningly there, yet intangible, a ghost in the room. I flung the manuscript again, firmly this time so that some sheets detached and fell away like a pigeon hit by a car. Was I so used to effect that cause was now invisible? I massaged my face with the leaves, inhaling their historic earthiness. In here somewhere was the answer – the reason I had just laughed. I felt I was knocking on the wall of a cave searching for hidden chambers, but every knock echoed. Every tap screamed treasure. I was confounded by the richness of the haul.

'. . . in Movement Two, although your choice of clause and subject is personal (indeed it should be something entirely germane to your persona) the employment of Zambian Belching is essential in psychic-transmutation of humour into its archetype . . .'

Each sentence refracted; Russian-dolled into infinite pinprick definitions upon which I couldn't focus. I kept glimpsing solutions without questions. Answers hovered beside me, transient and coy. If I turned and faced the problems, if I focused, they vanished.

I ransacked my utility cupboard in the hallway. The emergency bottle of Johnnie Walker! I broke it open and dropped the cap; began swigging wildly. I hated the taste of it. It did nothing for me except numb me, but that's exactly what was needed. A turning down of the high-frequency dials; just the bass left humming.

I forced myself to stay in the hallway for a good ten minutes. I worked steadily at the bottle, swilling down the brown fluid like a hardened drinker. In between gulps I stared at the manuscript on the sofa. I was a boxer eyeballing his opponent between rounds. Perhaps if I took one sentence, just one clause, a paragraph at most, maybe if I wrote it down in my own hand in my own jotter. Of course, this risked achieving the opposite purpose. I might focus more closely: more meaning locked out. A few more swigs would bring the numbness. It was worth the risk.

I swept up my jotter and edged into the lounge. I looked down at the manuscript, down at it – in all senses. Fiercely, almost sexually, I seized it. I copied out a part of Movement One, Waterman pen tearing through the paper. I thought of Hicks's entry in the visitors' book. The manic exclamation mark, the implacable aggression of red biro. Did he travel this same madman's corridor?

I read my scrawl aloud:

'STANCE
This is most important. We have Chrysippus and his donkey Naxys to thank for the herein numerical exactitude, and intrinsic hilarity.

'You will need to take the Drunken Donkey pose, hereafter DDP, or more directly the Stance. Your buttocks must thrust outwards so that the small of your back makes a 90 degree angle. Your feet should point inwards, toes opposite. The legs should be 81cm apart. Arms must be thrust forward, with forearms hanging limply at a 90 degree angle towards the surface of the performance area. You will notice that the small of the back and the arms form a Euclidean Quadric Paradox.

'Performing on a slope will require adjustment for accurate executions on the DDP/Stance.

'With your right hand, repeatedly grasp at three-second intervals as though you were reaching for a fig. Bring the hand to your mouth and repeat the manoeuvre at three-second intervals for the first eighteen seconds.

'This, combined with the first clause of the second part of the syntactical executions in Movement Two, is how you should commence the sixty-one seconds of the Primordial Architechtonic Synthesis, hereafter, PAS, or Pure Humour, or the Formula.'

I glanced at my pad, an entire page filled with a frantic imitation of my handwriting. I fetched a tape measure from the kitchen, chugging again and again at the whisky. My stomach protested, the walls of my lounge heaved.

I read it once more word by word, then began enacting these bizarre moves. I used my antique mirror for accuracy. I thrust my arse towards the wall. I contorted my legs as instructed. I started jumping around the lounge in this position. I thought of Chrysippus, the drunken donkey

Naxys. I jumped up onto the sofa and back down onto the laminate and made sure the insides of my feet landed on the zero and the 81 of the tape measure. I tried the whole thing several times over. Each landing became more aggressive. Ornaments fell from the mantelpiece. Sweat trickled down my back in a foetid stream. Instead of helping, monitoring myself in the mirror made the moves self-conscious, stiff. I hooked the mirror off the wall and slid it savagely across the laminate into the hallway. I wanted it to break. I wanted it to hit the skirting and shatter, just so something dramatic would happen.

I repeated the Stance over and over, maybe eight or nine times. Vomit rose in my throat and hair stuck to my face. The whisky was finished. There was something ridiculous about the empty bottle, but it was not as ridiculous as the feeling of the moves themselves. Try a different tack, do it in slow motion. I was about to attempt this when I glimpsed myself at a 45 degree angle in the dull grey of the television screen, my hand pinching at an imaginary wine-soaked fig. I pinched again. A misty, half-reflection – a translation of the move. I saw something. I saw for a second some light.

I fell backwards, electrocuted, belching a thick ball of porridgy vomit over my chin. It spread out over my chest and dripped onto my knees and the floor. My toes vibrated as an infinitesimal white-hot pin of humour ran through me. No language commented or broke it down, there was just the hotness and knowing it was there. Normally my perceptions manifested themselves in language. I'd see a printout, or hear a description of the humour, or occasionally perceive it as a gas or a whisper. But not now. I can only describe it as light and heat and not thought. The difference between music and literature. The chords of it came into me without interpretation – and they were atonal. This surprised me. *Purely atonal.* Humour in its ore. Even ugly, ungainly, unhewn. Yet dangerously powerful, undeniably that. Who says power is beautiful? Not many. It's an ugly rocky thing. I looked down at my shorts: a warm patch of urine soaked the front of them. Sitting into my chair, panting, I fell into mild shock. It was 4 a.m.

Two hours lost here: 6.30 a.m. and I had not managed to repeat the feat; not even a tremor or a glimpse. Nor had I written a single word in my pad. I had four sentences in total.

I drifted briefly into sleep. My dreams were violent, sexual, disordered – devoid of humour.

At seven or so, I picked up my pad and forced myself to write the bare bones of a feature plan. I just needed it to be good enough to fool that superficial tosspot Dominic. I wanted desperately to repeat the strange experience. I forced good sense to prevail. I knew I had to make the piece seem compelling, even though I no longer cared about it. Journalism, now? Truth be told, I did not care a wine-soaked fig for Dominic, Miranda, or anyone in that parasitical place – that amorphous criticism existing in the shadows of creativity; the shitty fumes of art. I had felt a laugh, the trace of a laugh, and nearly seen its source, the source of all laughter. No one would stop me exploring further. No one!

Somehow it came back to Bill Hicks. The only person on earth who could connect these dots would be Professor David Leavey. To get to him I needed the *Review*. This meant I needed Dominic to believe that this was the best feature he would ever commission; that he simply *must* arrange for me a rendezvous with the Professor. Yes, I would use them all and, when I had what I needed, drop everyone; perhaps even the Professor himself. I started fantasizing wild, evil things. I would die to understand what was happening to me. I would kill to learn more.

A noise issued from the bedroom – my alarm announcing sixteen minutes to eight. I threw my soiled shorts in the washing basket and climbed into the shower. Every five minutes or so I let out a scream. Dr Rowe had taught me this surrogate too. In places where one might emit whoops of joy, I used screaming. I screamed and screamed until my neighbour banged on the wall. I banged back. Hard. When I finished showering I rolled around on my bed like a washed dog, naked and howling into a towel.

I ate no breakfast.

I took no public transport.

I walked, wired, feeling quite insane, determined to see more of this white-hot light.

7

New Act

I was transfixed by my own nose. It's something people find hard to ignore. At times when I needed to be bland, that blunt awkward piece of cartilage always let me down.

One Friday evening: the Comedy Café, the City, London. James Dakota's set had been what I called 'class-stereotyping comedy drawing its faux force from dead tropes' and what Miranda rephrased as, 'typical upper-working-class, few-Penguin-Classics-in-the-hard-drive drivel'. Ninety per cent of his 'material' drew its Pavlovian laughs through banal name-checks such as hummus, balsamic vinegar, quail's eggs, the names 'Ollie and Jemima', Oxbridge, cherry tomatoes, IKEA; a set so riddled with easy clichés and gaping flaws it left me breathless, shocked at the crowd's susceptibility. Did I show it? I dared not. I watched disgusted as he floated off stage, riding after-applause and waving, victoriously parading. He pushed his way through tables stacked high with fried chicken, wedged chips and tequila-shot glasses. Troops of City-worker males cheered, quaffing at his cocktail of class-rants and genital humour.

This was the second time in as many months I'd witnessed him being received so well. He was just finishing his dilettante lap of honour when he caught sight of me. His body steeled and I knew I must react very carefully, or better still disappear. I straightened up. If only I could have smiled then, waved that emotional white flag in the normal human way. But I had to wait for him to make the call. My craven jotter in my hand, my ridiculous pale hair, and my damn nose – flat and repunchable. I had good reason to fear his fists.

James Dakota was the only comic on the circuit who had ever struck me in the face. I'd been shoved a few times, barged. Juliette Vere-Thompson (all Cheltenham Ladies' College and no punchlines) spat on my grey muslin jacket once, but only James Dakota had screwed his massive hand into a fist and laid me out cold. Six foot three of white working-class ex-builder who had read too much. We had a lot in common really, but no meeting of minds here. He was brimful with an outmoded half-baked Marxist hate. I'm sure he'd convinced himself I was one of 'the elite'. It would have been useless to plead my case with him; that I was an oppressed, sub-educated sub-editor, denied promotion for ten years; refused acknowledgement wherever I turned, no matter what I did; pointless to try and rationally explain that unleashing my no-holds-barred form of criticism, although it felt personal, was simply and necessarily accurate to the metaphysical core of those being reviewed. No. Take a breath. For pleading any of this would have been futile. Indeed on the night of the assault, a few months before this Comedy Café encounter, I never managed to utter a sound. Before a syllable of protest could issue from my demonized 'gob', his fists were in the air and blackness came swiftly after.

Maybe I'd deserved it that night. It was at a show called the Big Big Small Gig, held at the Mary Royal near Embankment – he wasn't even performing that night. He'd hunted me down – because of something I had written of course. It was a stressful time of year for us all, comics and critics alike, everyone jostling for notice, hoping to be selected for the Melbourne Festival. Well-reviewed gigs could get a comic a run at the Mondialle Theatre in downtown Melbourne. Incisive copy could land a journalist in a plush hotel on Swanston Street for a month telling the rest of the world who was hot and who was shit that year in Oz. Everyone upped their game. Performances heightened, strained – reviews with stinging clauses abounded. I crossed the critical line. Allowed myself to enjoy the venom, I mean. Two days before I had decimated a set of his which I endured at the Giggling Antelope, Wimbledon. Annette Singh of guffaw.co.uk emailed me on the day of publication congratulating me on this paragraph:

> 'James Dakota's oafish archery at such hackneyed and obvious middle-class targets in comedy, is like watching a Down's syndrome child fling excrement at a Venetian sculpture.'

The simile of course had been mostly Miranda's work. The insight, the bathetic comparison, the painful accuracy and cancerous correctness of the criticism: all mine. And I got the by-line to myself. When I received Annette's email of laced praise, I knew I'd gone too far. I had been intoxicated by thoughts of travelling to wonderful Melbourne, by ego, and I knew I was in danger.

It didn't take Dakota long to find out where I'd be that night. He entered the Mary Royal through the snug door clutching a copy of the *Review* and primed for violence. He roared, the crowd parted, and it was quickly done.

I didn't press charges, critics never do. We can't arm those we comment upon with anything, especially the realization that we're human. But, four months later, when we bumped into each at the Comedy Café, I knew straight away that more repercussions were due. Four months was too soon for another review, but would this occur to him, blinkered with rage? He would assume that I was there to exact some sort of printed revenge. I had a few vital seconds in which to let him know I was unarmed. When the heat was on, I was as much at peace being namby-pamby or sap as anyone else. I considered running, throwing my sissy pad down, and fleeing the club, possibly screaming. I'll admit this too: if James Dakota *had* been due for a fresh review, I would have vocally cancelled it before he got within ten metres of me. Yes. I was a normal Englishman without integrity when it comes to his job, just like millions of others.

So, as James Dakota strode through the fug and fake Marxism of the Comedy Café, I desperately tried signalling. I waved and nodded that I came in peace. I wanted to let him know I was there to crush the gay Indie-haired new act who had spent five minutes declaiming about Waitrose and *Big Brother*'s Jade Goody. But my nose failed me. It involuntarily invited James Dakota. (I shouldn't blame my mother for my nose, but I do: *did*. Mine was a bad birth. I was forced from the birth canal and into the unfunny world. My nose crushed against her pelvis, pressed downwards into a permanent sardonic nub. No, not a nub, a sneer, more a sort of inverted sneer. The nose of a vintner looking at a bottle of £2.99 Asda wine. That's funny – for me.)

'You fucking parasite cunt. I'm gonna acid your face, you cunt.'

'James. I'm not here to ...'

'It's a bloke's livelihood. See what your arms look like now. In five minutes they ain't gonna look like that.

They're gonna look like that spastic's over there.' He pointed to a disabled chap watching us in horror.

'Please, James.'

Out of the corner of my eye I saw club manager Hels Mellish laughing (a failed comedienne, with a back catalogue about clitorises, men and menstruation). My fountain pen fell from my hand, landing on its nib in a gruesome inky pool. He stamped on my pad crushing it into the blue ink, and kicking it under a table of shocked, but enthralled, City men. My paragraphs viciously dismantling the wannabe onstage were lost for ever. James Dakota brought his face up to mine. His Stella Artois breath was laboured, spittle-ridden. In the last moment, at the behest of a large African bouncer, he resisted full assault.

'You can fucking-well take that look off your face, you cunt,' he said. 'Or I will. With acid.'

But I couldn't take 'that look' off, and I never would. That had always been my problem.

It was a similar problem this morning after the night before with Leavey's manuscript. Dominic Wray was in fine spirits, steeped in them. Lucky for me, he stank so much of fine spirits that he failed to notice my hangover.

A long walk had given me a vital chance to steady my overt – I suppose symptoms is the right word. A veneer of normality would be crucial in this meeting. It took at least fifty minutes to walk from Clapham into the West End via

Vauxhall Bridge. I told myself this would be enough time to calm: but before it got better, it got much worse.

I had begun by checking my reflection in the windows of every parked car. I had a strange sense of being someone else, someone new and malevolent. Smoothing back my hair, I slowed to a stroll, trowelling off palmfuls of sweat, flinging them away in salty showers onto the cold dry pavement. I stopped and purchased a blackcurrant Lucozade from a newsagent, chugging the dark sugary liquid while still in the shop. I felt feverish, wobbly as I walked towards Vauxhall. My forehead burned. I checked in the wing mirror of a Land Rover – dilated pupils. I had to seem normal or all would be in jeopardy. If I could fix my outward appearance, perhaps my mind would level.

I rested by a battered old Ford Fiesta, inspecting myself in its window, now at full frontal, now at left profile. A sorry image of a man. Nearly forty, receding blondish hair and my hateful squashed nose.

Dominic would think the Zambia trip a one-off, a condescending gift bestowed upon the special child, but if he got a whiff it had transformed into some sort of tacit promotion, he'd drop the idea in a moment.

I posed in more car windows. At one point I considered bloodying my nose into disguise. Injury would damage me less than self-assurance. The lowest point. I considered turning back. I could phone in sick? It was true, I was ill.

I could hear the angry traffic of Vauxhall Bridge a few

metres away. I stumbled to a stop in one of those oddly serene oak-lined residential streets where the threat of stabbing and middle-class dog-walking happily co-exist. I moved my weight from heel to heel, rocking. The crisp winter breeze blew narrow and metallic, penetrated everything like a malignant auditor. The sky seemed too bright, chemically clear. A large Range Rover offered a chance of deluxe mirroring. Checking there were no voyeurs, I adopted the Leaveyian Stance. This was extremely dangerous, yet the sense of its danger encouraged me. Fuck it. Entropy. Just one taste, hit. A quick retest would keep me going all day. I thrust my buttocks outwards; dangled my arms. I jumped up and down with my feet in that peculiar rickets-damaged pose. Dry branches complained and creaked with winter, old bones above my head. I jumped around some more. And there it was. A shot of hot bile, but not unpleasant. The glow of its beginning. I froze. Shock, surprise that anything had happened – out in the open like this. I'd been convinced it would not work, not in public; yet – a shard, a razor of light, like swallowing a light bulb – but it does not break. Undeniable, implacable, live flesh being torn and eaten – but without pain. A sneeze that goes on and on – imagine that. I almost fell onto my backside. I straightened up, tried to think: normal. My body pulsed with spasms. A cramping twist went up through my guts pushing painfully against my bladder, my bowels, my lungs. It was all so free from words and ideas, just a burning, a knowing; a cruelly pure sensation of funny. I felt it in the same way I would a piece of Bruce or Hicks, yet free from all agents, all thought. I did not smile. My arms began twitching. My pelvis throbbed. I realized with horror I was about to piss myself. Leaning against the Range Rover I yanked out my penis. A copious stream of dark yellow urine, all booze and stress and bad thoughts. I failed to notice an approaching pair of schoolgirls. They passed me, pissing, dick in hand, saying out loud to myself, 'Bill Hicks, Bill Hicks, it's too pure, it can't be.' They ran away screaming.

It was another ten streets and a good few bridges before I once again felt anything close to calm.

I worked hard to annoy Miranda and stoke her negative impulses before the meeting. I needed Dominic diverted, and an angry Miranda was always good value. I called up Zambia websites, chatting uncharacteristically about my excitement at the thought of the trip. I discussed it with Chaz. Miranda listened. At first she took a back-slapping, flirty tack. She even made a few obscene remarks; hinting at what she called 'reward sex'. But the odours that clung to her, her garish, desperate choice of blazer kept me safe and focused. Shortly before our ten o'clock with Dominic, her salacious friendliness darkened. Nudges shifted into leering winks and smoothly into tutting. Annoyed, she accused me of 'uppityness'; reminding me we were 'a team', she was my boss as well as my 'fuck-buddy'. Ha. At ten sharp, Dominic had called us in with his strange fucked-in-the-Latin-room holler, leaning out of his office and pressing his gut against the blunt ridge of the glass partition. As we marched from our pod towards his lair, Miranda had panicked, gearing back into oiliness; touching me, tactilely claiming *her* protégé.

The meeting had begun unusually for a Dominic Wray.

'I have to say, Benjamin,' Dominic said, flinging his styrofoam cup at the wastepaper basket and missing, 'this is bloody good. Bloody good. Might make main.'

Thank you, sir, I thought. He was unshaven. Yesterday's shirt. Had Mrs Wray not wanted him home? Again? I looked for the framed picture of his two girls. It was face-down by his mouse mat. I thought of my own portrait of Becky. This is why I was here: not because of the Humour, or my problems, but because of love. I was the same.

'Fantastic!' said Miranda.

'You OK, Benny boy?' he said.

I felt a surge of vomit in my throat. Careful now. 'Yes. I walked in this morning. No Northern Line, you see. I'm a bit sweaty. And stressed. It's a good stress though, you see.' Yes. Two 'you see's. I'll never forget that.

There was an awkward pause while Dominic assessed my syntax. His face decided into smile. Vomit receded.

'Look at him, he's loving it!' exclaimed Dominic, testing a little more, pushing, but satisfied.

'We're both loving it!' said Miranda. It was too eager; she had brought something bad into the meeting: envy.

Dominic's gaze switched. He wished to play. This would serve my purpose. Miranda envious of Benjamin. *Miranda and Benjamin arguing. Jolly good show*. The twisted little games he could not resist.

He was falsely chipper, perhaps still slightly drunk, playful – cocky. He kept getting up and circling, acting the comedy connoisseur, all arms and eyebrows and pontification. Not once did he address Miranda directly. Relief – we were playing a game. After five minutes or so, she began fidgeting in her seat, her smile fixing crookedly like a stroke victim. Five minutes more, and her semblance of managerial pride had melted under Dominic's searing praise of me. The ugly side of her jealousy started leaking. Over-exclamations. False, piercing laughs. I would rather my no-laugh than that fake one. She was so transparent. It's one of the many things I loved about her. Dominic loved it too. You knew where you stood. If she thought you a cunt, you would be told matter-of-factly as you returned carrying coffee or a folder.

'This feels almost tailor-made, Dom,' I said. I was speaking – somehow words were peeping out like voles grown brave.

'Your turn, Miranda,' he said.

The scene for him was scripted. He'd probably planned the whole thing the night before. I imagined him laughing as he drank himself into oblivion playing solitaire and self-Googling in a Premier Inn.

'Made for the writing,' Miranda said.

'For the doing,' I said in a tone no one recognized, including me.

'The doing.' Dominic laughed. 'The doing . . .'

I watched the avarice ripple under Miranda's cheek-bones in pulsed clenches.

'Well what's the timing for us then?' she asked. The question poked out in an awkward yap, its plural pronoun glowing like a diamond on black cloth. It was the mistake that closed her game. I knew she'd move from this to explicit defence. She was more than capable, and oh, and she did.

Dominic smiled. 'Enanda has already called. Wants you in town by close of play Thursday, Benjamin. You'll have go-go via Joburg. Night flight. Business class.'

Miranda winced.

'It really is amazing,' I said, pleased for once at my default flatness.

'Don't shit your pants about it.' Dominic laughed. The laugh was cruel, it felt divine. Miranda joined in with a high-pitched macaque yelp. I felt safe. She was too good a journalist, his deputy, his main senator, his right-hand girl; no way would he send her. His dependency plus his malicious boredom were my shields.

'I really am excited, Dom,' I said. 'I promise.' Again, colourless. Good.

But then my body let me down.

Three fat beads of sweat geysered from my forehead. They converged into a torrent and trickled down the bridge of my flat nose. I quickly pinched away the runnel. Miranda, feline sharp, saw it all. Her paws flexed. Something else was in me. She knew it. She saw it then. This was more than just a career first; more than self-development. What was I hiding?

'Me too,' put in Miranda. 'Not as excited as Benjamin though.'

I nodded.

'Yes,' she continued, lips narrowing into teeth, 'I've never seen him like this, Dom. He's been mucking around with Chaz all morning, sending emails, running round the office. He's brimming with pride – aren't you, Benny?'

'You are? Good,' said Dominic. It was his turn to artificially smile.

'I just wanted to make sure—'

'Make sure, make sure?' Miranda cut me off. 'It's quite a biggie for rookie Benji-bot. I'm all in favour of you going on your own, babe, but the way you're shaking, you'd think you were running the front page. Ha! I'm sure that's what Chaz thought.' She did it with enough laughter and irony to simulate anodyne banter. Dominic smiled still, but that image, the idea of my rising to power, worked poisonously upon him.

'Chaz and he shook hands about it. Shook! Ha ha ha! More coffee anyone?'

Clever. Sneaky cow.

I watched Dominic play out the scene in his mind: Benjamin on his own, enjoying his hotel room, throwing his weight around with Enanda, the phone call to London from Dominic's cronies, the complaints, the ceding of power to an imbecile. I sat before him like a sick prince. I had one chance to counter Miranda's strike.

'It will disappoint, you know, the boring reality of that handshake,' I said. 'I emailed my mother – asked her to water my plants. And I asked Chaz if he wouldn't mind taking care of my cactus.' I paused. 'So, I'm ready.'

I'll admit it. I made myself more monotone, more devoid of warmth than usual. Miranda paled. It was the first time since I had worked there that I had protected myself. Not only that, I'd used her own brand of subterfuge: self-effacement. She looked shocked, momentarily floored. Dominic would never suspect idiot-genius Benjamin White of manipulating how he was perceived. It was the perfect counter-attack: part nerd, part zombie. It staunched Miranda's aggression. I could almost feel the cold card of my gold-embossed, priority lane boarding pass.

His patronizing smile returned. 'I know you're ready, Benja-bot – I've programmed you myself.' He laughed from his stomach, accidentally following through with a half-belch which came right at me, conveying a history of coffee, fried-egg sandwiches, and loneliness.

The energy evened. My body temperature stabilized as the meeting drifted back into functional talk of flights and deadlines. Miranda lowered her weapons and bit at her nails. I watched Dominic's mouth as he droned on enjoying his moment of patronage. He swivelled this way and that, opining and tilting in his chair, testicles and cock bulging obscenely against the seam of his grey flannel trousers. I indulged in a quick fantasy. Unleash a white dagger of humour upon him right at that moment. Maybe his face would split and twist into laughter like Becky's did in the dream. Would he be so regal then? It doesn't matter who you are, what you think you are, dignity melts when one's helpless with laughter. It levels us.

'Benjamin?'

I jumped from the fantasy.

'What are you doing with your leg?' Dominic was smiling, but there was an edge.

Miranda swivelled.

'Oh ... Cramp ... unfit.' I had been camply dangling my ankle in front of him.

'Are – are you feeling OK, Benjamin?' said Miranda. 'You look pale. Fetch yourself a coffee or water or something.'

'I'm OK. Thank you.' I would not leave her alone with him until my tickets and hotel were booked.

'Well I'd like one, wouldn't you, Dom?'

'It's OK, Mindy,' said Dom, 'we're nearly done.' Mindy. He said Mindy. She was finished.

They broke off into a fiery mini-tiff; witty, funny, yet underpinned with real spite. As I watched them, I locked my feet under my chair and silently reprimanded myself for losing focus. Now and again Miranda would say something so genuinely nasty that they would both laugh and I would watch their humour by numbers before me. Cold jibes and warm noises formed the lifts and dips in the music of their conversation. Yet, for the first time, I reflected on not how lucky they were, but how weak. They would never feel the substance of what I had felt a few hours before. They were cursed to a life of humour-snacking. I sat up slightly. These unaccustomed feelings of superiority were hazardous. What was happening? Not like me to look down on two normal, laughing adults. Envy was my usual stance; self-pity or longing. But not today. Something had shifted. I felt like an orphan who has just seen his birth certificate, his true status as prince or duke confirmed. They existed for me on a lower plane now. Again, dangerous. I squashed these reflections. Not out of any modesty (though these egocentric impulses did bother me), I'd had a lifetime of invisibility; no, it was fear that someone might notice my new confidence. I had a dread of what conspicuous self-belief might bring, the blockades it could erect. I had to stay level, unimportant – just grateful enough. Interesting though: this arrogance of mine, this assumption that what I had experienced was beyond them. I audited my logic. Why should it be only me who experienced this thing? Someone else might unleash it. I thought of all the mercenary unpaid comics who worked the circuit. What they would do if they knew. More reasons to remain covert.

'I could always go in support, if not as the primary,' said Miranda.

I snapped back into the debate. Miranda had abandoned all strategy. She was now outrightly foisting herself upon the project. If she persuaded Dominic and came with me to Livingstone, the real research would become impossible. I would have to bring her in on my discovery. No. That I was not willing to do.

'I really need you here,' said Dominic.

'I could go for the first forty-eight hours; until Benjamin's settled?' she said.

'No, Miranda,' I said firmly, suddenly.

She looked as though she'd been punched. 'I'm sorry?'

'Benjamin. Ha ha ha! Go on,' said Dom, delighted.

'I just think it is important that I finally do something on my own. I'm forty this year and I've never led a story ...'

'Benny, I ...'

'Let me finish. Please.' Miranda nearly fell off her chair as I continued. 'If I mess this story up, you need never give me another. But if you do not allow me to work on it alone, I ...'

'You'll what?' she said.

I was silent. Should I gamble?

'You'll what, Benjy boy ... Please, do tell us?' said Dom.

'If I can't go alone ... I shan't work on anything again.'

'You'll ...' she half-said.

'I'll leave. This morning. Keep my pay. Fuckers.'
Fuckers? Delight and horror.

Miranda's jaw fell fully open. Dominic's tightened – a

smile? This was risky. I had a fleeting image of Miranda naked, beneath me at the Christmas party, her holding onto me as I finished inside her. She knew I was essential. Dominic, however, he was arrogant enough to think anyone expendable. I hoped that my foul-mouthed resolution hit with his vicious sense of humour. He delighted in fall-outs, breakdowns.

'Hear, hear! Benny boy. Hear hear!' And he grasped my hand with his fat, wet palm and shook it firmly and I knew I had won.

'You cunt,' said Miranda. She stormed out of Dominic's glass cube slamming the logoed door hard enough for his Mondrian print to dislodge. There was an ironic cheer from Ali and Chaz's pod.

'Oh dear. It appears you've fucked her orf, Benjamin,' said Dominic, smiling oily and black.

Forty-eight hours later I would be eating roast chicken. In business class. Alone.

8

Pathos and Melancholy

The comic mode is thought a lower form by most. It doesn't matter whether it's a stand-up comedian plonked for the night in a 'serious' theatre, a volume of P.G. Wodehouse standing next to volumes of Proust, Aristophanes sitting with Sophocles – the comic form is considered lighter, less substantial. In humour's realm, practitioners and critics alike have a harder time of it. There's less greatness to go round, and any greatness achieved will be tarnished by the laughter. The assumption being that if one is laughing, it can't 'be great'. If one laughs, but then cries, or there's melancholy or there's pathos, that's OK, that's closer to art. But for the P.G.s, the Aristophanes, the Hickses, the idea of greatness enfeebles their art. Rilke said that criticism takes you away from art, and only love can make art true. So as a critic you try; yet every offering – sand, and you search and you search, but there is only insubstantial laughter, only fleeting noises of pleasure.

It's a human curse: finding more meaning in pain; we must be Kafka's insect, and never smile – perhaps I'm only talking about me. This is wrong, it's all wrong. Of course, *I* think it's wrong. I thought it before Leavey, and I believe it now. Laughter is light and automatic and good and this is its greatness; it just keeps some bad company, that's all. That's why Leavey sought its essence. And it *does* boil down. How it all boils down. And why shouldn't it? If poetry, plays and prose – why not wit?

Before I departed, I packed. I packed badly.

I packed a whole suitcase of useless things.

I packed the stuff of a man who might never come back.

I didn't go for my jabs. I kept the petty cash. I spent it wildly on fruit juices, chicken, and a single-malt whisky from Waitrose. In the forty-eight hours before my flight I holed up in my sealed nest and studied the manuscript. I didn't even bother collecting my malaria pills – an over-sight I would regret with both ends of my body.

Ridiculous, unsuitable objects ended up in my father's travel-worn brown leather suitcase. Books, sweaters, a guide to Southern France. I didn't remember packing any of it – especially the photograph. The one of her. The one of Becky.

I'd fetched the ancient suitcase from my parents' loft the previous day, refusing lunch before my mother had finished offering it. My father wanted to congratulate, toast success, but I brusquely made excuses; telling them I must work, lying about an early flight time. Cooper called my mobile phone that afternoon. I ignored it. Movement Two had hardened my addiction.

'The Syntactic Constructions in Forms of Humour.'

The Professor's paragraphs choked me: clouded with heavy clauses and dark ideas. They reminded me of a noisy new comic, Ben Hook, all vaunting attitude and no tuning. But thankfully Leavey had good material. Yes, the ungainly language spluttered and wheezed, but now and again I glimpsed the limpid thoughts beneath. I pushed myself into the hard unyielding jargon, and caught behind it a simple moonless beauty; caged things. I could nearly feel them through the iron bars of his over-thinking. I realize now this was exactly his point. His prose *was* overwrought, as was the world's humour. Once I stopped interpreting, language would mist away – a hidden code, solace in noise.

I stood before my mirror naked. I'd already lost weight, the first suggestions of a beard upon my face. I would grow it. Why not? Let the natural follicles burst through my skin and cover my face with wild bastard hair.

The flat stank eggy and sour: three full bin-bags in the kitchen, central heating rotting the remains of the chicken breast into a hot pulp.

The draw of Movement Two is that your own words and ideas remain. The beauty comes from the form, not the content. My 1992 attempt at a routine about the Centre, my mathematically perfect art about mental health, might breathe after all. I moved my legs apart and swung my genitals freely. I am a man, and I live. My body, my arse, my legs, my cock. I took the stance of Movement One. I tried pushing words and phrases into the modulations set down in Movement Two. I was yet to feel even the first burn of that white hard truth which would let me know I had it right. But I felt it close. Intuition, the cruel blade which had cut into my whole life, returned.

I seized the manuscript. I was about to reread Movement Two when I saw it. In my tumbled muddled suitcase of unchosen things I saw Becky – naked. *That* picture of Becky. How? I lifted up the worn faded image and inhaled it. Old books and food. It had been forgotten inside my Ainsley Harriott cookbook. For years she'd been pressed anonymously against the comic-turned-chef's recipe for Jamaican jerk chicken. I had no memory of packing her.

Placing the manuscript gently on the floor, I turned out the rest of the suitcase, rifling through the contents, desperate to stock-check my logic. Every item seemed silly, anachronistic. I thought back to the family-group shot cracked and face-down on my work desk. So here was my source. Here was my reason.

The photograph was taken in 1982, the year I 'graduated' from the Centre, the year we went to Venice. Both eighteen, and she so fucking beautiful it was like an illness. I *saw* her naked: her long legs, her armpits inexpertly stubbling, her firm breasts, her pale stomach, the thick dark knot of naive hair; and stretched out like a fine animal and letting me look, and I looked, and I grew silent and aroused.

Between 1974 and 1980 (courtesy of Miss Hathaway) my relationship with Becky had been in stasis. The Centre changed my world and my old life was stored away for a while. When I reached sixteen, I casually informed my parents I wished to stay on two more years at the Centre. It's hard to say which emotion presided, relief or hurt. We agreed I'd live at home for three nights a week, rather than just two. My father bought me my first car, an old grey Anglia, and this made it all easier. Becky and I had both chosen psychology and English literature for A level (I copied her) and it was natural we met and studied together on Wednesdays. I suppose I was OK company really. Fears of seeming ridiculous had made me a good listener and a timid, careful speaker. True, the Centre sheared the competitive edge from adolescence, but this absence of rivalry had made me quieter rather than more confident.

'Do you know what he did?' Becky said once, telling me a story about yet another boy who loved her.

'What?'

'He trod dog shit all the way through the house,' she gasped self-consciously with grown-up laughs, 'all the way from the front door to where he sat.'

'Oh.'

'Mum ... Mother was on her knees scrubbing. Dad just looked out into the garden. In a rage.'

'Priceless,' I said.

And she laughed harder at my discordant dull tone. I looked at her and she leant in to give me a maternal nuzzle. She had grown into a lithe, nearly sexual creature – black hair, green eyes, dark clothes and small French books.

'Flaubert.' she said, following my gaze.

'Good?'

'A twat.' She overplayed her self-assurance. I didn't mind. Her acting at womanhood was gauche; now sullen and biting, now crassly overdone.

Sometimes she would circle me in nightclothes or clad just in a bath towel, a studied impish look on her face.

'Let's draw each other!' Then she dressed clumsily.

The steady scratch of her Parker pen left me thrilled and breathless, her hair spilling onto my pages as we scribbled, forearms touching. Although things were strong and dangerous in me, it was still innocent. There was no badness, no cynicism. She always smelt of soap and twice I tried to kiss her, but nothing ever happened.

Another time I put down my pen and said, 'Kiss me.'

'What?'

'It's a dare.'

I knew she couldn't resist that, and for the tiniest moment, I felt her mouth and died.

The next year passed chummily enough. We finished revising for our A levels and sat the exams, her at the Sutton School for Girls, me at the Centre. Our collaboration was a success, both of us achieving As in English literature and psychology. It was Business French at Exeter for her, and journalism for me. But first, there was Venice.

On 19 August 1982, my father announced that a trip to Venice would be our reward; just the four of us, Uncle Jeff, Becky, my father and me. Thirteen-year-old Cooper was to stay at home with my mother. In my room I closed the door and punched the air. I shocked myself. I'd never managed an air-punch before. I tried repeating it; it came like a forced compliment.

Two weeks before the trip Martin dumped Becky for one of her best friends. She was devastated. The fucker had never loved her, just wanted to lose his virginity. We'd not seen eye to eye; I could tell not making fun of me was an effort for him. She had wanted sexual experiences too, but she loved him. Becky and I grew closer before the trip, sometimes spending hours: me listening, her crying. She declared I was the only man who understood. But I was her cousin, and that was the end of it. I knew these were merely the mutterings of a girl in trauma, but in the end, some force, some tendrils wound us close.

The afternoon before Venice we took all her photographs of Martin and drew phalluses going into his mouth and up his backside. I drew a gigantic cock ripping open the love-cheat's stomach. She laughed wildly, unfazed, relishing my flat, unamused face. When the sorrow got really bad, she spent time with my mother. I was never sure what to say, so I said nothing. I listened and watched, and it made me seem really tender. I did care of course. I really did. I loved her; but being honest, my stillness was sometimes put on. I appeared tuned in to her sadness, but in reality I was content. Glad he was off the scene. We spent the night before the trip watching a black-and-white film on television, our bare thighs touching.

The Venice break started predictably enough. Uncle Jeff and my father showed us around the usual galleries. My father told us what we should think and respect, while Uncle Jeff deputized with nods and leaflets and smiles. Becky and I were united in finding my father unfunny, and poor Uncle Jeff ridiculous in green explorer shorts plus wide-brimmed hat which accentuated his timid, carrot-shaped face. He was one of the good people, Uncle Jeff. I am sorry he died the way he did in 2002, but I'm glad he was gone before I did my thing.

After two or three days, a natural estrangement took hold. Uncle Jeff and my father would disappear to boozily consume art and music. Becky and I would walk and talk, but more often languidly watch Italian television in my hotel room, mocking it, mimicking the hammy gesticulations.

On the fourth morning she appeared in reception and told me she had not cried in the night. She went as far as hoping Martin and Melissa were happy. I was astounded. She was wearing a light printed green dress she had bought the day before in a small market near Campo. No breath, no air. The dress was loose, frivolous, see through in places, and had stolen the show at dinner the previous evening. She wore it again this morning, no doubt the memory of her splendour fresh in her mind. Perhaps that was why she smiled. She'd consoled herself with the thought that Martin had rejected all this, had spurned beauty and lost; but she was happy for them, she said.

Uncle Jeff and my father finally appeared. The four of us took a long, lazy street-side breakfast of dark red hams, speckled salamis, fine sweet pastries and wonderfully strong Savazzi ristrettos. Uncle Jeff and my father finished off with an 11 a.m. shot of grappa, slapping each other like teenagers, my father outsinging a passing gondolier.

At eleven thirty my father abruptly announced that they were off for an open-air recital of *The Four Seasons* on Burano. Uncle Jeff looked as surprised as we were, but, assenting, drained the dregs of a second grappa.

'We're gonna stay in town, Dad,' said Becky.

'Lots to get through – eh? That Italian telly won't watch itself,' said my father before Uncle Jeff could respond.

'No, Uncle Graham,' said Becky, 'not television actually.'

My father struck a mock-tragic posture across the jams. 'O Giuseppe, *o caro mio*, Giuseppe – I thinka I lova youa.

But I'ma leavin' yoooou, for Marioooo,' my father said, singing 'you' and 'Mario' in mock-baritone. He didn't even notice his stupid joke reminded Becky of her pain.

'Come on, Verdi. Let's get in the vaporetto,' said Uncle Jeff.

My father dusted some crumbs from his baggy cream trousers, then mouthed his apologies to Becky. Thinking it hilarious, he requested the bill in Spanish: *'La cuenta, por favor,'* then presented me with a large cotton serviette. I unfolded it, and inside were line drawings of Becky and me. I had not noticed him doodling during breakfast, but he had caricatured us with his fountain pen. The illustration had us as one body with two heads, both incredibly miserable. Becky smiled. I did not.

'Seriously though – are you two OK for lira?' he said.

'It's free, what we're doing today,' said Becky.

'Bloody glad to hear it,' said my father, and to the waiter, *'Muchas gracias,* Helmut, *merci* bouquet.'

Ignoring him, Becky addressed her father. 'We're going to follow that J.G. Links tour in your book, Dad, that *Venice for Pleasure* thing.'

'Wonderful!' said Uncle Jeff. 'Oh, you'll enjoy that. Your mother and I did it years ago. Oh, wonderful!'

She waited for the goons to clear off, then told me the real plan.

'Let's get a little drunk in your hotel room.'

I masked my lack of enthusiasm for this boozy scheme with my standard flatness.

We wheedled two litres of Valpolicella from an octoge-
narian lady who filled some plastic bottles with booze
using a petrol pump. It was a late August morning, yet
thick mist came in like a damp winter dusk. We followed
the lethal stone path and wooden stairwell up past the
Canal Endici back to my hotel room where we settled
quickly into drinking wine and playing pass the pigs. We
talked about Martin and nonsense and more Martin. An
Italian soap opera gently hummed in the background. We
grew bored, the game finished. I packed it away, but left
the two tiny plastic pigs on the tray. I sank into an ornate
red armchair which smelt of cereal and Venice. The hot
bad breeze from the Grand Canal outside my window
wafted up through the slats. I felt dulled and relaxed by a
glass and a half of wine. Becky sat on the bed gulping at
the booze. She jerked moods from sad to giggly and back
again. She pinned up her shoulder-length black hair with a
bright yellow clip, taking some time to position it. I saw
her bare breast through the arm of her green dress. Strands
of jet hair fell over her forehead as she flounced and playfully hit the wall with her fists and swallowed bitter red
liquid from a metal cup. She flung the small plastic pigs
around the tray even though we were no longer playing.
The green dress rode up around her knees and I saw the
thin white inside flesh of her thighs flexing and following
her muscles.

'I'll never love again,' she said, full of mock-drama.

'Let's not talk about him any more, Becky.'

She laughed, a short expulsion of noise. 'What would you know, Benjamin? You've never loved.'

Our eyes met and she laughed again the same way.

'Don't be cringey, Benny.'

'Stop laughing,' I said.

'Sorry,' she replied and wiped the red wetness from her lips, 'but romance at ten years old doesn't count.'

'I knew what I meant.'

'So did I, but we were ten. Now we're not. And we're cousins.'

'None of that means anything.'

'Really? It does to me. It does to most people. It would to my dad. It would to your dad.' She paused. 'It's a bit weird, Benjamin. And stop looking at me like that.'

'I'm not.'

'You always do it.'

'I do not, Becky.'

'Always have done.'

'Don't be mean.'

'You're my cousin. It's weird for you to feel that.'

'Feel what?'

'I'm not blind.'

'When you were with Martin ...'

'I love you, but you're odd. Stop.'

'Wait – you love me?'

'Not in that way. But this must stop. The way you look at me.'

'I do not.'

She tucked the stray strands into her hair and sighed. 'It doesn't matter, it really doesn't. What's important is that *you* are not a cunt.'

'He was. He was,' I agreed.

'And I still love him – in the other way. It's like an illness. I mean a sick feeling, actually like I could puke. I still fucking love him. I fucking love him. I just said that. My whole life is over at eighteen. Wanker.' She let out a compact sob. A finger of translucent green snot fired from her nose into her philtrum. I wanted to lick it away. She wiped her nose with her right hand. 'Even though he's a total bastard, I still want him, you know. Oh God, I want to vomit. Shall I puke? Why do I feel sick? He's probably fucking her right now.'

She laughed bitterly and flung herself back into the tangle of blankets. She sobbed for a few minutes and I sat with my hands on my knees watching her. Her head nuzzled into my pillow. My spit and my smell were in that pillow and now she was in it. I felt aroused and guilty and sad. Her sobs climbed and climbed then died to a heavy breath. I reached out my hand from my right knee, but drew it back and massaged my kneecap. She kicked her left leg at an imaginary bastard and the cotton folds of her dress billowed outwards, settling above her knees. I saw the compact white triangle of her underwear and the dark of her inside it. I felt hot and poisoned, wanted to fold inwards and scream; let it all out in an uncontrolled and wild way. I reached for my wine and gulped it down. When I turned back, she was in the same position and I saw her again. I wanted to see her naked, just to see her. It would be enough, electric and natural, like love.

The wine slowed me. Without it I might have touched her; had the confidence to soothe her, I mean. Instead I sat holding my knees, silent and alight and full of a good panic.

'That prick! What the fuck? What the fuck?' she screamed at the stuccoed ceiling.

The sounds of mild dispute drifted in through the flaky blue slats from the Grand Canal. A strained American voice vied with Italian money-making arguments. The sudden smell of sewer and fish blew in on the hot air, and I closed the window, more out of something to do. The wood and metal creaked shut and the atmosphere changed. We were sealed. We were in a thing.

She sat up and blew her nose on her dress, glaring at me in the hope I'd be disgusted.

'I'm sorry,' and she laughed.

She loved me and we were cousins. Her eyes were very red now. The yellow plastic clip had fallen out of her hair and neither of us could find it. I ran my hands over the cover and she searched under the bed, swearing foully at the loss. We crossed over each other and I searched by the pillows. She smelt of floral soap and mint and shampoo. She was the old Becky now, not bothered by indignity –

innocent and full and flirtatious; just wanting to be seen and loved and accepted. We gave up the search for the clip and she fell back onto the bed. I switched off the television and sat back in the red chair. The room shrank again. The ambience tightened up and focused.

'What?' she said.

'I think you're beautiful, Rebecca.'

'Christ.'

'He was an idiot, and you are beautiful.'

'You always say it, Benjamin. You always bloody look. For Christ's sake – must you stare? Don't make it weird. Let's have a nice atmosphere.'

This was news to me. Had I ever said it? I knew I did not look.

We sat for a few minutes in silence. Now I looked. She smiled.

'What?' she said.

'I don't feel ... usual,' I said.

'Usual?'

'Yeah.'

'Me neither,' she said.

There was a pause. Words did not serve themselves. The atmosphere had an internal, hidden purpose. I felt it must go somewhere, end in something. She felt it too, and looked away.

'Let's do something we'll remember,' I said.

I felt ill, good ill. Adrenalin ran through my stomach and groin in a searing twist. There was no panic on her face, nothing at all. We were close and familial and she knew me well. She could tell it would be something, but not that. She knew it would not be that.

'I don't want to go out exploring or anything, Benjamin,' she said, but she could see I didn't mean walks in Dorsoduro.

'I want to do something for you ... and for me,' I said.

'Pigs?' She laughed, and shook the tray.

'I think you're beautiful. I think we can never be more than cousins. And I think that you only love me as your cousin, but that you love me.'

'Like a brother,' she said. We clinked glasses and nearly leaned in and hugged, but there was more and we both knew it. It felt right to go on, it felt necessary.

'I want to make us something. For me there will never be anyone more beautiful than you.'

'Oh reeeeeally?' she mocked.

'But I know what you mean. I would never allow it. We are like brother and sister.'

'OK. Yes. If you say so.'

'You said it,' I told her and opened a cupboard, bringing out my Leica.

'A photo-shoot?' she said, laughing.

'Yes,' I said.

'Fun,' she said.

'Naked,' I said.

She laughed and then the laughter stopped. I closed the last window and switched on the lamp.

'I want to photograph you naked. To make your beauty into a real thing.'

'You're mad and talk shit. You're a perv.'

'You're beautiful and I love you, and always have, but we're brother and sister, so it's clean, but real. Do you understand?'

'You know I can't be that for you. I don't feel it.'

'You're not listening. You're my cousin, my sister.'

'Yes.'

'Then that's all, that's enough.'

'I don't think so.'

'We're children really,' I said – irony lost on my aluminium voice.

'I don't know. I couldn't.'

'Shy?'

'Just wrong.'

'But you can,' I said.

'Benjamin, I can't,' but I knew she could.

'My love is the same as when I was ten. It hasn't changed. It will always be the same.' This was the truth.

'Why would I get naked in front of you, Benjamin? Talk sense.'

'Fuck sense. To me you are yourself. Show yourself to someone who isn't him, who can't be anything like him, and who worships you.'

'Maybe I should photograph you?' she said.

I thought of my shapeless stomach and my ugly flat nose. 'OK.'

'I'm joking. I'm not a deviant like you,' she said. 'Why would I want to look at your skinny body, you weirdo?' But playfulness had replaced protest.

'I will take the photographs,' I said. 'Show yourself to someone who knows what you are and is full up with you. Someone who could die from looking and would treasure it for ever.'

'Don't die. How would I explain that? A corpse, and me nude. Very nice.'

'Like a painting by a Mannerist.'

She laughed as we thought of Uncle Jeff's didactic voice. I had made a joke, a rare thing. I wound on the camera. Its peremptory mechanical grind flinched her out of laughter.

'You're serious.'

'You didn't think I wasn't.'

'No.'

'Then that's all.'

Heat ran from my backside and into my crotch, my belly, my chest. It was like melting upwards.

'It's just nudity, it's nothing ... it's everything,' I said.

'Well it's nothing, because I won't do it. Why would I? What would I get from it?'

'You would get what I would get.'

'Which is?'

'A unique thing. Something dangerous and fun and cleansing.'

'Fuck off.' Her cheeks purpled. 'I'm not sure about the camera,' she said.

'Without it, it's just me looking and you naked.'

'True.'

'With it we're making something.'

'I see.'

'I adore you. What's your body like?'

She laughed.

I picked up the camera again. 'I'm ready for the first shot. Take off your dress.'

'No.'

'Do it,' I said.

It became more serious than we could be. More of her laughter. There was a long pause. The argument outside the window grew louder, penetrating the closed slats.

She looked around the room and then directly at me. Shuffling to the edge of the bed and bringing the cover with her, she slid her dress up to the top of her thighs. She leaned back, lifted her wine and drained the metal cup of its red acid in one smooth draught. Two beads of wine tickled either side of her chin. She wiped them away.

She said, 'OK. Yes.'

She stood up and removed the dress, standing naked now apart from white functional underwear. She was thinner than I had imagined. Her breasts were small above her ribs and white flesh, and I felt inexplicably sad for her smallness. The fire in me diminished, but still I felt hot and did not fully breathe. I lifted the camera and pressed it firmly against my brow. Through the viewfinder she became an object, and the danger quieted. I clicked the camera many times, capturing her defiance – unsure and beautiful. I edged closer bringing the red chair with me in loud scrapes. I wound on the camera with slow hard clicks. Her breathing quickened.

'If you touch me, this thing's over,' she said.

'If I touched you, I would die,' I said, and then pointed to her white underwear. 'Take them off.'

I replaced the photograph of Becky in the suitcase and collapsed into a diseased sob. I rarely wept, and when I did it was never deep, not like this. I kicked some of the motley items and wept some more. After a while it felt good to be naked and crying. I cleaned up my face and, looking in the mirror, was appalled at the sight of my red upset, furious at my cock, my balls, at maleness, and at the maleness I could not have. Women love a sense of humour, you see.

I picked up the manuscript and took the Stance.

'Life at the Centre was fucking maddening,' I began into the mirror, 'and when I say fucking maddening, I don't mean infuriating, I mean my best friend was an autistic rapist . . .'

A joke.

9

Doubling Up

Before garlic-roasted chicken, fine green beans and pesto mash in business class, two ego-shaking things occurred: one unlikely, one vile.

Ed Austen. The sneaky librarian shit. The absolute bastard elf.

I had dressed and packed, weeping like a man boxing up the possessions of a recently deceased love. When the tears were done, I felt better, purged, left only with traces of poisonous ego. It reminded me of vomiting during a Majorcan salmonella. The sweaty after-relief of a puking session is marred by the knowledge that another must surely follow. I hoped to hold it together long enough to meet Leavey. Under the aegis of this putative 'master', I told myself, I'd stabilize.

In the twenty-four hours that followed I perfected Movement Two. I even did some preliminary work on Three, Four, and Five: 'In-show Movement', 'Gaze', and 'Tics and Spasms'. There were many tantalizing gaps. The 'Nyanja Brow', The 'Lozi Thrust'. His gaps and obfuscations were playful, intentional – goading parries from an expert.

On the day of the flight I went to the airport via Senate House for a few more reference pieces. If Dominic emailed seeking an early draft I'd need something convincing. A few rudimentary texts would help. Also, another combing of the Safe Store seemed wise. Last time, in my excitement, I hadn't properly rifled.

As I left my stuff with Yanni I tossed out some polite chat. He seemed relieved at my return to form. I waved, a hard, confident salute, and took the damp-cardboard-smelling lift, half-leaping out on the fourth floor before the doors had finished opening.

'Benjamin, how . . .'

Nodding violently at Jules, I spryly wove through the shelves, drawing the volumes I needed with two pincered fingers and gaily piling them up on her desk. She stayed silent as book by book the stack grew. It took me less than thirty minutes to find the eleven leather-bound works I needed.

'Full of beans this morning,' she said, chiming her words like frozen peas dropped on china.

'I have every reason to be,' I said.

'In January too.'

'Why not, eh?'

'I agree,' she said, warming, 'I agree.'

I felt she had news too. I encouraged her with my eyes.

'I've ... I've taken up sculpture and pottery at home.'

My heart sank. 'Really? That's great.'

'Clay, engobe, potter's wheel, the lot.'

'So you're full of beans too.'

'I am. Clay beans.'

I watched the flaccid humour flop itself in front of her, quickly collapsing from its brittle internal structure. Her words flapped spastically like escaped budgies with clipped wings, and she continued for some time about the five main types of engobe. As she talked she inhaled contentedly, working steadily at the pile of books, clouds of fine grey dust puffing from each one and disappearing up my bored nostrils, a sort of dud literary snuff.

'My friend Gillian is a lesbian and she has a kiln.'

I loved Jules, I really did. 'The start of new things, Jules, the start of new things,' I said and did not smile, but she knew I would have if I could.

'Gosh! How very strange you should say that.'

'Strange?'

'Yes. Only this morning I was reading up about Polykleitos ... Herodotus reckons he commenced every work session with the same words – words that became legendary: "The start of new things must mould from the old."'

I found the phrase ridiculous. Could one even mould old? I feigned as much fascination with her Greek metal-worker as I could manage, politely asking a few more questions which she crisply answered. She worked her way through the pile of heavy books. With her slim mani-cured hand she smoothed away layers of yellow dust in clean, sweeping motions. I thought of her at home in her one-bedroom Ruislip flat, potter's wheel clamped between her untouched thighs, maidenly grip working at clay with every possible propriety.

'Just the eleven books today then, Benjamin?'

'Yes.'

'OK.'

She picked up the last work, a massive tome on the metaphysics of wit, slowly creaking it open, cracking its ancient blue leather spine, stroking the inside cover as though it were a baby's head. She carefully branded it with the ancient Senate House stamp. We were both terminal bibliophiles; both addicted to the contained, closed, per-ceivable beauty of these solid objects. We took a moment to admire the fine, processed stack.

'I might take one last look in the Safe Store,' I said, breaking the sweet, thick silence.

'The Safe Store?'

'Yeah, that manuscript's the reason I'm in such a good mood.'

'Oh ... The manuscript – I meant to ask about that.'

'Well – it's going to make my first feature.'

'Your first?'

'Yep – my first – happy fortieth, Benjamin White.'

'Oh – well, I'm so happy for you. Brilliant news, Benjamin.'

'Thank you.'

'You know Polykleitos was forty-two before he made *The Amazon* for Ephesus.'

She pushed the stack towards me with the flat of her hand.

'There you go,' she said in a whisper.

'Thank you,' I said.

An awkward pause.

'Oh gosh, I'm sorry,' she said, her face flushing behind massive plastic brown frames. 'The keys.' She dangled them apologetically. 'I'm all pottery and no memory! Ha!'

I blocked the anaemic witticism, then said, 'You sure you shouldn't check with Ed first?

'Ed Austen? Good God, no! Why ever should I?'

'He seemed to have put himself in charge of that room.'

'Well, it's his job to keep it orderly. He has full authority over the polishing. But I'm "in charge".'

'Oh. Well – I'm … I'm glad to hear it.'

'Me too.' She half smiled and straightened her hairy pink cardigan.

'Well, at least tell him I'm in there. I wouldn't want to startle him like last time,' I said. What I meant was – make sure I'm undisturbed.

'I'll send him an email, shall I?'

'His day off?'

'Well maybe a postcard then.'

'He's on holiday?' I was delighted.

'Yes. More "travelling" than holiday, he said.'

'Really?' I said, moving briskly away to the trade lift. I drew across the metal door and inserted my thumb into the button that glowed '8'.

'Where did he go?' I half asked.

'Zambia,' she said. 'The colonial city of Livingstone in fact.'

The lift heaved into life. It was some time before I removed my whitening thumb from the button.

My first experience of business class should have been amazing: the joy of luxury, blissful diversion from my plans. Instead, I spent the first five hours in torrid panic, resistant to all sleep drugs. I swallowed four times the dosage, drank quantities of whisky, but still my heart thudded and my mind worked black and spiteful.

My cabin was virtually empty. I had no neighbour exacerbating things. I tried watching something idiotic, *Mission Impossible*; then something French, *The Best Friend*. I attempted the introduction of a Saussure, but the words would not settle and without meaning to, I flung the book away. It thudded and slid out onto the gangway. A portly camp steward, eyebrow-pierced and covered in foundation, sprang into life, seizing the book and bringing it like a lap-dog surprised at its own obedience.

'Oooh! *The Ex ... pos ... ition of Struc ... tural Lingui ... sssstics in Jokes,*' he said slowly, taking the piss a bit.

'Yes.'

'Not very funny!'

I did not answer.

'Everything OK?' he said as he handed me the book.

'No. I am out of whisky.'

He scurried away, miffed. He reminded me of one of my brother's exes.

I often wonder if I'd have been better off as 'the gay son'. Perhaps Cooper got my happiness and my sexuality. The ripples that his own revelations caused were so minimal.

'I'm gay.' He announced it just like that when he was fifteen.

'And?' said my mother. It was the ultimate acceptance. To not even acknowledge it is a possible negative.

My father waded in. 'Come on, Coops, you're not exactly into rugby. You think I'm blind? Come here!' He kissed him; a mock-homoerotic kiss of acceptance. As though to say, Hey, son, your aberration is actually kinda cool. Or perhaps it was just that I had immunized them against disruption. The sobbings, the violence, the dropping off at special school, the passionate research – the rock of my revelation smashed into their pond, displaced every atom of liquid. Well – a queer son must have seemed refreshing. A gay one or one with special needs – which would you rather, Mr and Mrs White?

'Whisky, you said?' the steward was calling from his galley.

'Yessssss!' I said with a cruel cruel *s*.

The malice in my voice had been unequivocal, yet he returned with a JD and a face refreshed by a smile.

'Anything you need, just holler.'

'OK.'

'Just don't yell any "structural linguistics" at me, I'll have a panic attack.'

I felt weak, couldn't stop his diseased bon mot dancing up before me:

> *a deftly recalled polysyllabic term, used in*
> *quotidian surreal juxtaposition to his role. Camp delivery*
> *adding lightness and sociological minority skew to his*
> *expression; compounding the humour.*

My actual panic attack coincided with his hypothetical, old-lady-kitsch-value, joke attack. A bead of sweat discharged from my forehead, landing in my whisky with a plink. I dismissed the glittery oaf with a nod and resumed my paranoid Ed Austen thoughts. Was this paranoia though? What the hell might the imp be planning? There was no way *he* had the ability to see what this document held – impossible. At the very most he had realized the potential of meeting a comedic guru. But how could he have known he was alive? Or where to find him? Academic contacts? The London Research Centre? Yes, those fucking

Masonic nerds. Maybe he wanted Leavey for some sort of spiritual enrichment; the laying of hands upon a deity, to provoke inspiration. Hang on a moment. Hang on. Ed Austen might be unfunny and talentless, but thick he was not. He was a bright chap, very bright; yes, his Master's in Lacan or Jung, a first in psychoanalysis and humour. There was an outside chance he'd seen through the exuberance of Leavey's discourse – yes, the damn LRC ... he would have put in a call to them – assistant librarian at Senate packs a nepotistic punch when needed. But surely there was no chance he'd *felt* any of it. Even if he performed Movements One and Two correctly in his tragic little Acton lounge he would not *feel* their power. Only I could do that.

But wait – what if he performed it into a mirror – would that work?

Maybe.

Could he hit himself with it and gauge its potential that way? He wouldn't have had time to try the Stance in a comedy club. No ... wait. He might have. Monday nights were the Tittering Pony's Nonsense Night in Greenwich – a gig thick with racism and sambuca. I could call from the flight phone and find out whether he had played the gig. But who could I call – it was 2 a.m.? The promoters Josh and Colin would be smoking weed. Fuck. I was fucked and my breathing came heavy and wrong.

I clambered towards the flight toilet, slamming and locking the door like a scolded teenager. In the mirror was a man nearer fifty than forty. I felt the chance of a lifetime slipping away simply because some talentless little prick could use a photocopier.

'I should have had sexual intercourse with Becky.' The words came from nowhere. 'I should have fucked her,' I said. 'Made love to her. One night and I could have died and there would have been none of this. Love would have punctured all this. Imagine the feeling of her, of that moment. Fuck!'

'Are you all right in there?'

'Yes. I'm fine.'

'You sure?'

I banged on the door with my fist. There were no more enquiries.

I sat on the tiny toilet for a long time. The roaring noises of the flight somehow comforted. I cried – again. So this was it? No. I refused to crack up in an aeroplane lavatory. I dropped my self-counsel to a whisper: 'There is no way he could have got as far as you in that time. There is no one in the world as fast as you. The only advantage he could have is better inside info on Leavey's whereabouts.'

Yes. That was right. He may have used academics on the inside to locate Leavey; but his quest was bound to be dry and cerebral and egocentric. He'd probably be on the lookout for some sort of scoop; make himself look good on Guffaw.co.uk. Or wait – perhaps it's the other way round, I thought, he sees Leavey as the Grand Master. He's going on some sort of self-development quest, partly for him, partly to annoy me. The stupid little shit. If this Leavey document is what it seems (it was, it is) the Professor will see straight through him: a midget fake full of expectation and arrogance. He had knowledge. But I had the sight – and the document was created for a seer, not a pleb.

I brutally squeezed a bottle of Molton Brown hand soap. A fragrant creamy streak shot through the air and splattered on the ceiling. The glob drew itself into a glutinous stalactite, eventually breaking and dropping into my hair, a vanilla bird shit.

This was the moment the terrible resolve came upon me. I can isolate it that precisely. When the soap was still on the ceiling it had not started, but when it dropped into my hair, the thing began. That slapstick was a metaphor. The ridiculousness of me; my squashed nose and me on the toilet and my one expression of fist-clamped grief turned against me, the butt of that joke. This was the cold push, the sharp tip that ripped into the hull of me; and other people became less important than the Humour; than the Humour and me together. The will was in me. The will to *kill*, I mean; destroy and tear the weak meat from the bones of anyone normal who stood in my way.

Up until the discovery I suppose I was like anyone else. We dream our whole lives of our fantasy things: the published book; the platinum disc; the perfectly timed pregnancy. What's your thing? That you'd love more than anything, but know, even in your wildest fantasy, you will never have? The one that sits inert yet active; a dangerous hot kernel at the centre of your being which heats and jumps but never irrupts into your life because it is impossible. It's a comfortable, childish thing you play with as you stare from office or bus or van window.

Now imagine the odds fold in on themselves, the universe buckles for a nano-moment; you are pregnant with fraternal twins at thirty-five; your Lottery ticket comes in; all the women you could want, want you; you are the rock star, novelist, or Olympian; which is it? But it happens. See it there, feel the having of it. Then see one little fuckwit threatening to take it away; ruin it just for kicks. See people standing in your way. See the people who have mocked and blocked your road to it.

What would you do?

Of course you would.

So I resolved to do the same, you see. I would break. I would bury. I could feel his organs between my fingers, and I liked it.

I sat breathing, just breathing.

Were these just the ramblings of a man losing his temper? I waited for the fury to diminish. Black irrationality faded back into a simple task. The will to do away with Ed Austen became a logical, rational thing. I emerged from this lost state as someone else; someone no longer scared. No, not someone; but the only 'one', the 'chosen'. How megalomaniac that sounds, but I'm sorry, I was created for this; and I'd do all manner of wrongs to right it; I would destroy to create. Proof would come next. Already I felt its evidence, its certainty; I would run with it. I would go to my family, and then to the Comedy Store. And I would win; and they would all know it for ever.

A knock. 'Sir. Excuse me.'

'Yes,' I said.

'You really will have to take your seat now.'

How long had I been in that lavatory?

'Are you ill?'

Not any more. 'No!'

'Please, sir – there's turbulence.'

Yes, there is, I thought. Yes, there fucking-well is.

10

Three Acts and a Compère

Livingstone city is in fact barely a town. Its small airport consoled me.

I collected my suitcase from an ancient trolley and passed into the main hall of the terminal. It was hot and lazy and not like an airport, more a large branch of W.H. Smith's from the 1980s. People were kind and welcoming, and not in the usual cynical money-earning way; though of course they wanted that too. The Zambian idling speed is a smile. You feel calm within thirty minutes of arriving in that country. No grumpy people; even their mad tramps and youths smile when menacing. I spoke the few words of Nyanja I'd absorbed on the flight to some airport officials, and found myself giggled at. English was proudly used by all; not speaking it frustrated those who wished to display their conversational skills. I dragged my bag through passport control and out into a stuffy atrium. Friendly black hands greeted from all sides proffering various services in exchange for kwacha or an English chat or both.

'Hey, Delboy. You want taxi?' a fat man asked.

Not smiling when a nation's currency is grinning quickly becomes a problem. I declined the fat man with a surly nod. I know it seemed rude. I moved on through a throng of fat excited Americans, putative tour guides, and out into the narrow front part of the domed arrivals hall. It was bland and very beige – rickety ceiling fans, potted plastic plants, closed curio shops, pervasive smell of fried meat and body odour.

Bobby Enanda was easy to spot: a wide affable face, coffee-brown, not black, and a grin more First-in-economics than local international hack.

'You must be Benjamin.'

'Bobby?' I said.

'You look like crap.' He laughed. Incongruously, he had the thick accent of a white Afrikaner. That lilt which half hangs onto Europe with its violent fishhook consonants. 'Good journey?'

'I couldn't sleep.'

'No, it's shit, isn't it, man? Hungry?'

'Very.' I surprised myself. Yes, I was famished.

With a manly tug he took my suitcase and I followed like a diseased dog into a blindingly hot earth-scratch of a car park. I climbed into his dust-covered Toyota feeling drained and alien, but new.

Named with pomp after the Scottish explorer, Livingstone is refreshingly devoid of pretension. Perhaps because of my grand purpose, I had naively imagined monuments, history, shops, largeness, I suppose Britishness. Instead I found a modest splat of orange chalky buildings baked into humbleness by a scorching semi-desert. Weary locals shuffled up and down a central street as though one of them might drop from sunstroke at any moment. I found it eerily quiet for a city; metres of noise-lessness with the occasional cluster of activity around a vocal phone-card seller, or bus-ticket hawker. Yes, there was a museum and the odd campsite and nearly a hotel, but really I found just a placid gathering of hard-up humans around a main road.

We drove along Musi-a-Tunya, Bobby pointing out its basic features – a chemist, some clothes and rag shops, a MoneyGram, local eateries (some safe, some not), an incongruously gleaming Barclays Bank with a never-ending queue of suited, sweat-beaded Zambian men. The pavements were dusty, the roads actual dust. We left the town centre travelling south towards the Victoria Falls and the Zimbabwe border. Timid women congregated on corners, babies suckling empty breasts, travel-guide fruit on head. They peered into the truck as we passed seeming baffled by me, a phlegmatic European so interested in their town. After a while, we took a small dirt-track, slowing to five miles per hour. Mundane bright heat came in through the windows, sickening and malevolent and dry; burnt earth and faeces also in alternate wafts from small shacks, collapsed hovels, and abandoned dwellings. We drove for five or ten minutes more, eventually turning into a dusty avenue lined with withered baobab stumps. A sign handwritten with 'Mwanawasa Road' partly obscured a more official-looking 'Chiluba Way'.

'You know all about "Chiluba's way"?' Bobby said.

'What?'

'Nothing,' he said and chuckled. I had no concept of Zambian politics, I'd never heard of this character Chiluba, yet instantly the sharp vortex of Enanda's humour, the pun on 'way', spiralled up around me. Satire always comes at me like this. As a funnelled cloud, a rotating column which scoops up the atmosphere around its words. The proverbial chicken simply crosses the road. There is a laugh at his reason. It's dispersed and silly, tickly. If the chicken is a politician however, a vacuous celebrity, anyone on the receiving end of satire, it changes things. Rather – satire seeks to change things, real things, with the edge of its laugh. This is why satire's tornado-shaped. It wants to rip up and spin the elements, but at the same time its shape is ordered and focused.

'Chiluba's way,' I said. 'Nice one.'

Bobby Enanda was about thirty, handsome, muscular, short – not a hair on his shiny brown head. He'd driven the

Toyota hard, taking corners fiercely, yanking at the gear-stick, pulling and slapping the steering wheel, yet all the while smiling and relaxed. We both seemed relieved the other was male and reticent and not over-friendly. I knew Enanda's reputation – a Jekyll and Hyde egoist of a journalist. He never recovered from his Salinger scoop a few years before. Arrogance prompted him to quit the *Review* for six months in 2000. Of course, he came back with his tail between his rutting legs. But his humility had been destroyed. He was chock-full of his own talent and bitter and different. I knew how he felt.

'We've had a real result,' he said, skidding the Toyota to a halt outside a solitary white-brick building.

'Where are we?'

'My house.'

'Enanda House,' I said.

He checked if I was joking. I did not smile.

'Yes. Enanda House,' he said, unsure.

Enanda's two-storeyed plain abode was the only building on the dusty lane. I could see nothing on the horizon except a T-junction back onto Musi-a-Tunya towards the Falls. The day was yellow and the heat banked and rose from the ground in a hot dry blur. Again, the burnt smell, and the smell of scorched flesh.

Inside the house the air conditioning was icy. I became conscious of dirt and dust on my hands and clothes. I needed a shower. We walked along a cool tiled passageway into an English cottage-style kitchen busy with the smell of porridge and meat. At the stove an ancient Zambian lady stirred a pot as big as a man. She did not look up when we walked in, but crossed to the sink and lifted out a battered metal dish containing a thick mealy substance. She placed it on the table, gently inclining her head at Enanda in obeisance rather than greeting. Using a wooden ladle she filled two black ceramic bowls with the brown-gravy substance which steamed from the big pot. It smelt wonderful.

'*Nsima* and chicken,' he said, pulling out a small metal chair for me. 'You nasalize it. *NNNsima*. Otherwise it means something obscene.'

'It looks amazing,' I said to the old lady as I sat down.

She smiled coyly, but did not look up, and shuffled into the hallway.

'Take Mr White's bag up to the guest bedroom, Rose,' he said. I winced as the colonial irony of my surname twisted quickly through me – it again took a funnel shape. I hate the brash efficiency of satirical puns.

'We'll eat then you can have a nap, my man,' he said, tearing at the hot *nsima* porridge with his hands. I tried to do likewise but it was too hot and Enanda laughed as I shook the burns from my fingers.

'Yes. I am tired,' I said lamely.

'Quite a story this is turning out to be, guy,' he said through partly chewed chicken meat. 'It's like a Bill Hicks interview from the grave.'

'Bill Hicks. Yes.'

'Not even Enanda could arrange that one,' he said. I felt his knees touch mine as he spread his legs wide under the table. Legs and third-person selfing: we were going to clash.

'David Leavey,' I said, and looked at him.

'Your professor, isn't it?'

'Yes.'

'Thought that was bullshit, guy, but it's not.'

'Not bullshit?'

'It's a bit blown up.'

'Right.'

'He's not really on the run any more.'

'Not on the run?'

'The Yanks got bored with chasing him. He got bored with hiding – or got old and stopped giving a fuck. Piece of piss to find him, to be honest.'

'Brilliant,' I said, but flat enough for it to come across as ironic.

Awkward pause.

'You don't get very excited, do you, man?'

'You noticed.'

'It is an exciting story, guy – bloody impressive work, man. He's no Salinger – but it's a nice fucking piece.'

'I am thrilled – just tired.' I could not be bothered to give this prick my biography, my psychological history.

'I'm surprised old Miranda let you take it.'

'Me too.'

'Ol' Miranda.'

I knew straight away what was meant by his elision of the *d* from 'old', this mock informalizing of the adjective. A quick red rush which puffed its tawdry gas towards me at the salacious tone. In other words, he had fucked her at some point.

'As lazy as he's become – still should have been tricky to find him,' said Bobby – haughty, proud, 'but you're gonna cream your panties over why it wasn't. Cream, bro.'

'I don't understand.'

'He's become a tribesman; had some sort of fucked-up breakdown, man. Could be bullshit of course, being eccentric for the sake of it – but I reckon he's gone proper gaga ... Rose, some carrot juice, love ... I know one thing, the Simongans fucking love him, man.'

Simongans. Here was a word I knew. Movement Three. The Simongan Thrust. This was no coincidence. Leavey was here because it meant something. I knew that. I had felt things and I knew.

'Ya. He's some sort of fucked-up tribal chief, guy. You know. Gone native and all that shit. I tried a reconnaissance three days ago, but they were in the middle of some messed-up dancing and shit. Couldn't get at him direct. Sent a messenger.'

'But he's there.'

'He's there all right – totally up for your visit. Whole village is nuts.'

'How do you mean?'

'Not nuts, I mean – obsessed – like odd.'

'Odd. Odd how?'

'I don't know. Dressed up weird and shit.'

'It's Africa.'

'Hey, Mr Livingstone – I do know these tribes. I speak every fucking dialect, bro.' He ate messily as though to dominate through lip-smacking. 'No, they, er, they were wearing vegetables on their heads, man.'

'Wearing ...'

'Ya. Stuck on with something. Aubergines. Cut like ears – stuck onto their heads. Fucked-up, man.' He laughed weakly.

'What do you mean ears?'

'The messenger said it's some ritual with horses or something, but to be honest the other Simongan villages stay away. It freaks them out.'

'Donkeys?'

'Ya. Ya, maybe. Horses, donkeys – whatever. They wear vegetables.'

I ate some *nsima* and chicken thinking of Chrysippus and his drunk donkey, my blood racing.

'How did you find him?'

'He's still writing,' said Bobby, slightly bored now and belching.

'My God. I thought the manuscript was finished.'

'Not the manuscript. No. That is a fucking amazing thing, by the way. Hilarious, bro. Got great nut-job value. Makes Hicks look like a bit of a dickhead though. Never mind.'

'I see.'

'It's academic. He's pumping out Zambian anthropology and ethnography and shit. We got him through the ...'

'LRC.'

I had surprised him. 'Yes, Columbo, well done.'

'I thought as much.'

'You and one of your buddies, isn't it?'

Blood stopped, the world paused. 'You mean Ed Austen?'

'Fucking hell, guy, you have been stalking me, I swear.'

'Please don't tell me you've involved Ed Austen?' I said.

'Ya,' said Enanda. He seemed pleased. He knew this would happen.

'Where is he now?' I said.

'Hey – what's up, bro?'

'I'm here, you're working with me, and we should be careful, that's all.'

'Dude. He said he was a stand-up and he knew you and knew all about the project. You were on the later flight bringing extra materials.'

'And you believed him?'

'He was gonna go in anyway. I thought I'd midwife it. Be safer.'

'You trusted him?'

'Guy – I called London, I'm not an idiot.'

'Who?'

'Miranda said she knew him.'

'Bitch.'

He laughed. 'Ya. Great girl.'

'I don't want him near it.'

'Guy, it's hardly state secrets. It's a feature article on Bill Hicks.'

'It's more than that.'

'It is? I think you want it to be. There's no American government?'

'I just don't want him near it.'

'Oh my God. You're brewing an actual conspiracy theory.'

'He has to be removed from the field.'

'Ah. Tricky. Bro, don't be protective.'

'Bobby, what the fuck does "tricky" mean?'

'You're tricky,' he said, mopping juices from his plate.

'Don't play games with me.'

'More *nsima*?' He laughed. 'Chill out, guy.'

'Where the hell is he now?'

'Simonga, man. Miranda said it's cool, it's all hands on deck. And ...'

'And?'

'Hey, guy. London pays my salary.'

'He's a prick!' Spittle flew from my lip.

'She said Austen could help put another angle on it – plus ... the time-frame, you know ...'

'What do you mean the ... Dominic Wray's given me an open brief.'

'That's changed.'

'Changed?'

'. . . She wants you back home within forty-eight hours.'

'She wants? She fucking wants? Dominic's the Editor.'

'She wants you back home in two days, dude.'

'Cow.'

'Great fuck though.'

My sleep that night was disturbed.

I lay staring at the brown wood-panelled ceiling until 5 a.m. The air conditioning had been on all night, yet the sheets stuck firm. I washed, ate some cereal with goat's milk laid out for me by Rose, and waited for Bobby. He appeared at 7 a.m. with toothpaste stains on his lips and mischief in his eyes.

'Sleep well?'

'No,' I said.

'Hey – c'mon, man. How about "Good Morning", and we'll start again. Christ – you're making me feel bad.'

'Hmm.'

'Man, if he's that much of a problem we'll just get rid of him and bullshit Miranda – OK?'

'You don't understand.'

'Hey, bro, it's just an article. He might even help. Or we'll lose him. It's cool. Stop having a cardiac, man.'

'Stop reducing the situation.'

'Yes, let's build things right up.' Aggression crept into Bobby's voice.

We had exchanged less than one hundred words on

this fresh day, and I already wanted to drive my fist into his mouth.

'Can we just get out there?' I said.

'Of course, guy. I called Leavey on his mobile. We're due at eight.'

'He's a tribal chief with a mobile?'

'That's right.' Enanda laughed. 'I would say lighten up.'

A pause. So he knew everything about me. 'You phoned London.'

He looked sheepish.

'Miranda's given you my pathetic biography, has she?' I could have said laughable, I should have made a pun.

'She's just been emailing actually. Just do your thing and get home.'

'What if we don't get what I ... what we need?'

'Said she'd rather have a blank page than you under-mining her.'

'Cow.'

'What the hell did you do to piss her off like that, man?'

'I'll meet you in the car.'

'You didn't fuck her, did you?'

His coarseness was lame and produced no sensations.

We drove out onto Musi-a-Tunya. The day was already hot like it had a grudge. The sun kept rising and rising and the heat misted and brought back the smells of the day before. Simonga was less than twenty minutes from Bobby's house. Other than planning a loose schedule, we hardly spoke. Bobby was in league with Miranda. He could not be trusted.

We turned down a tiny unmarked track which finished at a dry, mud-cracked basin. Bobby swaggered from the Toyota and stood with his hands on his hips defying the heat. I joined him. For a moment there was nobody else; then a topless, toothless black man in tatty grey shorts and gleaming Nike trainers emerged from behind a dense wild-rosemary bush. He greeted us with enthusiastic waving and bowing. He smelled of sour spices.

'You must be Bobby. I was about to text you from my phone,' he said. His accent was gentle and lilting and he seemed proud of the ginger-cake-shaped device clutched in his right hand.

'This is Benjamin White,' said Bobby.

'Hello.' He clapped three times, squatted, then stood back up and hugged me. 'I'm ... well *he* calls me Colin.' He smiled as he released me from his embrace. I felt a keen rush of humour; his use of an overly mundane name; his awareness of how pedestrian it sounded in this African context. Pitched too with a self-effacing throwaway nod, a hug. Sublime. Learned.

'Leavey,' I said.

He giggled like a boy hiding a whoopie cushion. 'Leavey-Na is very keen to meet you.'

There was an interminable pause. He gaped at me. It was awkward.

I jolted as I noticed two pieces of dried aubergine on his

head. They were folded into leaf shapes and stuck onto his shining black skull with a kind of yellow sap. They were sun-baked almost to crisps, but the effect was unmistakable: ears. Donkey ears.

'I'm keen to meet him too,' I said, breaking the silence, 'and his assistant . . . Ed.'

Colin's face again grew wry.

'Something?' I said.

'Everything, Benjamin-Na. Potentially.' Belly laughter now; the smell of wild rosemary all around us.

We crossed the basin and climbed over a brow of ancient cattle dung. The Simongan village rose up before us; fifty or so small traditional mud huts; clay-brown circular structures with sheaved straw roofs – he called them mununga shacks. Colin seemed nervous when I inspected one of the dwellings. An unblinking eye appeared at a peephole in the closed mud door, then disappeared. Next to the door a large piece of baobab bark suspended on a length of string somehow moved in the breezelessness. This oval of wood was brightly decorated and in its centre was a chalked smiling face with a slim nose coloured-in solid white. There was a Lozi phrase underneath. I asked Colin for a translation but he laughed, prevaricated, moving me on with his cracked tired hands. I looked to Bobby. He uselessly shrugged and smirked.

We meandered through a maze of makeshift latrines, malodorous water pumps and mununga shacks of various sizes. There were no people. The ground was orange and stony and each step brought a musty cloud of clay-dust. Small patches of sorry-looking shrubs were fenced with rusty barbed wire decorated with red chillies, apparently to repel elephants and baboons. Occasionally Colin's phone beeped with an incoming text which he ignored.

'Waaahhhhaaaa.' Three hallooing children leapt at me, but an arm, their mother's perhaps, yanked them back nervously, and the door was firmly closed.

'You must excuse us,' said Colin, opening a wooden gate onto a barren garden with a very large hut at the foot of its path, 'normally we're extremely friendly.'

'Hey – they don't like us, Benjamin,' said Bobby with acid.

'They are just nervous. It is a great day for us,' said Colin.

'Great day?' I said.

'You'll see, Benjamin-Na,' he said, stopping and placing his hands on my shoulders. 'In time – you will see.'

We walked up a dusty pathway demarcated with what looked like rodent skulls. Although this hut was also bordered with barbed wire, no shrubs or plants grew. It wasn't until we were at the door that I noticed this building was brick and only daubed with mud to look like a mununga shack. It was also much bigger. Colin rapped the door three times, then sank in reverent genuflection before the threshold.

'Chrysippusa. Chrysippusassapapa, Chief,' he whispered. He clapped his hands; hillocks of bright mud had

240

accumulated between them dulling any slapping noise. Again I looked at Bobby. He snorted a derisive laugh.

The door slowly opened. A slim black girl, perhaps seventeen or eighteen, stood before me draped from head to toe in a long piece of embossed green fabric. It did not entirely cover her; here and there her dark flesh was revealed. Beneath the garment she was thin and grossly childlike with the body of a small boy. I thought of Becky and for a moment I could smell Venice and not baked clay and bush latrines.

'Hi,' she said. An American. The unexpected accent seemed absurd.

'Hello,' I said.

Bobby muttered something.

'Thank you, Colin,' she said.

Colin retreated like a dog with worms.

'I'm Melissa. And you're ... Well, you're Benjamin.'

'Yes. Yes, I am.'

'I'm pleased to meet you ... I'm ... honoured ... truly honoured.' She was calm and smiling, yet not quite deferential.

'You're honoured?'

'We all are, Benjamin.' She lifted an eyebrow. Reverence was not to be muddled with fawning.

She kissed my hand, allowing her tongue to protrude slightly and lick my knuckle. The green fabric fell away from her head revealing intricately braided hair crowned with two pieces of fresh aubergine.

'Come in.' Her lips still moist upon my knuckles.

'OK.'

'But not you. Thank you, Mr Enanda, but that's all for now.'

Bobby did not have a subtle mode when being rejected. 'Oh. I see. So, I'll just wait in the car, shall I?'

'No. Go home. Come back in two days.' It was not rudeness, but a kind of accustomed authority.

'What?' he said. 'Well what about Mr White's suitcase?'

She laughed.

'What?' Bobby was annoyed now. 'What, damn it, what?'

'Sorry,' but she could not control her laughter, 'I'm sorry.' She laughed for a good thirty seconds, Bobby heating with anger. She stopped, steadying herself against the rudimentary jamb, and then she quietly – brayed.

Enanda pouted and marched away, deeply offended. 'Fucking Americans. Fucking Yanks.'

Composing herself, Melissa pulled me in through the door. 'I'm Canadian,' she said, and lifted both her eyebrows into fierce triangular points. I felt a sharp jolt. The air thinned and my lungs worked hard; surely not at the obvious and uncreative undercutting of Americanness with Canadianness – a comedy standard. No, it was the eyebrows.

'What did you just do? With your ...?'

'In time.'

'What was that?'

'You won't need your suitcase, Benjamin,' she said, ignoring me and sealing us inside the hut.

'My . . . my passport?' My eyes were adjusting, but not my breath.

'It will all be taken care of.'

The hut was Tardis-large; easily the size of a stately home's gazebo. Partitioned too. In the centre what I thought was a latrine, turned out to be a clay spiral staircase into a tiny lower chamber. It took me another moment to realize the hut was lit by electricity. Must have a generator. That's it: focus on functional things, and then you'll stay calm, I told myself. The spot- and strip-lighting looked anachronistic, mocking.

'It's . . . It's very well equipped.'

'Follow me,' she said. Her tone remained blank.

Things grew more incongruous beyond the first partition. The gaudy embroidered screen concealed a lounge area: pale Habitat-style cushions; an old Hitachi television sat on a blue rug, a keyboard and PC in a pile, orange chalk stains on the dangling mouse; plug sockets too – bloody plug sockets! A Gaggia coffee maker, gently hissing. And a plug-in air freshener – Glade's version of Clean Linen pervaded.

'A generator,' she confirmed.

'I'm . . . Is . . .'

She took my hand. 'We knew. You know that. Don't you?'

'I don't understand.'

'Change into this and relax, you've got a big day ahead of you.' My hand was released and into it she placed a neatly folded square of chartreuse fabric. I shook it out to reveal a man's long garment, ornate V-neck and bright gold and red selvage. She called it a dashiki.

'It's not traditional to this part of Africa, but the hood's very good in the heat,' she said. 'Go on. Put it on.'

I stood stock-still.

'Come on.' She almost mocked now. 'You came all this way to get camera-shy about getting naked.'

'Naked?'

'You can leave your shorts on,' and she slightly gave it the cadence of the song 'You Can Leave Your Hat On'. The juxtaposition helped me. A pleasant buzz of humour.

'Right.'

'Strip, soldier.'

I removed my clothes down to my underwear.

'I'll take those.'

I slipped the dashiki over my head. The smooth bright green silk slid over my back and my chest in a dry cold wave. The garment hung pleasantly around my neck, caressing my ankles too. It smelt good and factory-new.

'You look great!' she said, and kissed me wetly on the lips. 'Coffee?'

There was something so completely erotic about her every move, her every tiny gesture – that this kiss, this saliva-transferring touch, was too much. My feelings folded in on themselves, went past anything salacious into a clean, composed readiness. She had me. She simply had me. I rested there.

The temperature inside the hut was pleasant. I thought of Bobby contained and sweating inside the Toyota heading back to Enanda House. I sat down on a small black leather pouf which could have come from my Granny Davids' lounge. Melissa made the coffee, then joined me. Don't touch me again, I thought.

We exchanged functional words about Livingstone. I relaxed a little, but not enough to recover from her kiss. I never fully made eye contact. She took my cup, stroked my hand again and rang an unseen bell.

'I'll see you this evening, my love,' she said, using the endearment neutrally as an aunt would. She smiled once more then disappeared behind a partition.

I sat for a time not knowing what I was supposed to do. Waiting. Insect noises – now I caught the buzz of the generator. The smells, the competition of Western caffeinated comfort with shit-spattered subsistence.

'Enanda House,' I said – giving a whispering mocking accent to the words. Huh – I had never realized that. I could use ironic inverted commas. I tried it with my fingers, lifting each one up like cartoon worms. Wow. Did that count as a joke? Just being here was …

… Then came a noise: a booming, rasping New York male voice. It filled me up.

'We had an American hippy girl here last week …'

'Hello?' I couldn't see anyone.

'We had a fat '70s-style hairy American hippy girl here last week, and she took off her clothes in my hut. You know what I said to her, Benjamin White?'

A pause. Still no sight of anyone. 'What?' I said.

'I said to her, "I'll say the same to you as I say to every other American: sort out your Bush administration."'

For a moment, the blunt cheap punchline vibrated only dully, a few molecules of red and strawberry-flavoured piece of tat, but it was followed by something, or rather someone, shocking. A man, an old man, emerged from behind a piece of hung gold cloth. He was naked apart from thick mauve face paint and two large hanging fabric ears which were glued to his head, and trailed down over his nipples all the way to his waist. He could have been a white man once, but his skin was charred and ruined. He walked towards me flapping his hands and genitals wildly. His scrotum was gigantic; something from a cancer documentary.

'Sort out your Bush administration,' he repeated. He flapped his hands as though his wrists were broken, then leaned within a few millimetres of my face raising his eyebrows into the same sharp triangular point I had just seen on Melissa. The pathetic joke shifted its energies, rushing in painfully, through and up and flooding, and then it felt ... good. I let out a snort. A mucus snort. Not a laugh, but still, a snort.

'I'm David Leavey,' he said.

'I know,' I said, unable to breathe. 'I know who you are.'

11

The Headliner

To describe the things that happened next, right up until walking on stage at the Comedy Store, Leicester Square, London, we must discard almost everything contained, labelled and real; do away with the consoling things of normal life. Instead, we must surrender ourselves to the ridiculous, to laughter and thus to death. I know now that laughter is a form of dying. Not just in the obvious, stand-up comedian sense; dying onstage as a phrase, as a metaphor. Getting zero laughter while onstage (or should I say for most, above-pub) feels a lot like your soul leaving your body, losing of self, forgetting of self in the serotonin crash of the non-laugh. My 1992 experience was brief, but enough. No senses remain, no thought; just the useless flesh-casing rooted to the spot and pinpricked with the sweaty Braille of your shame.

Watching others go down (which was most of my evenings) is akin to watching an Islamic stoning on YouTube. Morally wrong to sit there streaming it, but many still gruesomely pay attention. Perhaps, if you were there, sooner or later, you'd pick up your rock and have a throw.

Away from my familiar world of reviewing stand-ups, death and laughter continue to be inseparable. Take 'corpsing', for example. Not something I could ever feel, but something I witnessed a few times at Teddington Studios with my Press pass. The actor simply goes away. His body remains, but he's gone. Laughter takes him, transports him way beyond it being *OK* or an *in-joke*. It starts costing money, putting everyone behind schedule. Other performers become covertly then overtly irritated. The audience stops laughing and feels awkward and bladder-full and tired. But the corpser's laughter carries on. It redoubles in fact. The corpsing continues and it goes on until the very moment itself is dead for the world. Only then, like a sated, fat parasite, does the laughter move on.

Twenty-four hours later in the Simongan village: me, plus one hundred and eight shuddering, dribbling human beings convoked around a roaring midnight fire, an orange tent of flame in the unremitting African dark. The earth had rotated only once, but my universe had been utterly inverted. I perched on a small hand-carved stool to the right of Professor Leavey, who jumped and moved and rang his words through the night. On his left sat the violently convulsing Melissa Ferguson, student of ethnography, originally from Toronto, and, I suspected, the lover of Professor Leavey. Before us all, a large pyre burning bright with a straw effigy of Chrysippus's donkey at its centre. But this was not just a mock-pyre for mimed sacrifice; within a few minutes human flesh and straw would burn together.

The one hundred and eight Simongan elders were semicircled around the crackling flames, oblivious to the heat and progress of the fire. They were laughing; yet this was not really laughter; not consented steady dispersions of joy, more a ritual in death. They had gone from childlike attention to Leavey's words and moves into this. Less than a minute before the shaking and rocking. They had no eyes now, nor tongues; all had sucked their features into their skulls. Chests heaved arhythmically; bodies rocked and knocked into neighbours; individual pools of urine coalesced into a lake which lapped and hissed at the base of the fire.

Professor Leavey danced out the words, dribbling and entrancing himself as he spoke: '... and the goddamn doctor said, "No, Femmy Kaluba ... You cannot put in what you take out," and goddamn Femmy Kaluba said, "I cannot be put out by what I have put in ..." And the goddamn doctor said, "Take out what you can't put in," and goddamn Femmy Kaluba said, "I want to put it in, it's being out I want rid of ..."'

How old was this Guru Leavey, Leavey-Na? I would never know for sure. After the initial friendliness of his Bush administration joke, and a few polite cups of fine coffee, he'd become belligerent, physically violent in fact, remained hostile that whole first day, beating at me, speaking down to me. I suppose it was his way of provoking me. It was a test. I see that now. But back then it felt like madness, bullying; it was undeniably a gash on the back of my head which now is a small knobbly cicatrice.

'Bush administration! Crap, huh?' he had said, gulping scalding coffee then immediately pouring himself some more. 'But that's kind of irrelevant, wouldn't you agree?' and he'd raised that eyebrow to the same point again.

I neither nodded nor shook my head, unsure as to exactly what he meant. He wiped off his purple face-paint and slipped on a dashiki identical to mine except for the hood which was inlaid with gold. The first questions I wanted answered were the very discussions he refused point blank; what he called 'The World of Fucking Fucked Things'. He precluded all and everything like that in the first few minutes of our acquaintance.

'Let's get one thing straight,' he said, adjusting the green robe and again refilling our cups with Ethiopian Arabica, 'there are some things I will teach you. A few facts I'm obliged to tell you ... if you want. I will tell you how I knew you would come. I will tell you how I knew you'd found my manuscript. I'll fill in any nagging blanks you might have on this. I'm not telling you these things because I want to. I don't. Indeed, I'd be mightily impressed if you refused to ask. But of course, you won't refuse – because you're ... new.' He laughed, not a pleasant noise, and I sensed trouble. 'I fucking hate practical questions of any type. I only want to talk about the Movements. Do you see: I *will* only talk about the Movements. That's why you're here.'

I nodded.

'I'll fill in those other little banal blanks simply because they may distract you. But listen close, goddamnit! I will never talk about myself. I will not discuss a single syllable of my history. I will not talk about any person with whom I have attempted to work – including anyone working with me now, especially the Princeton girl, even more this bit of dog crap you walked through my camp – Ed Austen. If you ask me about my previous clients, this whole thing is over and I will bring pain to you. Yes, Lenny Bruce, it's true. Yes, the Monty Pythons too – and more than one of them. Bill Hicks. And those more cerebral types, still living, about whom you will learn nothing: David Foster-Wallace, Umberto Eco, Hugo Chávez. Who else? You'll never goddamn know. Why? Because material is unimportant. It doesn't matter shit. If you don't focus, the whole point of my work will be lost. This is the only time I will even speak about what I won't speak about. I won't talk about things outside the Movements. And that's all: OK?'

'OK,' I whispered.

'OK?'

'Yes.'

'It better be ... The dashiki becomes you, by the way.' He meant this as a joke, I think. I blocked him, just to see if it were possible.

We finished our fourth coffees. Melissa took me behind a blue partition in the far corner of the hut where a low iron bed and green lamp awaited me. Hung up on the orange clay wall were two more identical robes, and a clear bag containing toothbrush, toothpaste, soap and a flannel. My corner smelt of Glade's 'Vanilla Dream'. She showed me out of the hut, and gave a solemn silent tour of the village. I was left to relax before lunch; the lunch during which saucers would fly, and truths be told.

Watching Professor Leavey tell the 'Femmy Kaluba' story around the fire the following evening sort of proved his point. Perhaps story *was* irrelevant. That's what our lunch row had been about, you see. That's why *nsima* and goat meat ended up on the wall.

Woody Allen was right, Leavey had contended, as untouched food steamed before us. There is no such thing as substance or material, only pure 'ineffable funniness', and I could never hope to perfect one part of a single Movement until I freed myself from my pretensions. Naturally, I had protested at this, calmly at first and then aggressively; and aggression was a behaviour with which I was increasingly comfortable. He mocked the very core of my rigorous belief in disciplined and original creativity. If a comedian dares speak in facile clichés and worn-out stereotypes, then surely it's irrelevant whether or not the audience laughs.

'You're wrong,' he said through grinding teeth.

'No,' I said, a wilful toddler drawing on a wall, 'you're wrong.'

And that's when Leavey had slapped me – hard. The attack was so shocking, so unexpected, that it failed to properly register.

'Perhaps,' I said, 'if we could ...' No words; just stunned, stinging.

We waited. I caught my breath, he watched me catch my breath.

He started in a matter-of-fact tone. 'Your main block is intellectual arrogance.'

'Arrogance?'

'Even questioning that word is proof of your being it.'

I would have said over-confidence rather than arrogance – but still, maybe he had something. For years I'd prided myself in laying-low thought-hawkers such as Jay Conway; all those boy-band haircut 'career comedians' flogging obvious tat and stock imagery about the board-game *Guess Who*, American stereotypes, elitist universities and tzatziki – how I accurately contained and shrank and broke down these routines the next day when I declared them unoriginal (a word I single-handedly patented as the death-knell in British comedy). In postmodern humour, originality of discourse is the fundamental thing.

'I will always savage anything obvious. You won't slap that out of me.'

And the timing as I found myself slapped again was perfect; a harder strike this time; from reprimand into assault. My face glowed. I wanted to hit him back. His sudden physical attacks were so irrational that they bypassed shock, progressing straight into injury. If learning the Movements meant razing everything I had ever achieved or believed in, giving up all my dignity, I wasn't sure I wanted any part of it.

'As amazing as your abilities are, Mr White, your mistake is that of a fucking child's.'

'You're going too far.'

'You haven't even started, you fucking heathen. You are not fit to join the ranks of those who know. Who don't fret like faggots over a battered notebook.'

'That's not what ...'

'People laugh at *the being*, and only *the being*.' He spat on the wall. The phlegm was brown, dyed by coffee.

'Sounds a bit ... abstract to me,' I said, rubbing my cheek, staring at him.

'Listen, or this is going to get very unpleasant before you start to see the light: the illusion of substance has gotten hold of you, and it's very dangerous. It's an illusion that will suck you in, and you are bang in its vacuum, my man.'

'No. Bad material is ... bad.'

I held my ground, shaking my head. He shook his fist. I nodded.

He wanted me to admit that my theory about the primacy of material was 'more wrong than a serial killer's scrapbook'. His simile was exquisite. I see similes as wine and food. A fillet steak is the thought itself; Merlot is the imagery. And I could taste this one, but I would not concede; no way would I give in to the idea that the comedian's very words were irrelevant.

'Then it ends here,' he said. He would not discuss a single part of the Formula with me.

'I cannot simply assent for your convenience.' But maybe I wanted to. Still, I couldn't bring myself to shit on everything I had been up until that moment. Yes, this formula might have *felt* real, but all this new stuff: cheap pseudo-Buddhist self-help.

I took a deep breath, tried rephrasing. 'I won't delete myself to make your ramblings true.'

Another slap, and he returned the hand so that it hovered beside my cheek. I drew my palm into a fist, then relaxed, then again a fist, tighter this time.

'Yes. That's right,' he said, goading my knuckles, 'save me some time. Show me I was wrong to choose you, and then fuck off.'

'Choose me?'

'That's right, hack.'

'You didn't choose me. I found you. As "brilliant" as you might be ... my will ...'

'"Might be", you little asshole . . .'

'From a random list of books . . .'

'Random, huh . . .?'

'Yes. Random. What are you trying to say?'

'You think all this is an accident. Hack.'

'What do you mean?'

'Let's just say, I helped things along.'

'How do you mean?'

'Don't push it, writer.'

My blood pumped once around my head and stopped. The mechanisms of his acerbic put-downs into a binary code. Hack. Writer. 110011000. If I'm angry enough, the wit of others boils down into numbers.

'*I* found your . . . document . . . I.'

'Say pamphlet, say what you mean, you insulting middlebrow.'

'I found it. I couldn't give a fuck how you know, or knew. OK? Is this the test?'

'No.'

'Shall I leave then?'

'If you must. You're unique, but leave.'

'Just . . . stop speaking in code. You're trying to aggrandize yourself.'

'Oh that's good.'

'Make yourself more interesting.'

'No,' he said simply, 'not at all, you sub-undergraduate.'

'Look. I'm here. To learn. Stop trying to impress me with games, you tragic codger.'

It was the breed of insult he'd been waiting for. A put-down in his own voice. He launched at me with surprising speed. Just a half-hour before, we'd been sipping cups of African coffee, colourfully getting to know each other with intellectual chit-chat about comic writing. But as soon as we'd moved onto the real business, my stubborn love of material, the atmosphere had turned.

I tried forcing him onto his back with my feet, but he rolled me over like a fat insect, pushing his thumb against my nose until it made a sharp pop. His dashiki and mine became entangled. I saw his gross scrotum swaying in the hot enthusiasm of battle. He pinned my left shoulder to the floor and brought his knee up into my stomach strik-ing me with amazing force. I slammed into the Gaggia machine, espresso cups and saucers shattering on the hard clay floor.

I'm aware of some irony here. This ridiculous fight. Perhaps the only inherently comic thing I had ever been involved in. A farce. A slapstick scene. There was no laugh-ter. Believe me, none.

'Holy shit, what's going on, you guys?' Melissa; I could not see her.

Leavey had my throat pinned firm, choking me in even pulses. A shard of espresso saucer pierced then sliced into the back of my head.

'He's bleeding, David!' she said. 'For Christ's sake stop, he's bleeding!'

'No. He's not. He's not even breathing yet.'

'Please,' I forced out gutturally. It felt as though the shard were entering my brain.

'Comedy can never be art,' he said. 'We don't have time for you to be an *idiot* savant.' His joke melted away and the room dimmed. My breathing shallowed. The prospect of his breaking my neck suddenly seemed real.

'Listen to me, you atom. Listen to this, you baby. Listen to what the world of controllables means from now on: Jules Morris' sister was in contact.'

'Bill,' I spluttered. 'Hicks ...'

'You cocky shit.' He choked me harder for this impudence. 'On December 24th you received an email from Jules Morris. It wished you a Merry Christmas.'

This was true.

'It also made a lame joke about Chrysippus. About the students of humour in the Greek ages ...'

I had forgotten this detail.

'A week before, on December 17th, you received some junk mail selling you three leather-bound books; an Eco, a Foster-Wallace, and a biography of Graham Chapman ...'

Also correct. I spat white Tipp-Ex froth from my lips.

'On December 4th ...' I tuned out. My neck swelled and my consciousness faded. He was trying to dazzle me. Make me believe he'd herded me; controlled me. The truth was much simpler, I thought. I'd found the document, made enquiries through work and he knew I was coming. This was all part of an act to impress me. An act. Did he think I could be wooed with theatre? He could kick my arse around Africa, but I would not yield to his tacky pyrotechnics.

'There's no such thing as material or decisions or substance,' he said, moving back onto the one thing I cared a fuck about. 'I have found the pure thing. There is no question – truth has more beauty than language.'

Truth has more beauty than language: from which 'philosophy for beginners' had he ripped that? I tried showing scepticism with my eyes.

He released my throat and stepped away. I gasped and writhed.

Melissa scurried towards me proffering a glass. 'It's distilled water, drink it.'

'He's a bitch and midget,' said Leavey.

I gulped the cool, iodine-tasting liquid. For a moment, calm, then, sharp pain. He had kicked me in the ribs. I experienced it as happening to someone else. He was beating me out of myself.

Melissa screamed, 'For Christ's sake, David, you'll kill him.'

'He's dead anyway. Aren't you? You can't kill what never lived.'

'That's an original line.'

Toe punt in rib. He licked glutinous spittle from his lower lip. 'Comedy will never be literature, never be art. It'll never be what you're trying to make it. You're trying to make it something so that you're something. But you're nothing, and it's fuck-all but laughter. That's one of the four basic signs of the human soul. Instinctive and pre-linguistic: laughter.'

'I know this.'

'I know you know it. So it's fuck-all but that. Admit it. Admit that you know why.' He paused, looking down at me. He wanted to spit on me. I could tell. 'Admit that and that I've proved the truth of it.' He moved away.

I hoisted myself up onto my elbows. The room still pinpricked with darkness. My eyes swivelled. Melissa soothed my head. At Leavey's prompt she retreated behind a screen as though settling in for Act II. I think I heard gentle sobs and now and again she peeped out to make secret gestures, urging my assent. I simply shook my head at her.

The wordless respite went on for five minutes at least. 'I don't know it for sure,' I said, breaking the silence. 'It's much more than just laughter, I mean.'

'Shut up,' he returned quickly, coming straight back in and slapping me with a cupped hand. He squatted over me, right palm once again resuming its hover.

'I'm not trying to annoy you, Professor.'

'Ha!'

'I'm asking for proof.'

'Proof?'

'Yes.'

Another pause.

'Do you know what hormone your body is producing right now?' he said.

'Many,' I said.

'But one in particular. That stress hormone you know so well.'

Stress hormone? This was too specific. Surely a lucky guess. How could he know about the stress hormone research. It was the closest Dr Rowe had ever come to producing a chemical inhibiter and giving me a laugh. Had Leavey seen my medical records? So, maybe he had found me. Yeah – went online and shopped for a freak in the neuroscience archives. I remembered that Dr Rowe had published. I was hardly a state secret, an object of study in fact.

'That's correct,' I said without inflection.

'Serum cortisol,' he said.

'Yes. That's right. Serum cortisol.'

My mouth dried as he began quoting. 'One of the main ways in which the human being reduces stress, as evidenced by a decrease in serum cortisol levels, is through both voluntary and involuntary laughter.'

'So you've … read … Dr Rowe's paper. Well done.' I did not sound convincing.

'The great gelotologist and his gerbil Mr Benjamin White.'

'Fuck you.'

'Ha! You see, that's why some people laugh just before they die. Why some people, when they find their best buddy fucking their wife, they laugh. Isn't it?' He wiped a speck of globular saliva from his lip. 'You know what my

261

formula does, you mite? You mere collection of cells. It reduces serum cortisol till there's none left in the body. None. You laugh, or rather, they laugh, until the last little molecule of cortisol breaks down in the bloodstream.'

'And?' I said, checking my right nostril for blood.

'And nothing. A chemically stress-free human being is an impossibility, an abomination of our natures.' He stared at me, regrouping. 'You can produce all the stress hormone you want, Benjamin, but you can't reduce your base level. Not with laughter. Not with so much as a smirk.'

'Thank you, Professor Leavey, but I've been acquainted with my condition for some time.'

'I suggest you drop that tone now, and think about what I've just said.'

'I don't dispute any of that. The science of it, I mean.'

'That's all there is.'

'No. I mean that it's one thing to describe "funniness", scientifically if you must, but it's something else to dismiss the material – to make language irrelevant.' I swallowed mucus mixed with blood.

'You travelled the length of the globe to be a snivelling beetle shit and insult my choice of protégé, all my fucking work, and you bring this to me. A secondary-school child ...'

'... No ...'

'Hmm.' He laughed. 'Well, you've got yourself genius abilities all right, but you've also got the will of a donkey.

Little Chrysippusa-Na.' He coughed and moved off beyond a screen. 'Lesson Two.'

There was another long pause. Melissa gestured to me from behind her screen. I ignored her. Fabric rustling, tissue tearing, then, quite literally, an asinine noise. Leavey brayed. He brayed long and hard and – even though I know this should not be possible – he brayed with sarcasm, with harshly inflected irony.

I sat up fully, dabbing the daubs of thickening blood from the back of my head with my dashiki.

Leavey re-emerged with two plump turquoise cushions. He had the smile of a compunctious father, guilty after a vicious beating. I flinched as he reached in ternderly and stroked my hair.

'Forgive me, baby boy. We've gotten off on the wrong foot.'

'You think?'

'Yes. My foot went right in your fucking ribs, and I'm sorry.'

He used the witticism without any of his powers. I watched the double meaning of 'foot' fold neatly in on itself, rest for a moment and then dissolve like a pill in a hot drink.

'I'm passionate, and I *need* you to succeed,' he said, 'I actually *need* it.'

We waited until his smile shaped into something more genuine. 'Comedy can never be art because it lacks ... well ... what do you call it, Miss Ferguson?'

'Thingness,' came her timid reply. Had she ever seen him like this?

'Yes – "thingness", "thingness".' He swilled the word like wine approved by a junior sommelier. 'I find the term pleasing, if a little abstract, don't you?'

'It's OK. Yes.'

'But I will attack you if you sound pathetic and threaten everything.' His voice was even.

'Just one thing.'

'For Chrissake!'

I proceeded cautiously. 'Surely, well, surely comedy must have something solid – thingness.' He coloured, but bracing myself, head throbbing, I went on. 'A joke about Iraq is a thing, OK. A joke about a tub of organic coleslaw is a less important thing, because it impinges on the world so meagrely. Not only that but, well, when a symbol has so many users, a cliché, I mean, like the Argos store or a budget airline, then it ... it has diminished power; in comedy, I mean, organic coleslaw and Iraq might be equally funny, but it's lower quality just to toss out some mocking middle-class imagery ... It's, it's, it's ... lesser thinking.'

There was a long pause while he rubbed his chin, ironically considering my argument. Was he placated? Melissa emerged from behind the partition, ready to intervene.

'Thinking? Uh-huh. Thinking? Hmm ... If you don't respond to having your ass kicked by an old man – let's take a different approach.' He breathed in slowly.

'Now: Look ... at ... me. Do you want, Benjamin White, do you wish to perfect the Movements?'

'Yes.'

'You're sure?' He looked right into me for a moment. 'You've never felt any art like this?'

'Actually no, no I haven't.' I thought of Becky but dismissed the image, the nakedness.

'And you realize its potential power, should you perfect it?'

'Yes.'

'Then it is the most important thing you will ever know?'

'Yes.'

'Well. You see – this desire is at odds with the bullshit, and I'm sorry to use that word, but really it is bullshit you believe. The Movements prove my metaphysical truth.'

'Truth?' I said. 'Metaphysical?'

'Eric Morecambe, Lenny Bruce, Bill Hicks – do you think it matters what they said?'

I reflected. He still seemed calm. I risked an honest response. 'Yes, yes I do.'

'Well you're wrong. Their words were irrelevant.'

'Really? So if they'd just babbled nonsense words that would have worked. Just said *na na na. Ning ning ning*. Pah – no one would have laughed, Hicks especially.'

'Ha! A ... HA! But Hicks is the best comedian to *make* my case.'

'I can't agree. Are you suggesting him joking about

tapeworms or Essex shopping centres would have been better than his routines on George Bush?'

He was silent once more, looking at me like a puppy which has shat on a newspaper and not in the garden.

I said, 'You think he would have been just as good without a political dimension. You want me to admit that?'

'Yes, Benjamin. That's exactly what I want you to develop the intellect to concede. That's exactly why I just kicked your ass. To kick it out of you.'

I went to speak but he cut me off.

'Every bar, every college class, every little group of friends has their standard-issue snivelling left-wing fat opinionated prick of a buddy who trots out his liberal consensus stamped upon his soul during privileged schooling ...'

'Education has nothing—'

'Loathing inequality and detesting racism: it's such a fine thing to do, isn't it? So admirably "good". We're so proud of you, man, you read the – what is it you guys have? – the fucking *Guardian*. And before you even mount that high-horse, Mr White, I want to say how fully I subscribe to that fundamentally moral consensus. Of course taking an oppositional stance to injustice is the natural mode of human kindness.

'I'm not fucking saying it's a bad thing, don't shit your pants, you textbook liberal electron. I'm not saying it's *not* a good thing, Mr High-school Reactionary. I'm not even saying these "display liberals", with whom I happen to wholeheartedly agree, are misguided – I'm not saying they don't feel. I'm just saying that it's the boring standard. And good! I'm glad it is, but nonetheless standard-issue in the thought police – especially for your book-eating British middle class ... You see?'

I kept my head conspicuously still.

'OK, OK: why Hicks? Why should it be him? Why not your buddy you went to college with – why not the old hippy dude down at the bar? Why not your lefty uncle who belongs to the hardback book club? I tell you why, my closed-eyes protégé, and it ain't because they can't phrase it right either – because you know damn well they can – you've listened to them enough, you know a whole multi-tude of these people.' He blinked before delivering his coda. 'It's because Hicks was funny. Damn funny. *Im*materially, *a*-linguistically, fucking amusing.'

I gave him the pause he felt his theorizing clearly deserved. 'OK. Say I choose to take your point,' I said.

'Don't be obtuse.' He exhaled wearily, pushing out his next words in a suppressed angry wheeze. 'If you have to get such a hard-on over actual language, Mr White ... Melissa, can we have some more Band-Aids, please ... If you have to be that way, take this bullet in your skull: word order is mathematically more important than the words themselves. Concede.'

This I had to agree with. Whomever I reviewed, the theory of word geometry was undeniable. I thanked Melissa, sticking plasters on my elbow and head.

'So admit the rest then,' he said. 'It's simply the next step. Even if you don't quite believe it yet, please, say it. Say it and know that I wouldn't go all this way to bullshit you. I will teach you the proof, of course. But before you can inspect the essence you need to drop your attachment to the outcrops. I need to hear it, man. Hear that you believe that. Or at least hear you say it. I'll take that. Lie to me if you have to: just ... just admit there is no such thing as material.'

The pause was long and heavy.

'I'm willing to go with it ... to learn. I suppose. And then we'll see.'

'Listen, piss-fly, just say it. You've already felt a little bit of it, haven't you? Well, haven't you?'

I nodded slowly.

'Look. I'm no genius like you, Benjamin. I was just a little nerd with a degree who put together a few pieces of a jigsaw and stumbled on something huge – bigger than any art or material. Now you're thinking why am I doing this.'

I wasn't.

'Well, who wouldn't? Who wouldn't clean the dirt off a diamond they pulled from the earth? And that's what the material is, it's the dirt. This is beyond the system. It's the very scaffold that allows that system to be built. It was all there, man. Hidden. I tripped over the pieces of a jigsaw. I got lucky. A corner in Athens, a middle bit in Rome, but the main picture, the brushstrokes of it all, right here – in Africa. In pre-linguistic, primal story-telling Zambian tribelands. And so fucking funny. Too funny. Fatally funny. And I found it. And I've given up my whole fucking life trying to find someone who can carry it. There's a few willing, but none able. I just need one who can be the vessel and go all the fucking way. But lo and behold – he turns up with a little boy's hard-on over some Iraq gags. He turns up and spectacularly misses the fucking point. He turns up, with this gift, this immunity, protected, the only fucking one – and he won't give me a nod, even a fake nod, to proceed. What kind of ignorant bullshit is that? . . . So, I'm asking you one last time: admit it. Tell me it. Lie to me about it, and I'll show you something so magical, so powerful, you'll never believe in a material object ever again.'

We sat there staring at each other. The noises of the village children at play rose up then diminished.

'"There is no such thing as the material. Only the person",' I said as if by rote.

'Not very genuine, but I'll take it.'

'I can't do sarcasm.'

He slapped me gently on my right cheek and moved away. The mood had finally lightened, and with that the pain of my injuries came on in full.

I think even now, in here, in my final days, I cannot *fully* admit his proposition. So, making things real with actual words might be remarkably less important than I first believed, but it's not entirely true that words themselves are irrelevant; not in my opinion. It's taking the whole thing *ad absurdum* to suggest that babble could serve as well as language. It could not. No way. But of course, Professor Leavey had that one vital thing which put me in my place; that sublime structure which ensured I was humbled and quiet and prone: the Routine itself. The Movements, the Formula. It was a thing of undeniable power, a thing outside of language, beyond the specific; and, yes, material had no part of its beauty. I may not have remotely believed at first, but the truth was, by giving up my arrogant hold on the material, through temporarily allowing I could never write anything objectively amusing and nor could anyone else, I had found my entry point. Yes, yes, yes – for a moment at least it was true: humour, especially raw and in itself – stand-up in other words – had no *objective* substance to it. I allowed that. It had language, but no *stuff*. Perhaps that made me ridiculous, but I allowed that too, and by four o'clock on my first day I had perfected the Middle Movements and made significant headway into the rest.

Beside that fire on the second evening, I saw further proof. Each word was indeed 'a dependent', sometimes upon movement, sometimes upon the fall of another word. Each phrase clearly adhered itself to, say, a gesticulation.

Leavey bucked then quivered, his old body clicked and complained through the dance. He creakily executed the contortions and bends which, only a few hours before, had left us breathless and exhausted.

The fire died back into white embers as the last pieces of straw donkey expired in the flames. I knew the Movements, knew and felt all sixty-one seconds of them; although Leavey would of course perform only fifty, for obvious reasons. In forty-eight hours he had taught me the complete routine, but it wasn't until the second afternoon that we'd had a full practice run; well, much more than a practice run, an *execution* – and I pardon myself that particular pun.

Taken as segments the piece makes no sense; that's not the way to appreciate the true arc of it. That's the mistake I had been making in my study of the Movements; here an awful narrative, there a silly voice and pathetic move. That's what made independent study unfeasible. That's why writing it down is ultimately futile. You have to be guided into holding its humour, cradling it, and marinading your mind and body in it all at once. The alchemy is undeniable, even to a cynic, a cold spectator such as myself. Yes, when those hot Movements come together as one, logic dies in its fire.

The Simongan elders gradually recovered their senses. I was the only one who had not been in a trance. I'd snorted, my blood simmered and my mind heated and danced. I saw what it all was, but ultimately I was immune – the only such person Leavey had ever known. To him this meant I might be the first ever to perform the routine all the way through. Even with years of self-training, Leavey could only manage Movements One to Eight. He hadn't been reckless enough to attempt the whole thing.

'Anyone who experiences it is destroyed,' he said. 'If they were to survive, they would be vegetables. Unable to communicate.'

'I know,' I said. But how did I know? Perhaps I'd known it all along. Perhaps that's what I hoped for, what I wanted, the very thing which drew me in.

'Come with me,' he had said that afternoon.

I'd followed him to a small hut located fifty metres from the perimeter of the village. It was unlike the other shacks. The roof was flat, but by far the most striking architectural feature was a large pair of straw donkey ears that adorned the doorway. We were still a good ten metres from the hut when I heard the noises. Giggling, choking, then a scream, more giggling; another loud, piercing yell followed by maniacal cackling.

'You see,' said Leavey with mock academic serenity, motioning me towards the hut, 'Mr Ed Austen tried to usurp you before you arrived. Well, do you think I allowed that, or do you think I protected you, my Grand Project?'

'You need me. That's clear,' I said.

'You're wrong. I would have dropped you in a moment if Ed Austen's boasts had turned out to be true.'

'Boasts?'

'Remember the rules, Mr White.'

'And they apply to that . . . arsehole?'

'He was my project, if only for one morning.'

'What happened?'

He ignored me. We were at the door. He pushed it open

with his foot. 'Let's just say amateurs shouldn't go beyond Eight.'

We were greeted by a lithe man with light-brown skin, woolly hair and an impish grin; in one hand a rusty pail of water, in the other a battered old ladle.

'Leavey-Na.' He had a strange, high-pitched voice for a Zambian man.

'Robert. How is he?'

'The same, Chrysippusa Sire.'

'I see. Thank you, Robert, that'll be all.'

Robert left, dementedly winking.

The inside of the small hut was lit by candle lamps, bare except for a corroded wire-framed bed in the centre. Upon that bed lay a writhing, almost unrecognizable Ed Austen, or rather something that was once Ed Austen. How could someone lose so much weight, actual physical presence, in twenty-four hours? He wore only blue Y-fronts. His thin, pathetic body was glazed in a gossamer film of sweat. In place of eyes, pulsating and twitching, were blank white lumps of jelly edged with red. His swollen and bitten tongue wagged at us, snake-like, yet without a snake's grace; a reptile without dignity.

'Hello, Ed,' said Leavey.

Austen laughed, for it was a laugh of sorts, and opened his mouth unnaturally wide until bloodspots appeared at the corners.

'It's funny, Eddy boy, huh?' said Leavey.

Ed screamed, bucking and fitting like a dog with fatal sunstroke.

'What do you think?' said Leavey to me with a jovial smile.

'And that's Movements One to Eight?' I said.

'He didn't quite get to Eight. Made the most of Seven, but ...' He trailed off and we both watched the creature thrash and roll at invisible wit.

'Is he going to be OK?' I said it but I didn't mean it. Does that seem awful? For the first time in my life I was looking at a dying, suffering human, and instead of repulsion, fear or concern I felt nothing. Bollocks. Why lie now? What's the point? I didn't feel nothing. I felt aroused, excited. Glad.

'No. No, he most definitely won't be all right.'

'What?'

'Oh come on. You hate him, and he hates you. Do you give a shit?'

'We don't get on, but I doubt ... well I doubt he'd want to see me like that.'

He laughed hard, seeing straight through, right into my rotten centre. 'Treat others as you wish to be treated thyself? Is that it? Huh? Or maybe you do really feel pity and fear for your good friend. I underestimated you, brother Benjamin. Shall we save him?'

'Can we?'

'I think you know the answer to that.'

It was again that 'religious stoning' feeling; the

compelling urge to enjoy someone die onstage at the Comedy Café. Well, here was a being dying from the very opposite, too much laughter. And still I did not feel revulsion. Confidence lurched in me. I circled him. He seemed completely unaware. It was enthralling. As my eyes adjusted I saw clearly marks on his flesh; nicks and gashes where he'd likely flung himself from bed-frame to wall and back as his wit repeated the Humour on loop. And yet, I looked inside myself.

This is hard to explain: I may not be able to feel humour, or laugh, or empathetically share a moment of joy, but I have never had a problem with pity or knowing wrong from right. True – exclusion, knocks, loneliness all had a share in shaping my adult mind, but sadism? No. So when I looked at Ed Austen, who in fact could have been anyone, could have been the person I loved most; why did I feel an irrational urge to destroy him with Movements Nine and Ten? Maybe it's the same reason a few days later I went onto my other visits. This thing of which I'd felt a mere touch was my purpose. It was bigger than I could ever know. It was certainly more important than my life, my humble meandering existence. It demanded to be used. To take life with the use of it seemed suddenly logical, legitimate even. Something of such beauty should not be mounted on a wall like a samurai sword. It should be wielded. The people who are sundered by it will die smiling. And that's what I knew. Whatever you may think, whatever I may think, it's what

I instinctively felt. I felt the urge to consummate this art, and kill by laughter.

'You could be a fine Humorist, Benjamin.'

'A Humorist?' I said, but could not take my eyes from a green crusted glob of spittle on Ed's scabbed chin.

'Yes. The best.'

At the time I didn't think about the term Leavey had used. But he was right: 'Humorist' is a fine title. If you think about it, it means so much more than 'a purveyor of whim, wit and fancy'. It's more than a generic term for joker. The 'ist' suffix gives the noun agency, expertise, action. Anyone who is an *ist* is a connoisseur, not a lowly practitioner.

'How long will he live?' My eyes were still fixed on Ed.

'About five minutes more.'

'I don't understand.'

'Oh, I think you do.'

I looked at Professor Leavey and swallowed hard.

'You're gonna do a little show for him. Don't worry. You're immune. But you know that anyway.'

'Yes. At least I think I am.'

'You know you are. You cannot laugh. You're safe all right. Your life's a bit fucked because of how safe you've been.'

It was a reference to my mother and father. 'Yes. I couldn't please them. I couldn't.'

'What?'

276

'Make them happy.'

'Those two? I read about your parents.'

'That was the problem. All their damn happiness and I couldn't make them happy.'

'Happy? The word's dead. Every cliché lives in it. You have a gift, remember that.'

'I never forget it.'

Ed Austen made a noise. His chest was heaving; a thick brown liquid spilled out over his chin. Was he watching our little scene?

'Well then. It's all been leading here. It's why I've chosen you. I might be the one that dug up this damn diamond formula, but I can't even look at it, not all of it all at once. I need someone with the er . . .'

'Right goggles?'

He laughed. I'd made a joke. In all this shit, I'd made a joke. I saw the blandness of the noun 'goggles' mingle with the gravity of Ed's demise, my revelations. The bathos swept through me in a thick rush.

'You want me to do this on my own?'

'I'll start you off, but the reality is you have to do this alone. I have no choice in it. Unless you want me looking like him.' The silence grew heavy for a moment. He laughed. 'Maybe you'd like that. Huh? Like to take my place. Ha. You can be *a* Humorist, but not this one, Benny boy. I can't go that far. I need these people – my other work. But you'll be the first. The first person to grasp these rules and bend them . . . make the abstract concrete.' He spoke these last few words gazing into the distance with a fey expression I found indulgent.

'How?'

'Just as we practised. Just as I've shown you. As it's written, and has been since tribesmen drew pictures in the sand, and the donkey ate figs.'

This would be the first time I performed all the Movements straight through. Although we had only rehearsed Nine and Ten (Footwork and Guttural Noises) in isolation, I had already sensed the complete Formula. I certainly knew it. I retained every joke or routine I heard down to the last syllable. Recall would not be a problem. Just nerve. I kept my eyes fixed on Ed's writhing goblin body. The goose-fat balls for eyes, the double-jointed limbs in seizure. Leavey moved my legs apart, sculpting me into the Stance. He bent my arms into position like pipe-cleaners, all the while gently coaching me. We ran my agreed syntax one last time – the only routine I'd ever written, the one about the Centre, reworked so that certain words fell exactly with the all-important eyebrow, the Hicks Brow as Leavey called it. How I wish Leavey had talked to me about Hicks. Essential throat modulations were also recapped. Landing correctly and furrowing the brow with precision forces the voice to heel, wrap around the moves. By using the larynx correctly you can create the image of the Brow, the Lean, the Prance. That's how it's possible to use the Formula on a blind person, or someone simply not watching. It's immeasurably harder, but if intonations, timbre, and inflection are mathematically perfect, I could in theory perform the whole thing with Ed facing away from me. The chance of success is cut by about eighty per cent, but it's possible.

'Also, remember that Simongan Thrust. It's not just mathematical perfection. The true humour lies in the degree to which you thrust your pelvis beyond your feet, *plus* the sudden force with which you do it. Remember that. And don't forget to say "Gnughhh!", when you do so.'

'Yes,' I said, trembling a little. The Thrust had proved the most difficult to crack. I'm no dancer.

Leavey took hold of my shoulders and steadfastly bade me good luck before walking backwards through the doorway. It was locked from the outside with a gentle clunk.

The atmosphere shifted and focused and now I knew that nerves would not be a problem. I took a good look at Ed: he was finished anyway. The resolve came and so I went with it. I circled him a few times, before taking a position at the end of the bed. I wiggled my buttocks squarely into the Stance. I jumped up, hit the clay floor, cleared my throat, and resquared the Stance bringing up clouds of orange dust with my bare feet, a weightlifter savouring the moments before a clean jerk. Ed's neck spasmed violently and his milky eyes were on me, a quick obscene move, a twisted version of my own Owlhead phase all those years before.

'Life at the Centre was fucking maddening,' I began, and Ed's blind gaze was firm, not breaking until the thing was done. It was my first attempt at using humour. Yes the dance lurched with imprecision – but Leavey had done most of the thing for me. I was able to play and learn, a kitten with a half-dead mouse. Movements Three and Four I did twice. Ed popped, squirted, vomited, screamed. It's awful, really. I used the volume of his pain to mark my improvement. I took each Movement in very slow incremental steps; not proceeding until I felt fully focused and ready. After twenty minutes or so, I felt ready to close.

I snapped him into Movement Eight. He clicked his gaze onto me. He watched, and I mastered him, and he laughed until the blood ran from his ears, tears from his eyes. In the end, as his shallow breathing dimmed, as the final lungful leaked from him, there could be no doubt: Ed Austen was dead at the hands of the Humorist.

12

Complimentary Seats

The first of the complimentary seats was mine; a first-class adjustable flat-bed on South African Airways. I needed to disappear, so travelling home on the *Review*'s expense account was not an option. One text to Miranda from the Professor's mobile requesting 'Please do not look for me, but await instructions, Benjamin' took care of the office, keeping her on an ultimately fateful tenterhook.

Getting on at the Comedy Store the following Monday was also relatively straightforward. Not because of my connections and the respect I commanded, quite the opposite; due in fact to all comedians and club-bookers loathing me. They needed me, but they detested me, a necessary bug, the maggot who eats the gangrene from a wound. That's how they saw me. I used the Professor's mobile phone from the dry basin at the front of the village where I had one bar of signal. The Comedy Store's booking agent Fiona Merriman was in turns shocked and delighted as she granted me five minutes' stage-time at the Monday Gong Night. I had seen this barbarous event many times. The challenge: perform for as long as you can until the audience votes you off, their judgement sonorously confirmed by the gong.

'Where are you now, Benjamin? The line's crackly,' said Fiona, public school and unsexy.

'Abroad. Zambia.'

'Christ – they've got festivals everywhere now.'

'True,' I misled.

'Look ... it's ... I mean, it'll be great, don't get me wrong, good value, I mean, but are you sure?'

'I am.'

'Well, do you want to go on somewhere in the middle, or even ... near the end when the other comics have gone?'

'No. First. And announce it in *Time Out*.'

'You're mad.'

I'd never felt so sane. 'You don't need to clear it with Brian?' I said.

'Are you kidding? No offence, but Brian'll be there with bells on – or is that gongs?' Her joke, so limp in its imagistic linkings, dissolved before materializing.

Brian McFraley, Smirking Mule's New Act of the Year 1999, stopped performing comedy in 2001 shortly after my

257-word annihilation (edited by Miranda Love). He had subsequently carved himself a lucrative career in the Comederati booking and awards world. His hate for me, however, remained buffed and implacable.

So the date was set. Six days' time. I pulled a piece of paper from my pocket and memorized an address in Finchley. Leavey had arranged a safe house in which I could lie low, practise for a few days and ready myself for the Store. He'd been unaware of the other complimentary seats I had arranged; a private preview show – for my family. I screwed the piece of paper into a tight ball and flicked it into my plastic champagne flute. I extended my flat-bed to its full luxurious length and reflected. Considering what I was planning, indeed what I had just done, I felt strangely tranquil; apart from the recurring image of Ed's body burning in the flames. Dancing and chanting with the villagers as he burnt to a crisp was all very well, but the sight of flesh bubbling away – horrible, I wouldn't recommend it. I thought that organs swelling, popping and spilling sizzling contents was the stuff of gory novels, but it turned out to be true. The off-meat smell is still with me now, years later.

So yes, there was another phone call; covertly made.

'Sunday, yes, that's right,' I'd said to my mother.

'I see. I mean ... Well, it's not just the short notice, Benjamin ... anyway, I'm pretty sure Becky and Pierre have antenatal the next morning.'

'Tell them they have to cancel.'

'Pierre won't go for it, darling. Be realistic.'

'Tell him they must cancel. The two – the "three" of them are in danger if they don't.'

'You're scaring me, darling. And what about Cooper? He's going away with Gavin.'

'He must cancel. His life literally depends on it.'

'Cancel ... depends on it' said my mother, the perfunctory lightness still in her voice. 'Benjamin, what's going on? Tell me, for Christ's sake.'

'Like I said already. It's a thing of immense importance for the family. Immense. Missing this would be unthinkable – dangerous. I can't go into details on the phone. Just trust me, Mum.' I never said 'Mum'. 'I'm asking just once for the attention to be turned to me. One night. No ifs or buts. It's vitally important. It's the biggest thing this family will ever experience.'

'Oh good God, Benjamin. You're terrifying me. Benjamin? Benjamin!'

I was silent.

'... and ... what about Auntie Jemima? You can't rally around everyone for some sort of emergency and leave her out.'

I thought for a moment. I felt neutrality towards my timid aunt, even pity. She was still mourning poor Uncle Jeff; inessential to my plan, but then again she might raise an alarm before the Monday night portion of my scheme.

'Yes. Sorry. I wasn't thinking,' I said.

'Benjamin, she'll ...'

'Yes. So be it.' I cut her brutally.

'So be it? You sound like Yahweh.'

There was a pause. My mother's wit travelled down one continent and then another. A characterization. A mockery of my formal syntax through religious satire. 'Ha'. I thought the word '*Ha*'.

Her breathing grew wheezier belying her ringed neck, fatter in recent years. 'Benjamin. Darling. Please. What's going on?'

'You'll see. It's very important. For anyone who's not there, the consequences will be massive.'

'I'm going to put your father on … Graham! … Talk with your father.'

'No. I have to go.'

'Benjamin!'

'Sunday, 9 p.m. I love you.'

'I'm sorry?' she said.

I hung up. It was the first time I had ever said that.

'This better be good,' said Pierre, his conditioned grey mane swaying over his black roll-neck as he menaced with a vaguely Swiss lilt; the new alpha male, the silverback.

'Yes, come on, Benji, don't keep us in suspense!' said my father, a crystal glass of expensive sherry pinched between forefinger and thumb. The faces of the others lit up, waiting for his inevitable lightening of the atmosphere. 'You said our lives depended on it. Oh! My liege! My aorta is buggered. I'm dying!'

And there it was. And they all laughed, and I stood there. Well that was fine. Let's all laugh.

Pierre plonked gruffly onto the arm of Becky's chair. She refused eye contact with me, instead rubbing her eight-month swell meditatively. My father and mother squeezed into their brown leather two-seater like new lovers, all close and jokey and rosy-faced. Cooper had chosen his favourite backless stool, sitting erect like a meerkat, taller and more camp than ever. How had that fat benign ball of baby grown into such a knowing and charismatic sophisticate? He'd hogged both ends of the likeability scale; been the giggling chubby innocent *and* was now the lithe gregarious beacon. He smiled, extending his arm around a frumpy Auntie Jemima on the chaise longue. She looked gaunt today, lonely. Ready to go, I reasoned with myself. Mother leaned from the sofa and dimmed the lights. The room smelt of mulled wine and furniture polish and everyone was waiting.

'For Christ's sake, Benjamin. What is this?' said Pierre.

I looked at my mother and father for support. They did not react; so, they sanctioned his tone, this aggressive con-descension.

'Pierre,' I said blankly, 'shut the fuck up and listen, you pretentious Swiss prick.'

'Benjamin!' Mother and Father together, still grit-smiling.

'Yes?'

They were silent. Just their smiles as a shield against awkwardness.

'I see,' I said.

Pierre made to speak but was restrained by Becky. He squirmed and fumed, his face puce.

'I've gathered you all here today to tell you something extremely important. It's a story about what happened to me at the Centre. It's vital I share it . . .'

A whispering from Pierre. 'If you have brought us here just to tell us a story, and that is all, I will wallop, so help me God, I will wallop you.' 'Wallop', so strange in his accent, was humorous. I worked hard not to be affected.

'Hey, hey – c'mon, Pierre,' said my father, his scar of a smile unwavering.

'Listen. For sixty-one seconds. If you wish to "wallop me" at the end of that time, you may.'

Pierre grunted.

'Can you give me and *my* family sixty-one seconds of you not being Number One?'

'Don't push it,' he said.

'Well. Can you – give me one minute and one second?'

'Of course,' and he rubbed Becky's swell.

If I could have smirked sarcastically here, I would have.

'Anyone else? Do my nearest and dearest agree to listen to what I have to say for a meagre sixty-one seconds?'

A mixture of nods and yeses.

This was the first time in my adult life that my family had properly given me an audience. I stood there savouring and swilling their attention until it cloyed. Other than my lame joke on Cooper's fifth birthday, this was completely new. Yes, this would be a first and a last.

With that, I thrust out my buttocks; jumped up and down. I cracked and popped my arms into the position. It felt tight and precise and good. My mother's herringbone parquet floor had the same feel as the Finchley flat I had crashed in the previous evening, so the moves came metallic and clean. Gristly striations rippled on my neck. My lips grew taut. My body obeyed and all was firm and ready: the Stance. Pierre snorted, of course intended as derision, but the mucusy end of his mockery just got hooked by the Stance and ripped upwards. His snort bled into a giggle and that giggle dispersed into the room and into the lungs of the others. Their faces: unsure if they were laughing from awkwardness, or amusement, or something else, and I knew it was time to begin in earnest.

'Life at the Centre, was fucking maddening,' I said, lowering creamily into the Hicks Brow, 'and when I say fucking maddening, I don't mean annoying ...' and the Simongan Thrust, like a machine, digitally accurate.

My mother went first. As I flowed into the 'autistic' line and onto Dr Rowe and nitrous oxide, she, well I suppose she ejected from the two-seater. There was a shocking arc to her trajectory, a bit like a Buddhist monk defying gravity. She landed on all fours, her wrist snapping on impact with a turkey-bone crunch. The fracture compounded through her baggy flesh, the force popping her gold watch from her wrist. I reacted with the minutest vocal tremor which flecked my clauses on the Mental Health Act, but not enough to impair the progress of the Humour. My father reacted quickly with a spasm. The crack of my mother's wrist had disrupted the group's reaction, but not my hold. My mother held up her flapping ruined hand and for a moment my audience was unsure, yet still it fell into black laughter. Cooper hugged Auntie Jemima, who had opened her legs, allowing clear piss to gush down her tights and onto the parquet. My father slid onto the floor, Auntie Jemima's urine soaking into his grey pinstriped casuals. He emitted a powerful guffaw, twitching, laugh climbing and climbing into a dangerous, lacerating roar. I moved into the midway point of Movement Five, my robotic love for my A level knowledge, my masochistic thoughts on university education, and I conducted them, an orchestra of atonal screaming humans. Just as I finished the line about the St John's College I would never attend, I heard the tender meat of my father's throat giving way, and then his eyes were gone, white and mealy. He held onto my mother and both of them laughed hard, but soon her noises receded and her body slackened. Only thirty-two seconds in, perhaps because of her happy disposition, my mother's smile fixed and stilled, and she slid into a swimming-pool-chute pose, resting there in the piss with blood-tears on her cheeks. Her death prompted my father's biggest laugh yet. Cooper stood up. His effeminate whinnying built to a chimp crescendo, and his tick-shaped blemish, the mark I had inflicted, stretched with the laughter, the laughter I induced. He slapped Auntie Jemima's back, and then slapped it again. He kept slapping it, harder and harder, beating her like a rug. As I slid into the fortieth second, Auntie Jemima broke. I don't mean mentally, although she was having a right old giggle. I mean her shoulder bone cracked and came cleanly through her knitwear more quickly than any blood. Now the room laughed resolutely, and Cooper kept slapping and laughing. Auntie Jemima's noises changed as flesh and sinew folded and broke. I was full of a boyish fascination. Auntie Jemima died smiling, the first time she had smiled in a year. Cooper slapped the air and fell over the stool, his body in rigor before he hit my mother's yucca plant, dead in zombie pose. I turned to the remaining three. Forty-eight seconds gone. It was time for Movements Nine and Ten. I had finished Eight, leaping and bating, with some base words on masturbation. My father was a goldfish now, lying on the floor flapping and gasping in the shallow pool of the dead's piss. I was disappointed when he died (perhaps from a heart attack) before I could get into the fifty-first second. On reflection, it's no surprise he went during the all-important Movement Eight. That's the point of no return for everyone. The performer must move in such a way that it's inhuman, impish – Tolkienian. Surreal. Yes, that's the word, surreal. I bet that's why my father succumbed just then – I looked like a cartoon. I was the funniest thing he could ever imagine creating. But he never would. I had made it. He had seen it, but I had made it, and now my father, the great satirist Graham White, was dead.

Becky and Pierre: no surprise they lingered. This is why correct modulation and vocal pitch is paramount. Those who would not listen to the words themselves had to be hooked by sound alone. That's the power of the inflections, they bring in the inattentive, the blind, the ignorant – the Swiss.

They were fixed on me now. They both looked as Ed Austen had looked. Creatures rather than people, skinny faces, flesh stapled onto their skulls. Both had white barn eggs for eyes. No one should survive beyond Eight, and those who do transfigure; for a short while they become something higher. My Becky. I'd have liked to write here about poignant feelings of regret, of unrequited love, of compassion, of her white skin and red cheeks and black hair, and her vanilla smell. I'd like to have felt that if she had touched me this whole thing would have ended. I would have liked to report on the cold, sad doubt that coursed through me as I took her. But I felt exactly the same morbid satisfaction and artistic immersion that I felt when it came to the rest: Ed, the three hundred and twelve at the Store. The only difference was her beauty; its edges dulled by her late-thirties yielding to her forties. Her neck lurched and clicked. Her face, wind-tunnelled and glassy, was a Dadaist work of art. I wanted to lean in, just graze her lips with mine, but this would have stained my canvas, and the Formula's beauty trumped hers, so, unwavering, I commenced Nine.

I completed an aside on loneliness and began about the fling with Miranda, a combination of self-deprecation and loathing of the modern state of masculinity. On to the footwork and guttural noises of Movement Ten: a small symphony of semi-quavered phlegm and snort and footwork. Pierre gasped and roared and the bloodspots came as his lips tore and he was all teeth and screaming tears and fell unwillingly into death. Oh Becky. In truth, she died a few seconds before Pierre. Dead, she remained seated for a moment. Her arms hugged at something invisible, the way audiences sometimes embrace each other when the funnies reach a certain pitch. And that's when it happened – the disturbing yet aesthetic phenomenon about which I wrote to Leavey (I would love to have had a reply). At first, much like the others, she stiffened, her eyes popped, blood vessels mosaiced and her arms twisted and cracked and eventually she collapsed forwards into the swimming-pool-chute pose. But something happened after death; stranger than the usual post-mortem tears. I know I did not imagine this. On the punchline, 'And that gave me something to laugh about. For once,' her swollen pregnant belly spasmed. The tight black fabric of her maternity dress shuddered and jerked and I knew what I'd just seen. The foetus, the doomed babe, was laughing. The unborn thing had drawn itself up in fatal hilarity and shivered and laughed and perished. She had been dead already for three seconds when the final seismic contortion ran through the bump. Blood streamed down her legs, and the mess was bad.

So apart from myself, the only other being who heard my punchline was Becky's unborn child.

I took a few moments, surveying the room with a mixture of sadness and pride. As violent as their deaths had been, they looked like a family of sleepy Sunday lunchers. Only the copious urine and my mother's and aunt's compounded fractures spoiled the serene tableau.

Dabbing my forehead, I walked through to my mother's kitchen and hunted out some heavy-duty cleaner and strong Waitrose bin-bags. I wouldn't make a song and dance of clearing things up. There was no point. Besides it was already 10 p.m., and tomorrow was a big day.

13

The Closing Set

The worst thing about performing at the Comedy Store's Gong Night is the lack of privacy. Its sell-out popularity with performers and public alike means would-be comedians must lurk in amongst the audience: no dressing rooms, nowhere to hold the shit in your arse as you doubt yourself over and over. There can be anything up to thirty trembling, shifty rookies awaiting their execution before the gong. Observing the terrified amateurs pace up and down is a free bonus for the baleful audience. I had myself many times enjoyed floppy-haired talent voids and tousled Footlights arrivistes twitchingly awaiting their fate. Real first-timers were rare, however. In reality, most of the performers were lingerers, veterans of the unpaid circuit, some of them six or seven years in; using the Gong Night for a hit of specious glory. So you can imagine, it's a real treat when someone truly new climbs onto the stage. And that *is* the correct verb, 'climb'; the awkwardness of their clamber – ungainly tentative mounting of the boards, nervous wild glances, that fatal, oh so death-rattling pause before speech. These factors combine, placing stick firm and ready at gong before a single syllable is uttered.

It works like this: at the start of the evening ten members of the audience are selected and armed with red cards. When five or more cards are raised, the gong is struck. True newbies (I prefer the term for a novice bullfighter, *'novillero'*) rarely last longer than three or four seconds. Being dispatched that quickly is usually due to a critical pause after a blandly generic greeting. They leave too long between fake-happy 'hello' and their first foray into humour. They lethally overestimate the grace a British audience will grant. There's no doubt, the purpose of the night is entertainment-by-striving, and it does entertain, and failure comes often. That's why it's popular. Why I liked it. But tonight would be different. 'Liking' would have nothing to do with it.

'For fuck's sake. Do not do this,' said Miranda, gesturing to the stage, and lighting one cigarette with the dying stub of its predecessor. It was our first conversation since I'd disappeared in Zambia.

'Leave me alone. Don't watch. Go. Trust me.' I had not planned for her to be here. Word had spread quickly.

'Come back to the office with me. Right now. We'll

concoct something. We'll make a layout for the morning and Dom—'

'I'm doing this, Miranda. And I'm never coming back to that damn office.'

'Christ – you could just hang onto your job if you *think*. Do this, and you'll fuck it, babe. It'll put the seal on it as well.' Her face was lined, suddenly desperate and old.

'Good.'

'Fuck you then, Benjamin, good cunting luck.'

I stared at Miranda until she was uncomfortable. Her use of the C word in the present participle spun before me. I used it as a warm-up. Squeezing a swear word into a formal construction unusual to it. So, it was merely bathos again. Ha, I thought in monosyllable. Ha. She couldn't leave it, and leaned into me for one last try.

'I thought you said Ed Austen would be here.'

'He is.' I closed my eyes. 'In a way.'

'What the hell does that mean? Stop trying to make this a "big moment" – you're being a stupid bloody twat.'

I continued staring. If I could have hit her with a 'sardonic smile' I would have.

'OK. I really am done.' And she marched away to watch the show from the furthest corner. The corner in which she would very soon die.

As usual the night had sold out. Karen Tuborg, a pasty Glaswegian gag-hag, was on duty in the lightbox. Her skin was so pockmarked a blind person could have read poetry from it. Karen being on duty explained the unreasonably high central heating. The place kept filling, and the temperature rising. The budding comics tugged the scoop-necks of their bright Indie T-shirts. The low ceilings, the halogen lights, the cigarette smoke; a stale fug charged with emotion, a closeness you could scream into and never be heard.

And then the blackness.

Black, but a pinprick of white from a roaming spotlight scanning the room through the dense smoke, a metaphor for searching out talent in the infinite cosmos of wannabes and mindless fuckwits. The rolling rhythmic brass-band noise of the Comedy Store's jingle rose up and blasted from the 300-watt speakers; then the purples. The stage – thrust in mock-proscenium, polished and ready for its doomed matadors. The glow of the massive brass disc dominated. Gong Night had begun.

At this point the hopefuls, filed along the right flank of the audience, usually stiffened and paced and sipped at water, but not so much tonight. My stunt gave everyone something else to focus on other than their nerves. The seventeen rookies postponed their terror in favour of ogling Performer Number One: Benjamin White of the *Review*, British comedy's premier villain, delicately sipping at Evian, pacing evenly, ready for the stage.

In truth, I had been a little disappointed by the pedigree of performer turnout. I didn't know most of them. The *Time Out* advert had produced plenty of gossip and online speculation, but no real comedians at the event. I supposed they were all working, but I was bitterly let down that a few hadn't cancelled gigs to attend my spectacle. Perhaps some of these amateurs were serving as sentries for the bigger names. That would have to do. The biggest name in the queue of gong-death was performer Number Five, Miriam Hein, a comedienne I rather respected. She had a solidly playful fifteen minutes on voles and marmalade and Iran. She stood with her shoulder against the wall by the cigarette machine, and every time I met her gaze she told me I was mad in quirky facial gestures. Yes I am, I thought, and rather proud.

The British Press, however, did not disappoint. Liam Grey, the teenage hotshot from Guffaw.co.uk, pen poised, turgid in his boxers at the thought of brother turning against brother, and being electronically first to leave his critical droppings spattered on Google for eternity, a whitening dog stool of opinion. Mitch Bailey from the *London*, spectacles crushing aquiline nose, grey hair curlier at the prospect of the massacre; of course Magdalen College's Double-starred First and now the *Manchester Economy*'s Boyd Wallaby, so smug it seemed he might melt into intellectual caramel. The omnipresent, and omni-fucked, near-menopausal Holly Tyson of the *Commuter*, bedecked in powder-blue blouse and clown make-up. Even the *Morgan's What's Hot?* Penny Gleitzman was there, almost dissolving into gaseous form with cynical fizzy excitement. None of them could take their eyes off me. None of them, and not one gaze benevolent. They couldn't believe their luck, probably read the *Time Out* advert thinking it too good to be true, inundating Fiona Merriman with eager calls for confirmation. Yes, the most detested and feared man in the industry, the one whose opinions had disproportionate power to shape and decide, was about to be shaped and decided by his peers. Indeed.

The spotlight's pinprick of white widened into a crisp bright circle.

Brian McFraley's voice resounded through the venue. 'Ladies and gentlemen, boys and girls, welcome to the stage your host and compère for the evening, Matthew Hoooooptoooooon!'

And one last cannonade of jingle as the tiny northerner bounded on. He was dressed top to toe in black sparkly garments. His hair had been bleached by the 1980s, spiked by the 1990s. He gambolled grotesquely around the stage, waving and hallooing, a boyish grin on his wrinkled face, eyes all watery with acceptance and completion.

'Good evening, Comedy Store!' he belted in chipper Lancastrian.

'Hello!' the Pavlovians yapped back.

Matthew Hopton pranced and danced and explained the rules of the gong. He selected his ten judges, mocking each of them in turn with standard put-downs. Drunken stags in the front row were efficiently deemed 'wankers'; the bespectacled, bearded gentleman stage-left automatically labelled 'sex offender'. Each cliché was plucked gleaming from his leathery quiver of platitudes and he fired them out into the bull's eye of his drunken herd. After five minutes or so of mindless banter he produced his sequinned guitar from behind the sparkly curtain and told us that the competition would begin after a short song about the clitoris. And so it went. An embarrassing, out-dated, melodic ditty about not being able to find what these days most teenage boys could locate blindfolded.

'Ooh, I say, where is the clitoris? Ey? I've given up look-ing for it. But I ain't stopped singing about it!'

The song began, and how the audience howled. The lights dimmed now. The stage bathed more conspicuously in purple. Henry McMillan in the lightbox smoked a cigarette with Karen Tuborg, and they shared a private joke, both looking at me, almost pointing. Henry waved sarcastically. I met it with a thumbs-up, a gesture I whole-heartedly meant. They were no doubt sharing their joke with Brian McFraley in the soundbox at the back.

It was a shame about that bright lighting, so bright I couldn't glimpse Brian when I was onstage. They found him slumped in his booth.

'Oh the clit,
Where is it?
Let me look for it a bit ...
I'm in it for the hunt ...
Just to forage round your – nether regions ...
Oh the clit,
Oh the clit,

Where is it . . .?'

And on he sang. Ten minutes, but it felt like ten years, each gynaecological refrain pulling us back a year, the protracted asides slower than an old dog's illness, until I wanted to put *him* down. Apologies, to any family of Matthew Hopton, sincere apologies, but that's how I felt. I carried with me two and a half thousand years of comedic history, and was forced to watch my stage being defiled before I took it; an unforgivable heresy. Note the possessive determiner, *my* stage.

The stag party in the front row rolled with laughter, savouring every spittle-laced word. As sacrilegious as I knew it to be, I found myself dismissing once and for all Leavey's tenet that material is irrelevant in comedy. He'd misunderstood modern practice. Comedy isn't even the right word. It needs replacing. How about 'direct theatre'? One must think and *maybe* laugh. Laughs are irrelevant, originality all. That's why the Edinburgh Festival exists. It weeds out the original from the merely funny.

I itched to free the room of its mindlessness. Any last embers of nerves were doused by Hopton's vacuous sprays of filth. He knocked the groom (Gary, dressed as a nurse) on his head with the base of his guitar. The room roared in appreciation. The nurse-stag stood up and saluted the room before making his way to the Gents, turning back once and miming cunnilingus through V-fingers to the best man. Matthew finished his 'clit song' with a verse containing an unnecessary amount of labia. The guitar was restowed and, flushed with cheap glory, he came back to the microphone recapping the night's rules.

'Bollocks!' shouted the nurse-stag. He was by the cigarette machine unwrapping some Silk Cut.

'Thanks very much, nursie,' replied Matthew. 'Quiet down. I don't come to your place of work and knock the cocks out of your mouth.'

The room boiled into quick laughter, and the stag mouthed 'Fair game'. Yes, I thought, you are most definitely game, fair stag. I'd formed an epigram. I was warming up.

'Now. Ladies and gentlemen,' Hopton continued, 'it's time for the first comic to try and *beat the gong*!'

The jingle shelled through the room and the audience were wild.

'Remember, judges, when you've had enough ... stick your red card right up there. When I can see five, I'll hit the gong as hard as I fooking-well can, and it's all over. Do try'n be a bit supportive ladies and gentlemen. Some o' these guys are doing their first ever shows tonight ... So be nice!'

'Bollocks.'

'Cunts.'

'Wankers.'

And other choice welcomes snipered from the - darkness.

'Our first act tonight is very special indeed. And I don't mean in a disabled way ...'

Malign laughter ...

'He has never performed comedy before, *but* ... but ladies and gentlemen, he has worked as a comedy critic for the *Review* for over ten years ...'

Noises, gruesome noises, grew deafening – an Elizabethan hanging and quartering.

'Give him all your support, and at least give him ten seconds, cos I dunno about you, but I wanna fucking-well hear some of this ...'

The room's baneful roar redoubled. Although concentrating on warming my voice, I could not help for a moment remembering my devastating 196-word exposé of Matthew Hopton's intellect in 2001.

'Matthew Is a Total Vagina' – not my headline of course, Miranda's.

I moved towards the stage stairs. I could feel the poisonous delight of my fellow Press bearing down on me; the disbelieving stares of the fledgling comics. The lightbox and soundbox: gaping mouths, wide eyes. No one had thought I'd actually go through with this. I gave Miranda one last look. She gave one slow shake of her head. I cancelled it with a determined nod and she could do nothing but smile thinly.

'... so, ladies and gentlemen, boys and girls, wankers from Croydon ... welcome to the stage from the *Review* – he's been slagging off us comics for a decade – it's

Benjamin White!'

The jingle shot through the room melding with the malignant noises of the audience. I could not hear one decibel of welcome. The word 'jeer' was invented for this sound. I mounted the stage, tripping on the last stair. The first laughs, the wrong type. I had seen a hundred comics make the same mistake.

I walked up to the microphone and grasped it at the base. I pulled it from the stand, making sure I did not idiotically disconnect the cable. The room fell into a thick anticipatory silence.

'Good evening,' I said and licked my lips. No saliva. 'Hello.'

The tiniest cradle of grace before every known Anglo-Saxon expletive merged and came back in one stinking gust. Behind me Matthew Hopton calmed the audience with one hand, whilst his other maintained a steady grip on the gong's mallet. He wanted his pound of flesh, but a quick death would not be permitted. Well, that suited me.

'Yes. Hello,' I said yet again.

Another gap. I'd nearly fallen at the most dangerous gate, the first, but lucky for me, the cruel bastards wanted to see me writhe a bit. Must begin, but the paste of my mouth was almost cornflour now. The first card appeared. I couldn't see faces past the front three rows, but a laminated rectangle broke above the lights, floating blood-coloured. Of course, a second card, and then a third. It was only with the fourth that I began snapping out. I couldn't let all this mean nothing. Soon, my family would be discovered. I would not die. This, my only chance. That's when I saw the fifth judge. The nurse-stag himself. He stood beyond the lighting's purview by the cigarette machine; laughing maliciously, reaching for his red card. It was at his waist, horizontal, then rising. That's when I leapt, and it rose no further. Perhaps leap is too much, for it was not a jump, not even a precise squaring of the Stance, but more a shocking vault. My legs came down with such force it left Brian muting feedback from the microphone stand. Two cards instantly fell. Three hundred and twelve people: silent. I thrust out my buttocks. I could sense the mathematical funniness of it, the aggression of my legs, my curled fists juxtaposed with that African tribal-wife arse. Titters. Glorious, first-time-in-my-life titters from strangers. I needed no sprinting start. The blocks were kicked away.

'Life at the Centre was fucking maddening . . .'

The shape of this room made it much harder than in a Simongan hut, more difficult than at my parents' house. Here were strangers. Many not focused, some desperately drunk. And that horseshoe-shaped seating. But I made these impediments my fuel. Out of panic rather than precision, I amplified Movement One. The Stance was so grossly executed that it painfully clicked the base of my spine. I jerked my neck and the Hicks Brow came, no smoothness – flicks, hardness. Yet it was what the room needed, and they took it this way. I heard sharp in-breaths, flap-chairs clacking as occupants fell from them.

I had barely begun Movement Two when the first strange thing occurred. My Transition had lurched inelegantly, and no one really had the chance to laugh as such. This in itself was odd, but the really offputting thing, odour-wise as much as anything, was that the whole of the fourth row, every one of them without exception, vigorously shat themselves. I knew this because (stench and sounds apart) every person from 4a to 4y jumped up and checked their backsides with their hands. Almost in a dance they held their shitty digits aloft. Row three (and I imagine row five too, although I could not see) retched, then laughed. A kind of vomit laugh. Some even cackled through vomit; a cross between gargling and coughing. That's how the first surge came, not a pulse, or a gentle build, but a tsunami of laughter, too loud and overwhelming. When it sucked back for its second wave, the room died for a moment unable to sustain the backwash in-between laughs. It was this magnification of the Prelim Elements which caused the early deaths.

During Movement Three, just before the Mental Health Act section, all seventeen waiting comedians died. I moved my hand into the Bruce Twist 1.3. I delivered a clause on sectioning, moving again like raw silk into a further Hicks Brow. One by one, the comedians' mouths widened and they fell silently. And every one in the zombie pose. Not much urine, no screaming, hardly any blood, just melting into the rest as though their bones had been removed.

Perhaps they went this early because they were mechanically focused – they knew comedy. In front of their bodies, row two began expiring. A fat middle-aged American bled from his nose and fluid spread in a neat patterned cloud over his beige trousers. Two of his friends had eyes trickling with something, not quite tears, yet not pus. The American was leaking from his ears, his arse, his eyes. He frantically moved his hands over his body trying to hold in his essential juices. The final few comedians had dominoed now and were gone. Perhaps one or two lived on with broken limbs and whimpered a little, but by Movement Four, none so much as twitched. I had to use my ears and nose to monitor the rest of the room. During my bit about my A levels, the room somehow lost its cohesion and the laughs broke apart into silos and types. Here groans, there belly noises. The wheezes and screams went on like an atonal orgy. People hugging and squeezing, piss, shit and tears everywhere. I took thuds to be deaths, and screams as those getting close, and I felt quite light and good by the time I reached Movement Six.

A green light bathed the stage. For a moment I panicked. But it was all fine. It was simply Karen and Henry dying in the lightbox. One of Karen's withered breasts had hit a dimmer switch as she fitted and throbbed to the floor, gurgling on blood. I had not known one can laugh until the throat ruptures and bleeds like that. I continued drenched in green, resolute.

My second Simongan Thrust did not come off so well,

and I lost stage-left for a moment. The more obstructed parts of the horseshoe would need good acoustic work. I resonated my Lozi Horn Noise carefully, relieved when a group of teenage girls died quickly and violently with creamy eyeballs and urine-soaked, stick-thin legs. Three of them fell from their seats and went without dignity, legs spread, underwear on show. The link with Becky was strong but I pushed it away like unwanted bread in a bistro. I tried taking a moment outside myself, to savour and enjoy and mark it in my memory, but the concentration required was too great, and I dropped the egoism, bending my mind to Movement Seven.

It was as I began my sentence on Surrey that I saw the black cape. Floating out from the darkness, standing at the end of the dead, excrement-covered third row, was, unmistakably, Professor Leavey. He was clapping wildly, not enthusiastically, a breathless, raging, feral applause. His eyes had me, and he was showing his strength, proving he had not yet been taken, spurring me. The hood of his cloak fell away, his sleeves peeled back to his elbows.

'Bravo! Encore!' The voice was gristly and breaking.

I angled him the brunt of my Bruce Lean which came well during the beautiful clockwork of Movement Eight. Still he cheered, patting the backs of the dead. His eyes clicked like a 1950s fruit machine; bright as white petals in his dark, singed face. Still the applause. I began about Miranda, about the affair. I thought of her in her corner. I never saw her die, but afterwards, when I was lying to

WPC Lindsay Grebe, I made sure I had a good look. Her cheekbones had compound fractures, her eyes were gone completely. She'd held her bladder, but had no face left. Her laughter had been violent, though it looked as though she had fought the Humour.

I ignored a loud thud behind me. Hopton. He fell downstage grazing the gong as he went. The gentle, vibrating hum of stimulated steel somehow silhouetted the first stages of Movement Ten's 'gutturals'. Laughter was dimming back to giggles through to silence until there was nothing. The symmetrical ending had begun.

A few choking stalwarts remained, but the coughing sounded mixed with liquid. These were exceptions who would not survive outside the womb of the Formula; and they withered one by one as I turned off their air, and their air became mine. The loudest human noise remaining was Leavey's applause. I gurgled my Denouement Phlegm. I clicked and almost sprained my ankles with clean, hard footwork. Up came the final rising and falling, and then, but for the punchline and knee-drop, it was done.

'And I really had something to laugh about ... for once.'

Up into the air, down onto the knee. I hit the target hard, injuring my calf muscle. I contained the pain and undulated into a final Hicks Brow. A few juicy popping noises from the darkness, some gas and liquid. But still the clapping. Leavey clapped and clapped. His eyes were mosaics, and his tongue, almost gnashed through, hung uselessly from the right side of his mouth. The flesh on his face was like a bin-bag thrown into a fire, pulling and shrinking. He clapped too hard and one hand snapped. The other continued clapping thin air. I heard the husk of a 'Bravo' then his body obeyed the Formula he had made, drawing him into the Chute and slipping him gently from life. A final 'Bravo', and then Leavey was gone.

The Comedy Store's jingle softly playing was the only sound now. It ran on loop introducing nothing, mocking cruelly at the devastating scene.

And yet, there was one more noise: my own. It took me a moment to realize what it was. I was laughing. Not chuckling, but *laughing*. Warm, full, deep laughter. I held onto my stomach, tears running down my cheeks. I rocked back and forth on my heels, varying the pitch, playing with it, allowing it to come and go, feeling it take over and consume me, resting comfortably in the pauses before feeling it start again. I bellowed, looking around me, so happy, so genuinely happy, and I let it run through me. I let it run on and on, this laughter.

Acknowledgements

I would like to thank the network of family, friends and tolerant professionals who have supported and listened to me throughout.